"Oh, this gets . Carmichael. "He le r unlocked home and d when he came back, l l in the kitchen. Is that correct?"

"I know it doesn't look good," said Frances Noonan. "But remember, I know his family. You've all met Julia. Sarah, you met the man. He couldn't have done this, could he?"

Enid Carmichael watched Sarah intently. She was hesitating, that was for sure.

"You must have formed some type of opinion," Olivia Honeycut persisted, "some judgment of the situation."

Still the girl didn't answer. How could she not have an opinion?

"I only met them briefly," she finally said. "I honestly believe that man loved his wife and was trying desperately to change her mind about leaving."

"Desperate." Mrs. Carmichael latched on to the word. "What would a desperate man do?"

The Fog Ladies all turned to Sarah.

"I don't know," Sarah said. "I just don't know."

Praise for *The Fog Ladies, Book 1*

"A very specially crafted 'whodunnit' style mystery by an author with an impressive flair for originality and a distinctive narrative storytelling style all her own."

~Midwest Book Review

~*~

"An atmospheric, cozy mystery…an entertaining whodunit…with a light touch of interlaced humor."

~Lansing State Journal

~*~

"I was on the edge of my seat wondering when and how they would finally fit the pieces of the puzzle together… I had so much fun reading *The Fog Ladies.* Fans of cozy mysteries would do well to pick up a copy of this thoroughly entertaining book."

~Long and Short Reviews, Winner of *Long and Short Reviews'* Book of the Month

~*~

"The colorful characters are sure to enchant the reader, and the mystery will keep them guessing until the surprising finish. This San Francisco Cozy Murder Mystery is a suspenseful whodunnit."

~New York Journal of Books

The Fog Ladies: Family Matters

by

Susan McCormick

A San Francisco Cozy Murder Mystery, Book 2

This is a work of fiction. Names, characters, places, and incidents are either the product of the author's imagination or are used fictitiously, and any resemblance to actual persons living or dead, business establishments, events, or locales, is entirely coincidental.

The Fog Ladies: Family Matters

COPYRIGHT © 2020 by Susan McCormick

All rights reserved. No part of this book may be used or reproduced in any manner whatsoever without written permission of the author or The Wild Rose Press, Inc. except in the case of brief quotations embodied in critical articles or reviews.
Contact Information: info@thewildrosepress.com

Cover Art by *Kristian Norris*

The Wild Rose Press, Inc.
PO Box 708
Adams Basin, NY 14410-0708
Visit us at www.thewildrosepress.com

Publishing History
First Mystery Rose Edition, 2020
Trade Paperback ISBN 978-1-5092-3307-6
Digital ISBN 978-1-5092-3308-3

A San Francisco Cozy Murder Mystery, Book 2
Published in the United States of America

Dedication

To my family and to my silent but slobbery writing
companion, Albert the Newfoundland

**Other Wild Rose Press Titles by
Susan McCormick**

*The Fog Ladies ~ A San Francisco Cozy Murder
Mystery, Book 1*

Prologue

Shelley scrutinized the street before leaning in to unfasten Joey's car seat belt. No nefarious types lurked. She bent her upper body. The middle seat…they say the middle is the safest place for the baby. But hardest on the back. Joe had thrown out his back early on, and he refused to deal with the car seat. Women have stronger backs, he said. It's medically proven. So she hoisted little Joey in and out, anxious each time. Facing inward, concentrating on the baby, someone could easily come up behind her and she'd never know. And their street was not especially safe. She'd heard Mrs. Burkheimer had had her purse snatched the week before. Of course, Mrs. Burkheimer did carry around that enormous purse, dangling off her tiny arm. It's a wonder it survived this long.

An attractive nuisance, that's what the purse was. Shelley learned things down at the law firm. Even though she just sat at the front desk and directed people to the waiting area, the lawyers said she was part of the team. They were a large Philadelphia law firm, and they told her she was their face to the clients, the first thing people saw. It was a big responsibility, and they treated her with respect. Mr. Biffman sometimes told her about his cases. That's how she knew about attractive nuisances.

Well, she was sure her bottom hanging out of the

car was an attractive nuisance right now. Joe had gone into the building. He wanted to see the football game, and it had already started. She wanted him to dig a sandbox for Joey in their pea patch behind the building. She knew he wouldn't get to it this afternoon. She had reminded him all week, but he still acted like it was a surprise when she'd mentioned it that morning.

He was mad because she'd taken a long time to pick out the curtains. He said it was her fault he couldn't dig the sandbox today. She couldn't decide between the curtains with ducks and the curtains with bears. She thought he could distract Joey so she could concentrate. He didn't know what a big decision it was. The ducks were yellow, the bears were blue. If they ever had another child, though God knew she could barely convince him to have one, the blue bears would only work if they had another boy. They couldn't afford to keep buying new curtains. Unless they won the lottery like Joe always hoped, she would have to choose. The bears were a lot cuter than the ducks. But the ducks were more practical. Joe wouldn't understand so she couldn't ask him.

Joe didn't even keep Joey busy. The baby was colicky again. The doctor told her babies usually outgrew it by six months. Not Joey. Joey was nine months, and he still had these crying spells. It was probably never colic to start with. Joe was no use when the baby got like that. So she had to make up her mind with Joey screaming in her ear and Joe pacing back and forth muttering about kickoff.

Even if he hadn't had a football game, he would still bolt into the house. He hated it when Joey cried, and Joey cried almost every time they got in the car.

He'd arch his little back and screech and kick, and it was all Joe could do to get them home in one piece. He usually went right in, leaving her to the howling child. She was used to it.

Still, she felt nervous. She always looked around, making sure no hoodlums prowled the vicinity. Once two teenagers in low-cut trousers sauntered her way. She paused outside the car, pretending to check her watch, but they passed right by. They didn't notice her at all. Like she was invisible.

Today all she saw was a small man with curly hair, and she thought she recognized him. Probably a neighbor, though he was pretty well dressed for this neighborhood.

She leaned in, cooing to the screaming baby. His chubby face was bright red and wet from tears. Even his scalp was red, underneath his yellow hair. Shelley hummed a little song, and Joey started to quiet. She hadn't quite unfastened the first car seat strap when something brushed her leg. She jolted up, hitting her head on the door jam.

She saw the arm before the blow struck her head. She fell soundlessly into the car. Joey, too, was suddenly silent.

Chapter 1

"You wanted to come, now you deal with him. That car trip alone was hell with him screaming the whole way. I knew it would be. Now we've got five days of this, and you will see how much fun a vacation with a child is. If you hoped this would help our marriage, you're more of a fool than I thought."

Sarah James slid her book down an inch to see the woman spewing these remarks. She sat directly in front of Sarah, face-to-face. Sarah thought she would surely catch her spying, but the woman never glanced her way. Like Sarah, she lay on a lounge chair. But while Sarah truly lounged, relaxing back with the sun on her toes and a cool glass of iced tea dripping water as it rested against her shorts, this woman sat bolt upright in full clothes. She had *The Wall Street Journal* clenched in her hands, folded in half and unopened. Her husband stood next to her with a child struggling in his arms, a stricken look on his face. Sarah quickly turned back to her book.

It was a family resort. Around her were lots of families, lots of children struggling, screaming, misbehaving. And lots of parents watching with smiles, not shouting, not fretting, just enjoying their vacations.

Sarah didn't have children, wasn't even married, barely had a boyfriend. A patient of hers at the hospital had recommended this place as an inexpensive but beautiful spot, and Sarah had driven down from San Francisco for the weekend to celebrate the near end of her medical internship year. The resort was on the coast near Big Sur, and her patient was right. It was affordable and meant to be a place families could go in this otherwise high-priced area. The resort website boasted about the covered swimming pool, mini putt-putt golf course, and enormous playground, all of which existed, though a little shabbier than they appeared in the website photos. The two large shingled buildings had a worn but comfortable feeling, like the leather couch in Sarah's family room growing up. The air smelled of pine and a spice she couldn't put her finger on.

The setting was spectacular, on a bluff above the ocean. The warm, sunny weekend was certainly a treat. California coastal weather could be cloudy and cold in late May, and Sarah had anticipated a fog-obscured view. From where she reclined in the sun, she could see blue ocean beyond the fencing at the edge of the cliff and hear surf crashing on the rocks below. Seagulls circled overhead and swooped in to eat fallen scraps. Stairs and a short steep walk through a wind-bent cypress forest led down to a small beach. The beach was off limits to youngsters because of the violent sea. A set of double gates protected the stairs, and she needed her key card to pass through.

Sarah had spent the afternoon before on the beach, alone, reading her first non-medical book in a year. A novel! How luxurious to read a novel!

The year had taken its toll, and this beautiful spot made Sarah's eyes sting with tears. The patient who told her about the resort was a young woman with breast cancer. They met when Sarah was on her rotation in the intensive care unit and the woman was admitted for a pulmonary embolism, a blood clot to the lungs which could be fatal. She had four children, and her husband brought them to visit every day, the kids solemn and scared. When the woman left the hospital, the kids drew Sarah thank-you cards, and Sarah saw them smile for the first time. But they all met again when she came back with pneumonia. And she died.

As had many of Sarah's patients. A hospital sees death every day, sees people fighting illness, sees small miracles against the odds. For Sarah, this first year as a true doctor was full of agony and hope. Her fellow residents seemed to take the ups and downs in stride, cool, calm, unemotional. For the next two years of her training, Sarah wanted less emotion.

Laughing families played on either side of her. On her left four children all shared one lounge chair. They squirmed and shifted and squealed in delight. Four children. Just like her patient.

Across from her the man still stood with his writhing child. Controlling the boy was especially hard because one hand also held a bottle of beer. The resort did not sell alcohol. Sarah looked closer. The woman had a mini bottle of wine on the ground under her chair and a plastic cup half full. They must have brought their own.

The man's beer spilled as the boy jerked backwards. The man had a boyishly handsome face with small, round glasses. He turned his head to keep the boy's flailing arms from grabbing them.

"I'll take him to the pool. You sit here and read. We'll have fun in the pool," Sarah heard him say.

"Idiot." The woman made no attempt to say it quietly.

Sarah peeked up, relieved to see the man and the child had already left.

Chapter 2

People were so predictable. At first he watched them for weeks to get to know their patterns. Then he learned it wasn't necessary. People did pretty much the same thing every day, with little variation. If they were the type to forget things, they forgot things every day. If they were the type to be late, they were always late. If they stopped for coffee on Thursdays because the morning meeting was later that day, they stopped every Thursday. It was one of the only useful things his father had taught him. People never change.

Now he only watched for a few days. Enough to get the lay of the land. Enough to know their habits. Enough to make sure he hadn't been wrong. He was never wrong.

Chapter 3

Sarah saw the family at dinner that night. The resort's meals were part of the plan. A small dining room overlooked the ocean, but when Sarah arrived the sun had already set and outside the windows was blackness. As she settled in at the last open table, she was disheartened to see she again faced directly at the woman.

Beyond the family, a half wall divided the dining room from the kitchen. A chef in a white hat stood at a stove facing the diners. It was a nice touch for such a small resort. The dinner menu was limited, and at the moment the chef stood in one place stirring pots. He performed this simple task with energy and rhythm, like a drummer, and Sarah found his hands mesmerizing. A chair scraped, startling her.

The husband had dragged his seat next to his wife, so Sarah could see both their faces clearly. The woman's was turned away from her husband's, and her mouth was set in a line. The man took off his glasses and brushed his eyes, first with his hand, then with his napkin. The tables were close, close enough for Sarah to smell her rosewater perfume, close enough to hear every word despite the noisy room. From the slight slurring of the words and the woman's flushed face, Sarah realized they were both a little drunk.

"I'm almost done with this one. Then it will be

different. You'll see."

The man couldn't see his wife roll her eyes, but Sarah could.

"Where have I heard that before?" the woman hissed back. "Do you really expect me to believe that when you say it every time? You are going nowhere. I won't support you forever. You need a job."

"I have a job."

"Working part-time in a hospital x-ray file room is not a job. You don't even get full benefits. Thank God I make a decent living. We have a mortgage now. We have a son."

Their son sat in a high chair pushed close to the table next to his father. He appeared indifferent to the adults' conversation, but his plate of food sat in front of him untouched, like his parents'. His foot swung back and forth, knocking against the table. Water sloshed from a too full glass, a small amount with each kick.

"You know the hospital is only temporary."

"Temporary? You've been there *five years*. You need a real job."

"I'm a writer. That's a real job."

The woman shook her head, then scoffed. "Not for you."

The man took his wife's hands and tried to turn her toward him. "Andrea, you know I can do it. I've done it."

"That was *ten* years ago! And all you did was win a stupid contest. You couldn't even get published. You can't go on with this ridiculous dream. I can't go on."

Sarah shifted in her seat so she couldn't see them. She studied the resort proprietor, who greeted diners as they entered. The wife's voice rose and was hard to ignore.

"How do you think it feels to have to explain what you do? 'My husband sorts x-rays three days a week, but just you watch, he's going to make it big.' You still make minimum wage. What must people think? Natalie's husband is a banker. Nicole's husband is an engineer. Those are real jobs."

She paused and took a deep breath. Sarah took a deep breath.

"Yours is nothing." The woman spat it out. These words were clear, not slurred at all.

Sarah flinched. She searched for somewhere else to look, anywhere other than the couple. She fastened her eyes on the chef, still stirring his pots. He was as near to them as Sarah, and he leaned slightly to hear the man's soft voice.

"This book is different. This one is the one."

The woman's voice was soft now too. "We are not kids anymore. We have responsibilities. If it weren't for your mother taking care of Ben, I would have left long ago. You're never home and when you are, you're writing. I have to do everything. You didn't even know what size diapers to buy. I can't believe I ever agreed to start a family while you persist in this pathetic pipedream."

Sarah bent her head and busied herself breaking her roll into small pieces. When would her meal come?

"Andrea, please. So what if Nicole's husband is an engineer? Remember when we were in college and we all went camping, and he brought his calculus book? You used to think he was a nerd."

Her voice was tired. "I used to think a lot of things."

"And right before Ben was born, when you made your chocolate mousse and he wouldn't eat it because of the raw eggs? We laughed and laughed. Remember? We used to have such fun. When did you get so serious?"

"You haven't heard a word I've said, have you?" Her voice was loud again. "Anyway, that's it. I'm done. I told you before we came on this miserable trip. I'm not staying."

The boy kicked again, this time too hard. The glass teetered over and clunked onto their table. Water ran across the table and into his mother's lap. She jumped up with a shriek.

The proprietor hurried over to help. He reached to blot the water from the woman's lap with a large cloth napkin. She grabbed the napkin from his hand.

"What do you think you're doing?" she cried. "Don't touch me!"

"Andrea, he was only trying to help," her husband said.

"He's not helping. Get him away from me!"

"Andrea, shh."

"Don't tell me to shh." She turned on the man, but he was already backing away.

"Andrea, sit down, please." The woman's husband stood and took her hands again.

Two children dashed past them, and their parents hollered from across the room. Another table burst into "Happy Birthday." Sarah doubted anyone else knew what was happening in this corner.

"I love you, Andrea. We can make this work," the man pleaded.

"Too late. I told you it was too late, and I meant it."

12

"I love you. I love our life together. I love everything about you, your brain, your smile, your beauty, your humor. I always have and I always will."

"You are not living in reality," she said. She yanked her hands out of his, so forcefully that she fell to the side. Her husband was there in a flash, arms around her, holding her steady.

Sarah thought this might be it, that this instinctive reaction of kindness and caring would be the trigger for the woman to relent. The couple stood for a moment together. Sarah held her breath.

The woman broke free and strode toward the door.

"Andrea!" The man rushed after her, then pivoted back toward the boy, who slumped in the high chair with his head on his chest, his feet still.

The man caught Sarah's eyes. She was so engrossed she hadn't realized she was staring. She averted her eyes guiltily, but the man approached her.

"Could you watch my boy?" The man's little glasses were back on, and she couldn't see his eyes very well. His tone was urgent. "I'm so sorry to ask— I'll be right back. Could you watch my boy?"

He didn't wait for an answer, but just fled from the room.

As soon as his parents were out of the room, the boy began to scream.

"Mommmmmeeeee! Mommmmmmeeeee!"

The loud dining room quieted now, and people twisted in their seats to see the boy. Sarah felt strangely embarrassed, as if this were her son screaming. And she felt horrible for the little thing. He couldn't have been more than two. Maybe three. She shifted over to the chair next to him. He screamed even louder. He had piercing blue eyes that latched on to hers so she couldn't look away.

"Shh, shh, there, there." She unfastened his safety belt and lifted him out of his seat, slowly in case he was scared.

He wasn't scared, and he actually clung to her tightly, still calling out for "Mommy, Mommy." She held him close, shushing and there-there-ing. She didn't know what else to do, but it seemed to work, and eventually the boy stopped yelling. She rocked him slowly back and forth. "Mommy, Mommy," the boy kept saying, quietly now. Sarah gently stroked his soft hair.

This is what it feels like to have a child, Sarah thought. She knew that was ridiculous. There was a lot more to a child than the smell of baby shampoo, but this had to be one of the pluses. What she witnessed between the couple was definitely a minus. Sarah was twenty-eight years old and hadn't yet considered having children. College, medical school, internship. The long hours left little time for thoughts of a family.

She sat with the boy a long time, maybe thirty minutes, maybe longer. Most of the other diners left. The boy fell asleep and Sarah didn't want to wake him by standing. She wasn't worried. His parents couldn't have gone far because of the confines of the resort. She hoped they were talking. She felt quite relaxed sitting with this toddler in her lap. He had a dimple on one side that deepened as he smiled in his sleep. She was amazed at how adaptable he was, sleeping and smiling in a stranger's arms.

"You have a wonderful way with kids. Do you have children?"

Sarah jumped and the boy stirred but didn't wake. The chef stood beside Sarah. She hadn't heard him walk up. He wiped his hands on a towel tucked into the strings of his white apron. He had very large hands, though he was not tall.

"No," she said. "No children."

"Pity." His eyes lingered on Sarah. "Your black hair, green eyes, they'd be beautiful."

This was certainly uncomfortable. He was quite a bit older than she, probably in his forties. He seemed perfectly presentable, albeit a little silly in the chef's hat. If this was a pickup line, she didn't want to be rude, but the way he said it didn't seem like a come-on. In fact, without further conversation, he was gone.

No more than a minute later, the boy's mother appeared. She rushed over to Sarah and snatched the sleeping child away. He woke, startled, then clutched his arms around his mother's neck.

"What was your father thinking?" The stress was clear in her voice. "Thank you."

Sarah nodded.

The woman hugged the boy and smoothed his hair. She turned to Sarah and rolled her eyes. "Men."

Before Sarah could reply, she turned and left.

Chapter 4

Why did people even get married? This was what he couldn't figure out. Didn't they read the statistics? Half of all marriages end in divorce. Divorce. Lawyers, arguments, allegations, accusations, pain, financial ruin. And, if there were children, bitter custody battles, anguish, and heartbreak. For the child, lifelong intimacy issues and irreparable psychological problems. Divorce. Half of all marriages. Why would anyone put themselves in a situation with such bad odds? Why had he?

Love, that's what they'd say. He'd said it himself. Well, love was overrated.

Chapter 5

"How awful. Tut-tut. Just look at the little fellow. How could his father have done such a thing? He'll rot in hell for his deed."

Sarah glanced over from her mailbox. Harriet Flynn sounded more dismayed than usual.

"Now, now, Harriet, just because he's been arrested doesn't mean he actually did it." Frances Noonan leaned in to see the newspaper, squinting without her reading glasses.

"Of course he did it. Look at him," Enid Carmichael chimed in, tapping the paper with a long, crooked finger. "He's a killer if ever I saw one."

"Oh, I don't agree," Frances Noonan said. "I think he looks confused. Sarah, what do you think?"

Sarah closed her mailbox and put her mail in her bag. The three older women stood in the lobby of her apartment building, peering intently at a newspaper open on the table. The old wooden table was dark mahogany wood, well-oiled, and stood on a gleaming slate floor. The building was built in the 1920s. The room was large, with glass doors leading out to the street, an elevator with a shiny brass grate, and a stairway with deep red carpeting.

The ladies made quite a sight, Sarah thought, three older women of such disparate heights. Enid Carmichael towered over the other two, six feet tall and wearing high heels, as she often did. Sarah was amazed she'd never fallen, especially the way she charged around. Mrs. Carmichael had a large frame and dyed red hair, today an odd hue of orange. From this distance she didn't look older than the other ladies, but close up her smoker's skin and rheumy eyes confirmed every one of her eighty years.

Harriet Flynn was skinny and short. She didn't have to bend to see the paper. She seldom smiled and was definitely not smiling now. She wore a drab gray sweater that matched her drab gray hair. As if I'm any better at grooming, Sarah thought, with my hair hanging listlessly and without a proper haircut in months.

Frances Noonan was younger than the two other women, about seventy-five, and she was Sarah's favorite tenant in the building. She and Sarah were the same height, five feet eight inches, though Sarah had never realized this because Mrs. Noonan had always favored one leg by leaning or sitting. Since a recent hip replacement, Mrs. Noonan stood as tall and straight as Sarah herself, her carriage finally matching her level of energy.

Sarah had grown to know these women and the other people in her building well over the past year. She remembered her initial disappointment over her apartment. Her hospital provided housing for its medical residents, and Sarah hoped for one of the buildings close to the hospital where most of the residents lived. She imagined lots of camaraderie, with everyone working the same long hours and dealing with the same stressful situations.

Once she saw her Pacific Heights building, with its

elegant lobby and breathtaking rooftop views, she quickly realized she had a choice apartment. And the diversity of tenants gave her a respite from work she wouldn't have living with her colleagues.

The front door opened and Alma Gordon came in, one-year-old Baby Owen perched on her hip, her lilac bubble bath smell wafting in with her. She was in her seventies, yet she moved remarkably well. Olivia Honeycut followed with her walker, a grocery bag balanced in its shallow basket.

"I don't know how you would have managed if you hadn't bumped into me," Olivia Honeycut said in her low, gravelly voice. "These diapers are bulky. Good thing the heat wave is over."

"I never could have gone out yesterday," Alma Gordon replied. "It was close to one hundred degrees. In San Francisco in June! Give me this lovely fog any day. But I do okay. It's all a matter of balance. That yoga class has done me a world of good."

"Yoga, schmoga. Age will get you in the end. You'll end up with one of these. It's inevitable." Olivia Honeycut gestured to her walker.

These five ladies were the Fog Ladies, a group of women Sarah had come to love. Sarah gave the group their name because Frances Noonan told her that you could count on them like you could count on early morning fog. Every morning Sarah heard the weather report on the radio and every morning it was the same—early morning fog burning off by midday. San Francisco weather was a constant you could count on and so were the Fog Ladies.

Sarah was a Fog Lady now, too, invited in as they all grew closer over the year.

Enid Carmichael waved her large hand. "I have no patience for yoga. All that New Age-y music and whispery talk. Give me a good brisk walk any day."

"Yoga suits me just fine. Thank goodness they have childcare. Sometimes I do fall asleep during meditation time, though, and once they told me I snorted. Broke their mood. I blamed Baby Owen, said he was keeping me up nights."

Sarah had recommended the yoga class to Alma Gordon, and she was happy to hear she was going. Alma Gordon was short, the same height as Harriet Flynn, but the two were otherwise completely different. Mrs. Gordon was round, and Mrs. Flynn was all angles. Mrs. Gordon's hair was fluffy and white, Mrs. Flynn's bristly and steel gray. Mrs. Gordon was taking care of an abandoned baby, left over from one of the Fog Ladies' charity activities, waiting for his mother to return. Mrs. Flynn didn't believe in having children out of wedlock and had trouble speaking civilly to the teen mother when she was around.

Alma Gordon had told Sarah the baby made her feel creaky, and Sarah had told her she thought yoga could help. As Mrs. Gordon deftly shifted the baby to the other hip, Sarah was amazed at how agile she seemed. Looking again, Sarah saw a dreamy look in her eyes. And she was humming softly. Meek, nervous Mrs. Gordon—humming. This was more than yoga.

Sarah didn't have to wonder long. The elevator door opened, and Mr. Glenn stepped out. Mrs. Gordon stopped humming and turned toward him, her face crinkling into a smile. Baby Owen laughed and clapped his hands.

Mr. Glenn was stooped and bald and wore thick

glasses. But as he held out his finger for Baby Owen to grab, he seemed taller and more animated than Sarah had ever seen him. His wife, Bessie, died before Sarah moved into the apartment building, and as long as Sarah had known him, Mr. Glenn seemed serious and sad. But not today.

"I was just telling them about my snorting during yoga," Alma Gordon said.

"Those young whippersnappers don't know how easy it is to nod off when you're our age." Mr. Glenn patted his ample stomach and yawned. "Maybe I should come to your class and show them some true snoring."

"Oh, that would be a sight," Olivia Honeycut said. "A man at yoga class."

"There are lots of men, Olivia. Almost half the class," Alma Gordon said.

"Why on earth would a man want to go to yoga class?" Enid Carmichael said. "In my day, men went to men's clubs and used medicine balls and lifted weights."

"Like Jack LaLanne. Now there was a fine specimen," Olivia Honeycut said.

"One shouldn't flaunt one's body," Harriet Flynn said. "That skimpy outfit. Unseemly."

"The man in the newspaper goes to yoga," Frances Noonan said.

"What man?" Alma Gordon asked.

"The man who killed his wife," Enid Carmichael said.

"We don't know for sure that he did it," Mrs. Noonan said.

"Stabbed her with the kitchen shears. He'll rot in hell," Mrs. Flynn said.

"Murder? Are you talking about murder?" Mrs. Honeycut's raspy voice accentuated the word.

"Yes, indeed. Murder. It's all right here." Mrs. Carmichael picked up the paper. She pulled a pair of glasses from her pocket and squinted at the print. "'San Francisco police have arrested a thirty-one-year-old man in connection with the slaying of his wife. Paul Blackwell was jailed last night after police received a nine-one-one call from a neighbor who heard screams. Police found Andrea Blackwell, thirty-two, in the kitchen of the couple's Marina home. She had been stabbed with a pair of scissors. The couple's child was sleeping and unharmed and has been taken in by Child Protective Services. Blackwell states that he had been at YOGA'"—Mrs. Carmichael emphasized the word— "'which he did every Tuesday night. However, a police spokesman said the yoga class had been canceled due to a faulty air conditioner, and that Mr. Blackwell was covered with blood when police arrived.'"

Mrs. Carmichael stopped reading and put the paper down. "There," she said with satisfaction, "it's an open and shut case."

"The poor child," Mrs. Noonan said. "Look at those eyes."

Sarah set her bag on the slate floor and joined the ladies at the table. She bent to see the photograph. Staring at her in black and white was the family from the ocean resort, the handsome man with the small, round glasses, his unsmiling wife, and the little boy with the piercing eyes.

Chapter 6

"Sarah? Sarah? You look a little green, dear," Olivia Honeycut said.

"Yes, Sarah, she's right, you don't look good. Did you eat breakfast today?" Frances Noonan asked.

"It's the picture, you ninnies," said Enid Carmichael. "Sarah, do you know them? The killer? Do you know the killer?"

Sarah could hear the excitement in her voice. Mrs. Carmichael loved other people's troubles, other people's business, other people's misery.

"Oh, dear." Alma Gordon pulled Baby Owen in close. "Do you know them, Sarah?"

Sarah's mouth was dry. She licked her lips. "Did you say her name was Andrea?"

"Yep," said Mrs. Carmichael, "Andrea Blackwell."

"I know them," said Sarah.

It had been less than a month, and Sarah remembered every detail. She especially remembered the little boy's smell and the man's pleading voice, "Andrea, I love you."

Sarah told them about her weekend at the resort. She tried to leave out the nastiness but found she didn't have much to say about the couple that wasn't unpleasant. Could a marriage get so ugly that a man would resort to murder?

The next day's paper had more details. Andrea

Blackwell worked for an investment firm and had a large insurance policy, one million dollars, payable to her husband. He was in custody and the child had been turned over to his grandmother, who had watched him regularly while his parents worked. The man's coworkers in the hospital's radiology records room expressed disbelief that he could have committed the crime.

Sarah, too, struggled to believe it. She had only met him briefly, but he made an impression. The man had worked in the radiology department at her very own hospital. She had never seen him. She headed down there, into the bowels of the building, drawn by some urge she could not explain. The room was enormous, with multiple workstations with large computer screens and paper folders with colored tabs stacked high. From the counter barrier, Sarah craned her neck to try to see more.

Despite being in the basement, the room was well-lit, tidy, and surprisingly cheerful. A radio played a soft tune in the background. A young woman came to help her, and Sarah made up some excuse about an outside film and gave a pretend patient's name. The woman could not, of course, find the image. She was helpful and apologetic and did not give any indication that one of her fellow workers had been arrested for murder. Sarah couldn't bring herself to ask any questions. It was an unsatisfactory experience, but what had she expected?

She knew what she expected. She expected something to show there had been a mistake. The man she met could not be a murderer.

She remembered how quick he was to hold his wife

steady when she fell. Could someone so loving and protective go on to kill her?

At home that night, she stood in the lobby and scanned the newspaper on the table, searching for more about the killing. The elevator door opened, and Frances Noonan stepped out, her cat, Camouflage, tucked under one arm.

"Are you reading about that man again?" she asked.

Sarah nodded. She picked up the paper and read aloud. "'Preliminary autopsy results show Andrea Blackwell died from multiple stab wounds to the upper body inflicted by a pair of scissors. The scissors were recovered at the scene and fingerprint data matches those of her husband, Paul Blackwell, who is currently in custody for the crime. Authorities say he has remained silent since his arrest. The couple's young child remains with his grandmother, Julia Bentley Blackwell.'"

"Julia Bentley?" Frances Noonan stepped closer.

"Julia Bentley Blackwell."

"I know a Julia Bentley." Mrs. Noonan knelt to put the cat down and he settled at their feet, sprawled across Mrs. Noonan's sturdy shoes. "If she's the daughter of Fred and Grace Bentley. Bill worked under Fred Bentley when he first started at the police department."

Mrs. Noonan had been married to a police officer. Sarah had heard her tell many stories about him. He died not in the line of duty but after retirement, hit by a car while crossing Lombard Street on his daily walk down to the waterfront.

"Fred Bentley was a man of great integrity and

courage. He stood up to the brass and put an end to a nasty cover-up in North Beach, put his job on the line because his immediate boss was involved in the scandal. Bill admired him tremendously. Fred showed all the young cops that good wins out."

"Does your Julia Bentley still live in San Francisco?" Sarah asked.

"Oh, heavens, I don't know. Fred retired long before Bill. I lost track of their family. I did work with Grace once on a raffle through the SFPD Wives' Guild. That was years ago. Thirty years ago, perhaps even forty. My, time flies. She was lovely, a beautiful woman and every bit as honest as her husband. There was a discrepancy in the raffle monies, and she wouldn't let it rest until she made sure every cent was accounted for. Turned out, it was my own arithmetic error which caused the turmoil. Oh, I was embarrassed. But she was very gracious, said she just wanted to be sure the fund got all the money coming to it."

"And their daughter's name was Julia?" Sarah said.

"Yes, Julia. She and I spent a summer volunteering with the juvenile offenders. If this is their daughter, then she is as proper and upstanding as her parents. She must be beside herself."

"Because her son's been accused of murder?" Sarah asked.

"Or because he *is* a murderer." Mrs. Noonan lowered her voice, though no one else was present.

"What? I met him, I saw how he was with his boy, how much he loved his wife. He couldn't be a murderer!"

"Murderers might not be murderers until something sets them off. Crimes of passion."

Sarah's stomach tightened, remembering the man's pleading voice.

"I don't want Enid to think I agree with her," Mrs. Noonan continued, "and I know you met the man and I defer to your judgment, but my husband always said that if there is a domestic crime, the spouse did it."

"Oh, Mrs. Noonan, how can you say that? What a stereotype!"

"I know, I know, that's exactly what I'd say to Bill. But time after time it turned out to be true. If you were placing odds, you'd put your money on the spouse."

"Wagering is a sin."

Sarah jumped. Harriet Flynn and Olivia Honeycut stood just inside the lobby.

"Mrs. Flynn! You startled me! How long have you been there?" Sarah said.

"Long enough to know you're talking about that murderer again. Of course the husband did it. One million dollars. Money is the root of all evil."

The elevator door opened, and Enid Carmichael dashed out, pulled by her Bichon Frise, Snowball. The dog was tiny but strong, and Mrs. Carmichael flew across the lobby like a kite behind the leash.

The small dog saw the cat tucked under the table and u-turned toward him. Mrs. Carmichael came to a halt within inches of Mrs. Noonan, who swept Camouflage into her arms.

The scene was so typical that no one commented. Only Sarah seemed flustered by these near misses. Her heart pounded, but Mrs. Noonan exuded calm, as always, standing still and petting the cat under the chin.

Enid Carmichael nodded to the others, then her eyes lighted on the story in the paper.

"Any news on your killer?" Mrs. Carmichael asked.

"Innocent until proven guilty." Frances Noonan winked at Sarah.

"Lambs are innocent. This man is not," said Harriet Flynn. "It's the breakup of the family, no family values, no respect. What's society coming to?"

Sarah couldn't stand it any longer, this flippant chitchat about another man's life. She blurted out, "Mrs. Noonan knows his family! They're good people! With values!"

The women turned to Mrs. Noonan, and Sarah was relieved to see her thoughtful expression as she stroked Camouflage's fur. Finally, she addressed them. "Ladies, Sarah's right. I know this man's mother and his grandparents. They are as honorable as they come. There may be more to this than money and passion—"

"And a dead-end job and a wife with a rising career," said Mrs. Carmichael.

"Jealousy. A sin," said Mrs. Flynn.

"And the loss of manhood manifest by his wife's lack of respect and his unusual choice of exercise," said Mrs. Honeycut.

"Vanity. A sin," said Mrs. Flynn.

"Ladies, ladies, please," said Mrs. Noonan. "This is not just some man we're reading about in the newspaper. Sarah met him. She got a feeling about him. I know his family. I think we should offer our support. If nothing else, we can be a comfort to his mother. But there may be more to this killing than a desperate husband."

"Oh, I hope so," said Mrs. Carmichael gleefully. "When do we get to meet the killer?"

Chapter 7

Julia Bentley Blackwell was very close to Frances Noonan's own age. "I always thought of her as younger," Mrs. Noonan explained to Sarah. "She was in graduate school on the East Coast when I knew her parents. We worked together a whole summer. She was on break from school and living a completely different life from me. I was a married woman, cooking and ironing and planning for a family. I always thought of her as carefree and young. But *I* was young too. I just didn't realize it."

Mrs. Noonan eyed Sarah, sitting next to her at the kitchen table, dipping a chocolate cookie into a glass of milk. Sarah seemed so young, but she was older than Frances Noonan had been when she met Julia.

"I didn't even call her 'Miss Bentley.' I called her Julia. That's how much older I thought I was."

Sarah eyed her quizzically.

"We were from a different era than you are, dear. Our parents were definitely of a different era, and they taught us well. This was long before 'Ms.' was popular. Everyone was 'Mrs.' or 'Miss.' It was a form of civility, of respect. The country was in crisis and we held on to these courtesies, they held us together. We were comfortable speaking this way. In this building, we Fog Ladies, we just kept it up, even now."

Mrs. Noonan thoughtfully sipped her milk. "The

first person I met here, when Bill and I moved in all those years ago, the first person I met was so old I couldn't believe she was living on her own. Miss Carroll. That's how she introduced herself, what I called her as long as I knew her. It was months before I learned her first name. Margaret. Margaret Carroll."

Mrs. Noonan studied Sarah. Not a wrinkle. Fingers straight and not bent by arthritis. The whites of her eyes white, not yellow. Well, white with red blood vessels from not enough sleep. Anyway, the point was, in retrospect, Miss Carroll turned out to not be so old. Turned out she was only sixty-five. Which seemed ancient then, when Frances Noonan and Julia were young. Now sixty-five just seemed normal.

Mrs. Noonan found Julia Blackwell easily. She was listed in Mrs. Noonan's old telephone company-issued paper telephone book under Blackwell, Julia B. An address was given on Russian Hill. Could she simply call her out of the blue?

After much thought and discussion with the Fog Ladies, Mrs. Noonan left a long message on the answering machine, saying that she was an old family friend, that she remembered Julia from their summer together, that she had read about the murder in the newspaper, and that she was very good with children if Julia needed babysitting relief in order to help her son. She hung up wishing the machine would give her some reaction, some assurance the message would be received in the spirit she intended.

Her answer came within a few hours. Julia Blackwell called back to say she indeed remembered her and that she would be grateful for any help Mrs. Noonan could offer. Mrs. Noonan told her several Fog

Ladies had babysitting experience. The two women agreed to meet the next day.

Mrs. Noonan was happy when Alma Gordon suggested she join her. Mrs. Gordon had transformed Baby Owen from a sad, silent waif into a bubbly toddler. She had a way with babies.

Enid Carmichael somehow assumed she would be coming too. Frances was appalled at the thought and kicked herself for asking the ladies if anyone else would like to go. She hadn't meant Enid Carmichael. Olivia Honeycut, who had grandchildren, would be useful, though she was sometimes too outspoken. Even Harriet Flynn, with her holier than thou preachings, was preferable to Enid Carmichael.

Of course Enid would want to come. This was murder, after all. Enid Carmichael thrived on gossip and excitement. She'd been that way as long as Frances had known her. People never change, Frances's husband, Bill, always said. He was certainly right about Enid Carmichael.

The Fog Ladies had been meeting more than a decade, the group growing larger as each woman became a widow, except for Enid, who just glommed on. First, Alma Gordon's husband died of a coronary. Then her own Bill, hit by a car crossing Lombard Street on his morning walk. She always thought he would die in the line of duty. She never expected that kind of a telephone call once he retired.

Then Philip Flynn—a stroke. And Chester Honeycut—lung cancer. Muriel Bridge, who had died herself the year before, became a widow when her husband died of pneumonia following gallbladder surgery. Five men, all dying before the wives.

The Fog Ladies had turned to each other for comfort and for company. After more than forty years of marriage, it was an adjustment to be alone. Having these women during the day was a godsend. If only the hours between ten p.m. and four a.m. could be filled as well.

Oh, how she missed Bill. His smell, of wintergreen breath mints and coffee, his smile, showing teeth that got more crooked as he grew older, his solidness that softened over the years with all her baked goods, her molasses cookies being his all-time favorite. The Fog Ladies ate her cookies now. Though she hadn't made the molasses ones since Bill died.

Enid Carmichael was not a widow. She had been divorced forever, divorced and bitter at first, but that, at least, had mellowed. Knowing everything about everybody, she latched on to the growing group instantly, even before they knew they were a group. Enid was one of them. Still, she didn't know diddly-squat about children.

In the end, as far as meeting Julia Blackwell was concerned, Mrs. Noonan diplomatically explained that since Enid had no interest in actually babysitting the tyke, there was no real reason for her to come, and Mrs. Carmichael grudgingly stayed behind.

Julia Blackwell's apartment was in a large brick building on Russian Hill. Parking was difficult, and Mrs. Noonan's car was not small. She circled the block several times, up and down a steep hill, waiting for a space to open up. Each time they turned the corner at the top of the hill, the San Francisco Bay opened up in front of them, blue today, with several sail boats and one large container ship they tracked with each circle of

the block. Just as Mrs. Noonan was giving up, a van pulled away from a spot directly in front of the building. She had been concentrating so much on finding parking that she hadn't noticed the van was from a local television station. Alma Gordon pointed it out.

"I bet that's about the killing. Poor woman," Frances said.

Julia Blackwell answered on the intercom with an anxious voice, and Frances heard it relax when they announced themselves. The woman still squeaked when Frances pressed her apartment doorbell, and it wasn't until the door was shut and they were seated with tea that she seemed to calm down.

"They won't let us alone. At all hours of the day. Cameras, questions. Poor Ben. This last group got into the building and actually came to the door and had the camera rolling when I opened it. Got Ben on film. I thought it was you and stupidly opened the door without thinking. Poor child. He's only two and a half, but that's old enough to know something has happened to his parents."

Ben was set up in an adjacent room which they could see through a set of French doors. He was surrounded by toys, but he sat on the floor watching them. He had a stuffed giraffe in his arms and one thumb in his mouth.

"They haven't let him visit his father. I've been there, to the jail, a few times, but they won't let Ben go. It's probably just as well. Paul is in an awful state. I don't know if he could pull it together, even for Ben."

Julia Blackwell was crying and wiped her eyes with a handkerchief. She turned her head away from the boy so he couldn't see. Mrs. Noonan wanted to hug her but didn't want Ben to get alarmed. She sat in silence, placing her hand over Julia's. Finally, Alma Gordon spoke.

"Do you need help with Ben?" she asked. "I am taking care of a toddler myself, younger than Ben. I know how tiring it can be. Frances and I would like to help if we can."

"You're so kind. Your call caught me off guard. All I've had is media calls, police calls, and crank calls. Since Ben was born, I've taken care of him during the day, and I must admit, I have let my social obligations go. I've been so wrapped up in Paul and Andrea's lives, I haven't seen some of my own friends in years. Many have died or moved away from the city." She paused to gaze toward Ben, then leaned toward the ladies.

"Frances, when we were young, my parents talked about you and Bill so much I felt like you were part of the family. Meeting you again now reminds me of all the stories my mother told about the Wives' Guild. She used to say that no matter how undesirable the task, she could count on you to volunteer with a smile. I can see what she means. And I remember you at the juvenile detention center, tackling that huge sixteen-year-old when he threatened that other boy with his pen to his neck. You just shoved against him somehow and the crisis was over, and he even laughed that you would try it."

"How funny, I haven't thought of that in years." Mrs. Noonan smiled. "All I was thinking at the time was if someone gets hurt on my watch, my Bill will have hell to pay."

Julia Blackwell nodded. "Well, I always admired

you. I just stood there petrified. I can definitely use your help. I can't tell you how relieved I've been since you called. You can imagine how much I have to do now, to try to get help for Paul. It is very hard to manage with Ben, not to mention not being able to talk in front of him."

"You can count on us," Mrs. Noonan said. "We'll introduce ourselves to the lad, see how things go, then we can set up a schedule. You let us know what you need. We have several ladies who can help out, not just Alma and me."

"And then there's Baby Owen," Alma Gordon said. "He will be pleased to see a boy close to his own age. He's stuck being around us old folks all the time."

"Is he your grandson? There are a lot of us watching these little fellas," Julia said.

"Oh, no," Mrs. Gordon laughed. "Sylvia, my daughter, doesn't have children. She didn't meet Harold until she was older. I guess too old for babies."

"It's never too late. My husband and I thought we couldn't have children. Paul came along when I was in my forties. You never know, you may be blessed with grandchildren yet."

"Wouldn't that be something," Mrs. Gordon said wistfully.

"Who is Owen, then, if he's not your grandson?"

"Oh, such a long story," Mrs. Gordon said.

"We were helping with the 'high risk youth' through a program at the hospital," Mrs. Noonan said.

"We used to help in the newborn nursery," Mrs. Gordon said. "I loved that. Little bundles of pink and blue and everyone so happy. Why we had to change to Chantrelle, I don't know."

"It was my fault." Mrs. Noonan knew it was her fault, but wouldn't she do exactly the same thing again? "I thought we could be of use. The hospital needed volunteers to help the social workers with the teenagers, the ones with troubles like drugs or abuse or depression. Chantrelle was sixteen and had a baby, and we were supposed to give our support and set a good example and try to keep her in school and teach parenting skills."

"What did I say about you taking on the undesirable tasks?" said Julia.

"I don't think we accomplished even one of those things, come to think of it," said Mrs. Gordon.

"Well, we did give our support," said Mrs. Noonan. "And we still are, if you count Baby Owen."

"So Owen is this girl's child?" Julia asked. "Do you watch him while she's in school?"

Mrs. Noonan didn't say anything, and Mrs. Gordon certainly didn't say anything. The silence grew. Mrs. Noonan saw Mrs. Gordon shift uncomfortably in her seat, eyes down.

"Well, no, not exactly," Mrs. Noonan finally said.

Julia Blackwell stared from her to a silent Alma Gordon.

Mrs. Noonan decided she'd just better out with it. "I think we should tell you straight up, or you will think we go around offering our services and then stealing babies."

"Oh, dear. Oh, dear," said Mrs. Gordon.

"I wouldn't think that," Julia Blackwell said. Mrs. Noonan saw her eyes dart over to Ben.

"We got to know each other very well," Mrs. Noonan explained. "Chantrelle and Baby Owen even stayed with Alma for a while. So she knew how good Alma was with children."

"Then, after they'd moved out, she left him one day, just left him at my doorstep," Mrs. Gordon said. "I kept thinking she'd come back, that she only needed a break. But she hasn't yet."

"My. Oh, my," said Julia Blackwell. "Well, she'll probably turn up still. Don't you think? How long has it been?"

Mrs. Noonan looked at Mrs. Gordon for help, but Mrs. Gordon was inspecting her shoes.

"Has it been a long time?" Julia persisted.

Mrs. Noonan spoke quietly. "It's been months. We tried to find Chantrelle. We didn't have any luck. Alma is afraid to tell anyone official for fear they will take Baby Owen and put him in a foster home. So we keep hoping Chantrelle will turn up."

What must this woman think? What was Alma Gordon thinking? Had they done the right thing?

Julia Blackwell nodded vigorously. "I understand. I completely understand. Ben spent a night in Child Protective Services before they could track me down to come get him. Of all days, I cut my hand, stupidly, holding a bagel to cut it in half. Thought I'd cut a tendon. Had to go to the emergency room. Took most of the night and when I got home there was a note on my door." She paused and her eyes filled with tears.

"A note. From the police department. You'd think, being a policeman's daughter, that I would understand about tragedy. I had no idea." She stopped again. She glanced at Ben, but he had turned his back.

"Tragedy. Paul. Andrea. And Ben. They had found a temporary foster family to take Ben overnight and that's where I picked him up. I'm sure most foster homes are nice. This one was not."

The ladies all looked over at Ben. He made a noise, a quiet singsong noise. Julia Blackwell tiptoed to the French doors. As she opened them, his song became clear, a repeated refrain.

"MommyDaddyNannaBen."

Chapter 8

Alma Gordon and Frances Noonan stayed a while
longer, meeting Ben and playing with him for a short
time. Alma had never seen a child with eyes so blue.
She admired his giraffe, and he handed it to her without
a word. He did not seem troubled when Julia Blackwell
told him he might go to Mrs. Gordon's house to meet
another boy.

The ladies agreed they would try it that week.
Alma and Frances went home, and Alma collected
Baby Owen from Mr. Glenn, who reported that Owen
was babbling up a storm.

"We mostly talked baseball." Mr. Glenn waved his
arm toward the TV with the Giants' ball game.

Baby Owen was on all fours and pulled himself up
using Mr. Glenn's legs. Mr. Glenn bowed down to take
his hand because Owen couldn't stand yet without
toppling unexpectedly. Mrs. Gordon's heart squeezed,
seeing Mr. Glenn bent over with the child's tiny hand in
his meaty one, talking with her as if this was the most
natural thing in the world. Two old people who had
enjoyed love once, now with a second love. And a
baby.

She reached over to touch his unshaven cheek, but
Owen tugged him back into the room and Mr. Glenn
had already turned away.

"Did he know any stats, Albert?" Mrs. Gordon

asked. She didn't know what a stat was, but she'd heard Mr. Glenn mention the word to Jonathan Martin, a lawyer who lived next door to her.

"Not yet, not yet. But I'll get him up to speed. Lionel and I used to love to watch the ball games together. He knew all the teams, all the players, all the game situations."

Mrs. Gordon heard the melancholy in his voice. Lionel had given the Glenns so much trouble when he was a teen. Before his teen years, he was just another child in the building. There were several kids then, not like now. Some came through the teen years fine. Others, like the Carmichael's daughter and the Glenn's son, had challenges. The police even came once. Mrs. Gordon remembered the whole building in turmoil when Lionel went missing. Bessie was beside herself, and Mr. Glenn took time off work. The husbands went with him to search San Francisco's scarier neighborhoods where a teen might go. A teen with drug problems.

Oh, what a time. Lionel eventually disowned his parents and ran off to Oregon. The Glenns never saw him again. Mrs. Gordon's daughter, Sylvia, had been a few years older. A few years made so much difference when you were young. Sylvia had come through her teen years unscathed, but Mrs. Gordon knew it was just luck of the draw.

"Someday, I'll take Owen to the games just like Lionel. We caught a ball once, Lionel and I. It's still here, somewhere, maybe."

Mrs. Gordon followed his gaze around the apartment. It wasn't the cleanest. All the apartments had hardwood floors, and Mr. Glenn's was bare, which would be fine if there weren't dust bunnies in each corner and crunched up tortilla chips on the floor. How had those gotten there already? They had gone through the day before and "baby-proofed" the apartment for Owen, and Mrs. Gordon had taken the opportunity to vacuum and sweep, saying it was for the crawling baby. She brushed off piles of dusty magazines and set them in one of her extra baskets. She folded the cadre of sweaters that lay everywhere, hiding the tattered ones on the bottom of the stack on the shelf in the closet. Mr. Glenn set glass objects out of reach and covered the electrical outlets with baby-safe protection. He didn't object to anything she did, even when she plucked a holey undershirt out of the laundry basket and used it to oil the table.

Bessie Glenn's precious violin lay in its open case on a chair in the corner. Mrs. Gordon didn't know what to do, how to bring it up. Mr. Glenn loved Bessie and her death haunted him for years. Her violin was still there, unmoved, ready to be played, as if Bessie might appear at any moment.

As she stood staring at it, Mr. Glenn came behind her and circled her in his arms. He hugged her tight and without a word gently closed the case and placed it high up on top of the bookcase.

Now here was this man, stooped sideways, walking slow step by slow step to accommodate a toddler. Her toddler.

Her horoscope that morning said, "Good fortune is yours today." Mrs. Gordon knew when she read it and she knew it now that good fortune was hers every day.

"His diaper's new and he ate a big lunch. Should be ready for a nap now," Mr. Glenn said. "Me, too, soon as the game's over."

Mr. Glenn gave her a kiss as he turned over the baby. He kissed the baby too. "Remember what I told you. Don't talk about no-hitters."

"No," said Baby Owen.

"Shh," said Mr. Glenn.

Mrs. Gordon walked slowly to the elevator. She didn't have to lean so far to hold Baby Owen's hand. Back upstairs, she settled him in her lap on the couch. Who would teach Ben about baseball if Paul Blackwell stayed in jail? And Baby Owen? Mr. Glenn was so good with him. Her mind conjured the image of Big Owen, Baby Owen's father, and she shivered. She hugged the baby and thought how cruel life could be to children.

They started out so innocent and hopeful. But with each sharp rebuke, each careless word, they learned to be cautious. In Baby Owen's case, his mother, Chantrelle, simply had no idea what to do and no patience for a baby. She didn't know about hugging and coddling and kissing and sweet talk. Big Owen was even worse, a lumbering, overweight, overgrown boy with a mean face and a mouth full of chewing tobacco and reprimands. When Mrs. Gordon first met Baby Owen, he was silent and withdrawn. It was weeks before she saw him smile.

He certainly smiled now. He sat on her hip, his wet fist gripping her collar. He hid his head in her elbow, then peeked up at her, laughing, laughing. Then he ducked his head and did it again. Each time she feigned surprise, setting off extra fits of glee. It definitely took two to play this game.

Chantrelle would never have played this game.

Mrs. Gordon sighed, a familiar heaviness closing in. What if Chantrelle returned? What if she wanted Baby Owen back?

Chapter 9

Sarah's last month as a first-year medical resident was grueling. She was on the medicine wards, with a wide variety of patients and diseases. Ninety-year-olds with pneumonia, sixty-year-olds with liver failure, fifty-year-olds with bleeding ulcers. The wards were busy, the patients were sick, and Sarah thought she herself might get an ulcer from all the stress. Even though she knew stress didn't cause ulcers, just aspirin, NSAIDs, and a bacterium, *Helicobacter pylori*. Her stomach felt tied in knots all the time, like when she finally convinced a woman that her pancreatitis stemmed from too much alcohol, only to have her ask Sarah to keep this information from her concerned husband. Like when she had to tell a mother her twenty-one-year-old son, a delightful young man in his last year of college, would need dialysis for the foreseeable future, and maybe a kidney transplant.

She chided herself over this last patient. When she explained about dialysis, his mother cried. Then Sarah's throat tightened and she was grateful she had finished talking. All she could do was put her hand on his mother's. She couldn't speak. She felt uncomfortable remembering this, and she hoped they hadn't known she was on the verge of crying too.

If her patients saw tears, how would they take her seriously and have confidence in her recommendations?

She had to get her emotions in check.

The month finally ended, and she celebrated with her friend Helen, a fellow medical resident. Their internship year was over. They were now officially second-year residents.

She and Helen both had a Sunday off before starting their new rotations and the new year on Monday. Sarah wished she had a full weekend like her resort weekend the month before. That seemed like a lifetime ago.

Not the murder, though. Sarah thought about that all the time. What if she'd had to tell her twenty-one-year-old's mother that he was a murderer? Kidney disease was better.

Sarah and Helen had hardly seen each other over the past month because Helen had been in the ICU, the intensive care unit, with its notoriously difficult hours. Before that, Helen had been on the cardiology floor, so she had had two hard months in a row.

They met for lunch at an old Italian restaurant on Chestnut Street in the Marina. Chilly fingers of fog floated in from the Bay. Fog in San Francisco was not like the rare fog Sarah remembered growing up in Virginia. Fog there was thick and stationary, the typical pea soup type of fog. San Francisco fog was always in motion, swirling patches of fog here, billows of fog there, seeping, oozing, creeping through the atmosphere.

Sarah shivered. Fog horns sounded as she pulled open the door to the restaurant. Classic San Francisco weather for the end of June.

Helen was already seated and waved to her from a back table in the cozy restaurant. She looked as put together as always in a black turtleneck, her short blonde hair falling gracefully around her delicate features. Sarah pushed her own long hair out of her face, blown by the wind and moist from fog, never a good combination.

Sarah and Helen had met a year earlier, at the intern orientation picnic. Helen and her husband were from Boston, and Scott was finishing his PhD thesis in Japanese history from San Francisco, traveling back to the East Coast when needed. Helen had tried unsuccessfully to match into residency programs in Boston, so it was "because of her" that Scott had to complete his PhD long distance.

Scott was in Boston now. Sarah and Helen planned lunch and an afternoon movie in the old movie house down the street.

"Don't get too full," Helen said as Sarah sat. "Look what I made for the movie." She pulled out a gallon-sized plastic baggy filled with caramel corn. "I have this great recipe, but Scott likes the stuff too much, so he won't ever let me make it."

Sarah laughed. Poor Scott struggled with his weight. Helen always had a big appetite, and now that she was pregnant, she ate constantly. She was still tiny, making her beach ball-like belly more obvious. The last time Sarah noticed, it was more like a basketball. When had she gotten so big?

Helen sniffed the bag. "I put extra peanuts in. My own special touch."

"You know who would love this? Andy." As soon as Sarah said his name, her heart jumped. Andy Middleton had moved into her building earlier that year and shared an apartment with his brother, Mike, down

46

the hall from Sarah. Andy and Sarah started dating soon after they met. But, as Sarah had known almost from the beginning, a few months later he left on a yearlong journey to Asia to photograph elephants. He had taken a leave of absence from his job at the San Francisco Chronicle and had only been gone a few months. It seemed like forever. He was mostly out of cell phone range, and Sarah kept track of him through his brother and e-mail, and even that communication came in spurts.

"Andy loves caramel corn and he loves peanuts. And I wish he were here." Sarah had always known he was leaving and tried not to get too attached to him, but every reminder was difficult. She couldn't look at a picture of an elephant without Andy's whole presence flooding back.

Helen nodded. "I made enough for him, too, I think."

Sarah changed the subject. "I need to save some room. This place has such big portions, I'll have to get a doggy bag."

"Not me," Helen said. "I'm starving."

Sarah ordered spinach ravioli and Helen had lasagna, which came in a huge oval dish, large enough to feed two. She ate it all, along with salad, bread, and olive oil.

"I can't believe you can eat all that," Sarah said, breathing heavily after half a plate of ravioli. The bus boy started to take her plate away.

"If Scott were here, I'd get some of his bread, so can I have yours?" Helen asked.

"Have at it. I am stuffed," Sarah said.

Helen reached over so quickly, she knocked over

her water glass. "Oops. Sorry," she giggled as the bus boy whipped out a towel and dried the table.

Sarah immediately thought of the little boy from the resort, kicking his water glass over. Somehow she imagined Helen and Scott there, bickering as badly as that little boy's parents.

"How is Scott doing?" She was sorry immediately. Helen's happy mood disappeared. She ducked her head and turned her face to the side.

"I don't think he wants to be a father," Helen said quietly, her face still turned. "Even after all this time. He never talks about it except to say how much things will change. For him. I know the brunt of the work will fall to Scott. And now…"

Helen's voice trailed off. Sarah waited.

"We had a huge fight before he left," was all Helen said.

"I'm so sorry." Sarah took both Helen's hands in hers. She thought of the little boy who sat in her arms so trustingly. She thought of Baby Owen, full of fun and joy.

"This is a baby," she said. "A part of him. Of you. He'll come around soon. This is one of the most wonderful, special times in your lives."

Helen nodded slowly. "I feel like it is. I can only hope and pray Scott does too."

The next day Sarah started an elective rotation, gastroenterology. Elective rotations were easy, easy hours, no overnight call, no weekend hours, no direct patient care responsibilities. She would even have a week of vacation, which she intended to take at home, sleeping in every day. She would work in the clinic with an attending physician, see his patients with him and follow him to the inpatient hospital wards as a consultant, not as the primary doctor of record. She had one elective in her internship year, pulmonary, and this was her second. The thought of an entire month of set hours and dinner at home instead of on the run at the hospital made her giddy.

And a little guilty. Helen was going from the ICU to the medicine wards, which Sarah had just finished. A third hard rotation. Poor Helen. She was saving her easy rotations for the end of her pregnancy.

Sarah liked gastroenterology, with its variety of diseases such as inflammatory bowel disease, hepatitis, and gastroesophageal reflux disease, all of which she saw her first day. She liked the attending doctor, an older man with a great sense of humor. He made the patients laugh, he made Sarah laugh, and he still seemed competent and caring.

Except with one patient who had pancreatic cancer and was not responding to chemotherapy. Her attending danced around the terrible prognosis even when the patient pushed him. Her attending didn't look him in the eye but kept his gaze on the computer CT images in front of him. He left the room to get the patient's printed prescription for pain medicine, and the man turned to Sarah.

"My wife has always wanted us to see the Taj Mahal. She says we need to go now. I'm still working, I feel fine. I think I have a few years left, and the doc hasn't said otherwise. What do you think?"

Sarah looked right at him and told herself he hadn't seen her blink back tears. She touched his arm and nodded toward the images on the screen. "I think you should see the Taj Mahal," she said.

The man began to cry, as if he'd been holding on to these tears for so long they were ready to spill over unchecked now. "Why couldn't the doc have told me that?" he said. "Why am I still working? She also wants to see the Great Wall of China. I told her someday we will. Will we?"

Sarah handed him the box of tissues. He blew his nose and wiped his eyes.

"You won't feel as well in a few months," Sarah said. "Someday is now."

Sarah got home early her first night, before six, drained from this last patient. Her attending wasn't drained, but she was.

She had known the boy was coming. She still came to a halt when she saw him in the lobby, the little boy with the blue eyes. Something about his eyes drew her in, and she couldn't look away.

He gaped at her, his expression confused. Then he grabbed the dress of the woman he was with and screamed, "Mommmmmmeeeee, Mommmmmmeeeee!"

The woman bent and hugged the little boy, who was now crying. "Ben, Ben, shh, shh, it's all right." To Sarah, she said, "I'm so sorry. He's been through a lot."

Sarah didn't know what to say. Should she tell this woman she knew who the boy was, knew about what happened? Should she slink away and not cause the boy more pain? She didn't have time to decide because the elevator door opened with a ding, and Enid Carmichael strode out, her fidgety dog in her arms.

"Sarah," she shouted from across the lobby, "perfect timing." She motioned for Sarah to come over. As Sarah got close, she whispered, again loudly, "This is that boy you know. From the newspaper. And his grandmother. Maybe you can introduce me?"

Sarah glanced back at the boy and his grandmother, embarrassed. They had clearly heard every word.

Sarah stepped toward the woman. "I met your son and his family on vacation, down in Big Sur. I think this little guy might recognize me."

"Oh, my," the woman said. "I was there too. I don't remember you. I'm Julia Blackwell."

"You were there?" Sarah said. "I didn't see you either. I was only there for the weekend."

"Oh, I came after that. My son called and asked me to come and help out with Ben. He wanted some time alone with his wife. I suppose you met her too?"

Before Sarah could answer, Mrs. Carmichael stepped in, her leathery hand extended. "I'm Enid Carmichael. A friend of Frances Noonan's. I'd be happy to help out…" She peered down at Ben. "I'm not good with kids. Anything else, though, you just let me know."

"Thank you, that's very kind." Julia Blackwell leaned and took Ben's hand. "It's getting late for us. We need to go now. Very nice to meet you."

Before the door closed behind them, Mrs. Carmichael bellowed, "So, that's the murderer's mother, huh?"

Chapter 10

Enid Carmichael watched Julia Blackwell and the child walk down the front steps and out of sight. That boy must have been upstairs for his practice visit with Frances Noonan and Alma Gordon. She hadn't seen them come in!

Enid grabbed Sarah's arm and led her to the elevator. "We'll find out all about the visit. See if they learned more about the killing." Sarah tried to disengage her arm, none too discreetly, so Mrs. Carmichael held firm. The girl might be able to remember more details from the resort. Mrs. Carmichael knew a sugar coating when she heard one. She wanted the juicy details, not just the bare minimum. Why didn't Sarah just tell them everything?

Mrs. Carmichael paused before she knocked on Mrs. Noonan's door. Her good hearing could pick out Fog Ladies voices from inside. Frances Noonan and Alma Gordon, even Olivia Honeycut. What were they all doing here?

"I wanted Julia to meet Mrs. Honeycut, in case she is needed to watch Ben," Frances Noonan said, holding the door open wide. Sarah slid in ahead of her, but Enid made sure to get to the living room first. Mrs. Noonan had a very comfortable wing back chair, and Enid needed a comfortable chair much more than young Sarah.

"You didn't call me," Mrs. Carmichael said. "I had to go to the lobby to meet her myself."

"I thought you made it clear you didn't do babysitting," Olivia Honeycut rasped.

"Hmph." Mrs. Carmichael searched around for something to eat. Usually Mrs. Noonan had a tart or a pie or cookies at least. An empty plate held crumbs, nothing more. The tot must have eaten everything.

"Tea?" Frances Noonan asked.

It was no use asking for coffee, especially with Sarah here. Frances didn't drink coffee. More importantly, Sarah thought Enid had given it up due to severe heartburn and palpitations. Well, she had given it up. She'd given up those luscious Starbucks lattes. They were too expensive anyway. And Enid's own drip coffee didn't count. She'd had her allotted cups this morning, and Sarah need not know anything about it.

"No, thank you, Frances. No tea." Mrs. Carmichael relaxed back. She would like a chair like this. She sniffed, "Even if I don't babysit, I still would have liked to meet her. So, tell me everything."

"Well," said Mrs. Noonan, lowering herself to the edge of her flowery couch, "things do sound dreadful."

"The man is guilty, that's all there is to it." Olivia Honeycut slid over to make room for Mrs. Noonan.

"Oh, do tell, do tell." Mrs. Carmichael clapped her hands in excitement. How had she missed this?

"Olivia, we don't know anything. You're jumping to conclusions," said Frances Noonan.

"We know he lied about where he was," said Olivia Honeycut. "And that he has no alibi. If Harriet Flynn were here, she'd say his goose was cooked."

"Where is Harriet?" Mrs. Carmichael peered

around.

"She's not much into babysitting." Alma Gordon spoke from the corner, where she sat with that baby. He dropped clothes pins into a glass milk bottle. Clank, clank, clank. How did Alma stand it? If she had a plastic milk jug like the rest of the world, the noise wouldn't be so jarring.

Mrs. Noonan's cat, Camouflage, sat near them, seemingly oblivious to the obnoxious noise. Mrs. Carmichael's dog would never be so placid. That cacophony would rile him up, deservedly so.

Mrs. Carmichael turned back to her ally, Olivia Honeycut. "Well, tell me more. If he wasn't at yoga, which would be a ridiculous place to be anyway, where was he? And why did he pretend to be at yoga? Couldn't he think up a more manly place to be? Couldn't he say he was at a bar? Shooting pool? Doing things men do?"

"I'm so sorry you missed the discussion with his mother so you could have asked her yourself," Mrs. Noonan said. Mrs. Carmichael saw her wink at Sarah, who stood by the couch.

"I'm sorry too," Mrs. Carmichael huffed. "Wasn't invited. So, did you pin her down?"

"Gracious, Enid, you'd think we were the police. We are trying to *help*, remember?" said Mrs. Noonan.

"If he's guilty, he's guilty. Not much we can do about that. Just help out with the boy, I guess," said Mrs. Honeycut.

Sarah spoke quietly. "Is it pretty clear, then? Does it look like he did it? What did his mother say?"

"Well, to start with, Paul is pretty distraught," Mrs. Noonan said. "His wife is dead and he found her. He says the screams the neighbor heard were his. The scene was gruesome."

Enid Carmichael was beside herself. "Oh, I can't believe I missed this. You ladies should have called me!"

"Shh, Enid, please," Alma Gordon said.

Mrs. Noonan continued. "The police can only determine the time of death to within an hour or two, partly because of the hot weather that night. Apparently they use a drop in body temperature to pinpoint things, but in this case it was not helpful. So they look at rigor mortis and a discoloration of the skin, but they can't say for certain. So the police think Andrea was alive and screaming when the nine-one-one call was placed, and that Paul didn't have time to set the scene up the way he wanted or to get his alibi in place."

"Yep. That sounds about right," said Mrs. Carmichael. Frances Noonan was deluding herself if she believed this guy was innocent. "That's why he has that hokey yoga alibi."

"That's what the police think," said Mrs. Noonan. "But, of course, Paul says she was dead when he got home. He told the police he was at yoga because that's what he told his wife. He said he was so shocked he couldn't think, and when they asked him where he was, he just told them what he had told her. He didn't know they weren't having a class that night."

"Why would he ever say yoga? Especially if he didn't go?" Mrs. Carmichael asked.

"Usually he did go. About half the time, at least. But sometimes he didn't, and that's what happened that night."

"So where does he say he was really?" Mrs.

Carmichael asked.

"In the park," Mrs. Honeycut said. "He says he was sitting in the park and no one saw him."

"Oh, come on. In the park? Is he kidding?" Mrs. Carmichael looked around for confirmation.

"He wasn't just sitting in the park," said Mrs. Noonan. "He was writing."

"Writing?" said Sarah. "He was writing in the park?"

"Yes. He told his mother that he didn't like to write at home because it made his wife mad. So instead of going to yoga, which he'd been doing every Tuesday night for years, he would go to the park and write. Especially now that it's summer."

"That's the stupidest thing I ever heard," said Mrs. Carmichael. "What a lame-brain alibi. He said he was sitting in a park in San Francisco on a sweltering evening? Writing? Couldn't he come up with anything better?"

"Apparently not. And that's the problem," said Mrs. Noonan.

Mrs. Honeycut added, "Either he did it and he can't think fast enough or he didn't do it and no one's going to believe him."

"Wait a minute," said Sarah. "How does he know no one saw him? Someone might have seen him."

"Nope. He told his mother that he can't think when it's noisy, so he finds the most deserted area of the park and sits there. He said he's never seen anyone," said Mrs. Gordon.

"What a crock of a story," said Mrs. Carmichael. "He did it. You'd think he could have thought up something better for a million dollars."

"That's another thing," Mrs. Honeycut said. "He claims he didn't even know his wife had the insurance policy. Said it was through her work and she never told him. Nonetheless, he's the beneficiary."

"Who else would have done it? Is there anyone else on the policy?" asked Sarah.

"Just the boy. Ben," said Mrs. Gordon.

"No one else could have done it," said Mrs. Honeycut. "The door wasn't forced. There was no sign of a struggle. It's not like she opened the door to a stranger at night."

"You heard what Julia said. Paul doesn't lock the door when he goes to yoga. He said the lock makes a loud noise when it turns, so they keep the door unlocked so he won't wake his wife in case she goes to sleep before he comes back," said Mrs. Noonan. "It sounds preposterous, I know. But that's what he told his mother."

"Oh, this gets better all the time," said Mrs. Carmichael. "He left his wife and child in their unlocked home and went to sit in a park at night, and when he came back, he found his wife in a bloody pool in the kitchen. Is that correct?"

"I know it doesn't look good," said Frances Noonan. "But remember, I know his family. You've all met Julia. Sarah, you met the man. He couldn't have done this, could he?"

Enid Carmichael watched Sarah intently. She was hesitating, that was for sure.

"You must have formed some type of opinion," Olivia Honeycut persisted, "some judgment of the situation."

Still the girl didn't answer. How could she not have

an opinion?

"I only met them briefly," she finally said. "I honestly believe that man loved his wife and was trying desperately to change her mind about leaving."

"Desperate." Mrs. Carmichael latched on to the word. "What would a desperate man do?"

The Fog Ladies all turned to Sarah.

"I don't know," Sarah said. "I just don't know."

Chapter 11

Alma Gordon watched Julia Blackwell push the "play" button on her ancient answering machine.

"Listen to this," Julia Blackwell said as the machine spoke. "Mrs. Blackwell, this is Spencer Tremaine—"

"Spencer Tremaine?" Alma Gordon croaked. "*The* Spencer Tremaine?"

"Shh. I want to hear this," said Frances Noonan.

"—and I'd like to talk to you about your son's case. I'd like to speak to both of you about representing him. I think he needs a top-notch defense, and I would be interested in leading the team. Juries don't like men who kill the mother of their child. I think you'd be remiss not to call me. You can reach me through my San Francisco office."

Mrs. Blackwell punched the button again, hitting it so hard the machine fell off the table. "What do you think of that?"

Alma Gordon, Frances Noonan, and Harriet Flynn all jumped forward to try to catch the machine, but it caught on its cord and slowly dangled to and fro. They had come to pick up Ben, who was now in his bedroom retrieving his sand bucket and shovel. They would drop Mrs. Flynn at her doctor's office, which was in the Sunset District near Ocean Beach. While they waited for her, they were going to make a sandcastle. Baby

Owen had his own bucket and squatted on the floor with the bucket in his hands.

"Was that really Spencer Tremaine?" Mrs. Gordon asked.

"Sounds much different than on television," Mrs. Noonan said.

"Who's Spencer Tremaine?" Mrs. Flynn asked.

"Who's Spencer Tremaine?" said Mrs. Gordon, aghast. "Who's Spencer Tremaine? Didn't you follow the Baker Beach killings?"

"Why would I ever follow the Baker Beach killings? Ladies of ill repute, murdered and left on a nudist beach—why would I ever subject myself to such tawdry goings on?"

"Well, Spencer Tremaine was the lawyer who represented the killer. Got him off, if you can believe it. The whole case hinged on a technical issue—"

"No search warrant," said Mrs. Noonan.

"Yes, no search warrant." Mrs. Gordon knew everything about the case. "The police said they didn't need one, as the evidence was in full view through the window. Mr. Tremaine successfully argued that to see inside the house, the police needed to step onto private property through a latched gate and even climb into the bushes to see through the window. Thus, when Mr. Butts opened the door and they rushed in to seize the incriminating objects, they were conducting an illegal search. So the jury was never told about the evidence."

"He said the Fourth Amendment assures a right to privacy within one's home and protects against unreasonable search and seizure. So, Mr. Butts walked free," Mrs. Noonan said.

"What incriminating objects?" said Mrs. Flynn.

"Oh, you don't want to know," said Mrs. Noonan.

"Ladies' undergarments, a bloody rope, and handcuffs," said Mrs. Gordon at the same time. How had she remembered all this?

"And this Mr. Butts is out there because of Spencer Tremaine?" Mrs. Flynn asked. "Why would you want to have anything to do with him? A man who makes deals with the devil is no better than the devil himself."

"Yes, that's how part of me feels," said Julia Blackwell.

"Part?" said Mrs. Flynn.

"Well," said Julia, "when Spencer Tremaine took that Baker Beach case, people could not understand it. It seemed so open and shut. The man was certainly guilty, at least in the public's eyes."

"So why would you ever want to associate with someone who willingly defends such a fiend?"

"Because now Mr. Butts is free," said Julia Blackwell. "My Paul could be free."

If he takes the case, Alma Gordon thought, I might get to meet Spencer Tremaine.

"Will you come with me?" asked Julia.

Alma Gordon whipped her head around, words about to spill out. Of course she would go! She'd get to meet the great man himself!

"Frances, you are very levelheaded," Julia Blackwell continued. "Will you come with me? You'll know if this is right."

Mrs. Gordon shut her mouth.

"You already know this is not right," said Mrs. Flynn. "This Spencer Tremaine will meet his maker in the end."

Chapter 12

Frances Noonan studied Julia Blackwell. She wanted Frances to meet with the skilled but unprincipled lawyer. A mother, hoping, praying for a miracle.

"Of course I'll come," she said.

The man was actually available the next day. His office was in Embarcadero Center, a group of towering dark buildings in the Financial District with offices, restaurants and shops. The office itself was light and airy, with an oriental rug, several deep leather chairs and an enormous glass-topped desk, completely bare save for one thin file.

They were ushered into the office by a tall blonde woman with stylish glasses. Spencer Tremaine stood from the desk and came around to greet them. He was shorter than he appeared on television, but his voice was full and confident. He launched into his spiel as soon as they sat, murmuring about what a difficult time it was, but how they needed to act quickly to control the information getting to the media to stem the tide of public opinion. He had a large team at the ready if Mrs. Blackwell and her son, whom he would visit at the jail later that day, agreed to let him take their case. A situation like this was delicate, and finding just the right approach was of utmost importance in allowing the matter to conclude in a satisfactory way for all concerned. He had experience and a reputation as someone who could not be dealt with lightly. He had connections and endless resources all prepared to begin work today to facilitate a speedy resolution.

And then there was the matter of the fee. Such talent did not come cheap, but you get what you pay for, and after all, you will soon have insurance money to soften any financial hardship.

"If you decide on another lawyer, another firm, and then the case is lost," he said in his smooth voice, "will you wonder what might have been if you'd only gone with the best?"

Mrs. Noonan thought this was going a little far. His presentation was impressive, but now he was preying on their vulnerabilities.

Spencer Tremaine wasn't finished yet. He came right over to Julia Blackwell and took her hand in his. Mrs. Noonan saw her soften.

"What's important here is to get your son out of jail and back on his feet so he can make a life for himself and his son. So they can be a family again."

Chapter 13

Family. What was a family?

It was one of her drinking days. He was too young then. He hadn't yet learned how to predict it. He could only think about his new red yo-yo and the trick he learned to do. He had figured it out all by himself, no one had shown him. His father was away that weekend, and his mother was in one of her cleaning moods. She didn't want to see the yo-yo, and he had to show someone. He didn't dare take it to school because Mrs. Bender confiscated toys. Just last week his friend, Buster, lost his super-high-fly airplane to her drawer.

So he brought Buster home after school. He was so excited about showing off his trick he forgot to tell Buster to take off his shoes. Before they were halfway up the stairs, his mother was on them. She stood in the hallway in her see-through pink bathrobe, screaming up at them about the dirt on her clean floors. Her shrill voice slurred and started to shake, her words not making sense, not about the dirt anymore but about his father not coming home that day after all. Buster ran down the stairs and out the door. Buster never said a word to him about it. But it was a long time before they played again.

Chapter 14

Frances Noonan couldn't help laughing as she relayed the conversation with the lawyer to the Fog Ladies, including Sarah. Sarah seemed to have a lot of free time this month, Mrs. Noonan noticed.

"Unfortunately, I think his hard sell worked. Julia is strongly considering his proposal."

Harriet Flynn crossed herself. "She needs our prayers."

"She needs more than that," Enid Carmichael said. "Her son's going to prison, and this lawyer's going to eat up all her life savings."

"What was he like?" asked Alma Gordon. "Did his hair glow like it does on TV?" She looked far too dreamy, Mrs. Noonan thought.

"I didn't think you cared about hair, Alma. Mr. Glenn's not got much up top," said Mrs. Carmichael.

"Enid!" said Mrs. Noonan. "What a dreadful thing to say." Where was Enid's filter?

"Ladies, ladies," said Olivia Honeycut. "You're straying from the point. Which is, how does he think he can get Paul Blackwell off?"

They all turned back to Mrs. Noonan. "He's short on answers at the moment," she told them. "He preached a lot of fancy words, but he didn't say anything concrete. Oh, I hope Julia steers clear of him. I didn't get a very good feeling. Even his young office woman made me uncomfortable. She was a beauty, could have been a model, I'm sure, but there she sat in his front room, sitting and staring and not doing anything at all. It was unnerving."

"Beauty is wasted on the youth," said Mrs. Honeycut.

"Beauty is skin deep, and it sounds like this one didn't have much between the ears," said Mrs. Carmichael.

"Beauty leads to trouble," said Mrs. Flynn.

"I think *this man* is trouble," said Mrs. Noonan. "I only hope Julia thinks so too."

Alma Gordon stayed back when the ladies left. "What else, Frances, what else? What was he wearing? Did you get to see that sleek glass desk they show on television? Tell me again about his hair."

Frances smiled as she set out saucers and a second plate of sugar cookies. She would try to remember every detail to tell her friend. "What kind of tea would you like?"

"Oh, no, no thank you, Frances," Alma said. "I can't stay. Mr. Glenn is taking me bowling. Can you imagine? Bowling. I just wanted to hear a little more."

Frances Noonan turned off the kettle and sighed. Tea for one was fine, but a far cry from tea for two. No, she could not imagine bowling.

Chapter 15

Sarah hesitated before knocking on Helen and Scott's door. Helen had been all smiles when she issued the dinner invitation, yet Sarah wondered if something was wrong. Helen was on the medicine wards. Usually the wards were so exhausting that even on a day off like this Saturday was for her, having someone over to dinner was too much. Plus, Helen had morning sickness, so she had extra reason to want to take it easy.

She was still her same perky self, and Sarah marveled at her energy. Brushing her teeth in the residents' room after vomiting, Helen looked immaculate as always, if a little green. "It's a good thing I didn't have this all along, or I'd be pretty peeved by now," she had said, smiling all the while.

Sarah had eaten many dinners with Helen and Scott. Scott was a wonderful cook, and Sarah loved each new dish he concocted. He started cooking the year before, when Helen began her internship year. Helen said it was darned embarrassing remembering what she'd cooked for him all that time she was in medical school, given the talent he turned out to have.

His meals seemed simple. Sarah once tried to copy a tomato pasta dish because Scott promised it was impossible to go wrong with just five ingredients. But hers tasted nothing like his, her pasta all gummy and the sauce too thin and with none of the flavor of Scott's.

So she gave up and looked forward to returning to his kitchen.

Standing outside the door, Sarah remembered what Scott said the last time she visited.

"I'm going to be the one taking care of the thing, so I hope it naps so I can get my thesis done."

Even Helen couldn't hide her hurt feelings. "Not 'thing,' Scott. Baby." She'd said it so sadly.

Sarah took a deep breath. All was quiet inside the apartment. As she knocked, she heard a sharp, indecipherable bark from Scott. Then silence, then Helen opened the door with her usual smile.

They sat down to eat almost immediately. Scott served chicken salad with almonds, perfect for the summery day, and a cold raspberry soup. He told Sarah the soup had only three ingredients, but she passed on his offer to write out the recipe.

They talked about the changes to come. Scott's PhD was not going well, and he was rushing to finish research before Helen's due date.

"I feel like I'm going to be the sole caretaker, what with your guys' hours," he said.

Sarah thought about Ben, with his grandmother to watch him. Both Helen's and Scott's parents were dead. Helen's were killed in a boating accident when she was a sophomore in college. She met Scott at a group for students who had lost a parent and was amazed to find they had both lost two parents and were also only children. It was a strong bond. Helen said without Scott she would have fallen apart when her parents died.

Sarah understood completely. Her own mother died when she was in high school and her father when she was in college. Her brother, Tim, who lived in

Washington, DC, was her lifeblood. Losing her mother to ovarian cancer had changed her life. It was part of the reason she was a doctor. It was also why she clung to the Fog Ladies like she did. And why she was such good friends with Helen. Being without family was hard.

"What about day care?" Sarah asked. "Would you two have objections to something like that?"

Helen stared at her hands. "Scott looked into it. It would cost almost my entire salary."

"What? For day care?" Sarah asked.

"Not your entire salary," Scott said. "But two thirds of it. Two kids in day care is too expensive for us."

"Two kids?" Sarah said.

Neither Helen nor Scott responded right away. Then Helen nodded slowly. "Yes. Twins. Two kids."

"Oh." Sarah let out a huge sigh.

"I missed my first ultrasound, I had a patient crashing and had to cancel it. Then I had to cancel it again. I never got around to rescheduling it until my OB said I absolutely had to have it at twenty weeks. We've known for a while but haven't told anyone. It was quite a surprise."

"It's still a surprise," said Scott. "It's all a surprise."

Helen was worried enough when she told the program director she was pregnant. Now twins! No wonder she hadn't said anything. Helen and Sarah were the only female interns in their class of nine. Of the three women in the third-year class and four in the new intern class, none had children. If Helen got sick or needed bed rest, one of the other residents would have to cover her duties. Her news would not be greeted with enthusiasm.

Scott certainly did not look enthusiastic. He sat glumly across from Sarah, his body hunched away from Helen. For once, Helen wasn't eating. Her raspberry soup was untouched, her chicken salad just pushed around on her plate.

"I may have met a murderer," Sarah said, desperate for something to talk about other than the babies, to add life to this dead conversation.

Chapter 16

"Sarah, what was the name of that resort you went to in Big Sur? Where you met the Blackwells?" Alma Gordon walked with Sarah into the building later that same night. She noted how Sarah slowed to match her gait. The girl was so conscientious.

"Gosh, it seems like such a long time ago, but I was there the last week of May. It's called Paradise Cove. And it truly is a paradise. The rooms are huge, and they're all suites, I think because it's family oriented. The food is pretty good, considering they've got a captive audience. And the setting is spectacular. Gardens and a pool and the cliffs and the ocean. I don't know how they do it for the prices."

"It sounds wonderful," Mrs. Gordon said.

"Just thinking about it makes me want to go back. It was a pretty easy weekend trip."

"I was thinking of going myself. It sounds like it would be appropriate for Baby Owen, and Mr. Glenn and I were thinking of taking a trip together." Mrs. Gordon peeked up at Sarah to gauge her response.

Sarah didn't miss a beat, bless her heart. She just smiled at Mrs. Gordon and said, "I think you both would love it."

Sarah told her it was a small resort and she might have to leave a message to make her reservation, and it did take a few calls to get through. Sarah also asked her to see if there were two rooms available. Mrs. Gordon was surprised when Sarah suggested that they all go together, but it made perfect sense. Sarah wanted to go back. Mrs. Gordon didn't drive, and Mr. Glenn had not been looking forward to driving on those twisty roads. He said his reflexes weren't up to it. Sarah had borrowed Frances Noonan's car when she went the first time, and she said she'd feel better about taking the car again if it wasn't just for herself. Mr. Glenn offered his car, but Sarah couldn't drive a stick shift. She said she was on an easy rotation that month and any weekend would work. The resort had room for them the last weekend of July, which sounded perfect.

Frances Noonan arrived with oatmeal cookies as Mrs. Gordon finished her packing. Her horoscope that morning read, "Food plays a role today," and she eyed the cookies hungrily.

"Hope I made enough. I know what an appetite Mr. Glenn has. He ate an entire blueberry pie himself last week, kept shaving off another piece, another piece. That man sure can eat," Mrs. Noonan said with a smile.

As she spoke, Mr. Glenn stepped out of Alma's bathroom, her various pill bottles in his hand. Mrs. Noonan's back was to him as she set the cookie plate on the counter. Mrs. Gordon stood helplessly between them as Mrs. Noonan continued talking.

"He ate that leftover roasted chicken I was saving for Sarah, just kept picking at it until it was gone. And the last time the ladies came, he ate all the apple muffins himself, six of them, before the ladies even arrived. I had to serve coffee cake instead, remember?"

Mrs. Noonan turned around. Mrs. Gordon saw her smile evaporate. Mr. Glenn stood there, his portly shape on full display in his undershirt.

"Oh, oh. Sorry," said Mrs. Noonan.

"Oh, dear. Oh, dear," said Mrs. Gordon.

Mr. Glenn, bless him, was unabashed. "You are absolutely right, Frances. I hope you have more because those cookies look delicious."

Frances Noonan smiled and said she did, and she'd be happy to send them with another plate. "It gives me no end of pleasure to bake for someone who appreciates it so."

Mrs. Gordon thought this should smooth things over. She piped up anyway to change the subject. "And I appreciate you, too, Albert, for helping with my pills." She turned to Mrs. Noonan. "I can't open the bottles myself, so he's putting all my pills in this little box for our trip." She held up a yellow plastic daily pill container.

But Frances didn't look at it. She was already at the door, and her voice sounded flat when she said, "I'll get those cookies." She didn't look at Alma when she handed them over a few minutes later. Oh, dear. Had they offended her somehow? Shouldn't it be Albert who was offended?

They packed the cookies in the car along with all the baby gear. Mrs. Gordon thought Mrs. Noonan might come out to say good-bye, but she did not.

The weather was agreeably perfect as they left San Francisco. The sun was shining and it was almost seventy degrees by ten o'clock, very warm for the city. Mrs. Gordon rolled down the back windows of the old car, and Baby Owen turned his head to the wind and cried out with glee.

They stopped for a short visit with Mrs. Gordon's

daughter, Sylvia, and her husband, Harold, in Sunnyvale. The top of Mr. Glenn's head glistened in the heat, and he had to mop his brow with one of Baby Owen's spit up cloths. Poor man wasn't meant for this kind of heat.

Sylvia and Harold had been married less than two years, but you'd never know it. Mrs. Gordon admired their easy, comfortable relationship. You'd think they'd known each other their whole lives. They even looked alike, with dark hair and glasses and big, toothy smiles. Constant smiles.

Sylvia produced some water toys for Baby Owen, a beach ball and a blow-up turtle for him to ride in at the swimming pool.

"That turtle took me all morning to blow up. It was impossible. Treat it with care." Harold said it with a smile, of course.

"I had no problem at all with the beach ball." Sylvia grinned at him. "I think you'd better head to the gym more often, build up those lungs."

"But can you do this?" Harold hoisted Baby Owen onto his shoulders.

"Nope," Sylvia said. "Can't do that. But watch out, he's spitting up into your hair."

"Oh, dear, she's right." Mrs. Gordon hurried over to him. "And Mr. Glenn has the spit up cloth. Oh, dear."

Harold just laughed. He brought the baby around front and swiped his wet hair with his hand.

"Here you go, honey." Sylvia handed him a wet towel. They stood there beaming like newlyweds. Ah, youth.

Although Sylvia and Harold weren't young. They

were both in their forties. Sylvia had waited to get married. "I'm waiting for the right man, not just any man," she'd always said. And she seemed to have gotten him.

They lived in a 1950s era Eichler house, all sliding glass doors and natural wood. The house had belonged to Alma's older sister and her husband, and Sylvia moved in when they died. The house was perfect for children, with an inner courtyard as well as a front and back yard, but Baby Owen was the only child other than Sylvia to play there. Radiant heat warmed the floor for Owen's crawling legs. All the homes were surrounded by tall fences, left over from the original design of the neighborhood. Even so, Sylvia and Harold knew their neighbors well.

Sylvia was a landscape designer and her front yard was immaculate, with orange and lemon trees and bougainvillea that spilled over the fence. Harold was a junior high science teacher. They met when Sylvia's twelve-year-old neighbor asked her to give a talk for his class on edible plants. Sylvia suspected the boy's mother, Kate, of setting the whole thing up, but Kate claimed innocence. They married six months after they met, and the young neighbor had a special place in the ceremony.

Mrs. Gordon looked at the two of them now, with Baby Owen swinging on Harold's bent arm. How sad they wouldn't have children of their own. Sylvia had wanted children, but she gave up on that idea years ago. She was very practical, her Sylvia.

Sylvia sent them on their way with glass bottles of iced tea. The good weather held until they finished the drinks. Then, as they came over the summit on

Highway 17, the skies turned gray, and by the time they got to Monterey they could barely see the ocean because of the fog. Thank goodness Sarah was driving. The curves and the cliffs would be treacherous enough in good weather, let alone the poor visibility they had today. Mr. Glenn could never have done it. He looked a little pale even in the passenger seat.

And poor Baby Owen. It was a long trip for him, and thankfully he slept through most of it, nestled into his car seat, his head lolling to the side like a wilted flower. But toward the end, and it was her own fault for giving him apple juice instead of milk, he threw up, all of a sudden with no warning.

With no place to pull over on the narrow, twisty road, they drove on. Mrs. Gordon tried her best to sop up the sour fluid with their beach towel. She rolled the windows down again, even though the air was now cold.

An actual drizzle greeted them when they pulled into the resort in the midafternoon. They all opened their doors and climbed out at once, breathing in the fresh, wet, vomitless air. Sarah somehow still seemed composed, and she actually apologized for the weather, saying she hoped she hadn't oversold the place, especially if they were going to be indoors the whole weekend.

"That's what I planned anyway," Mr. Glenn said. "This is my first trip with Alma, after all." He gave her a little squeeze on the arm.

Mrs. Gordon was mortified. What would Sarah think?

But there was Sarah, smiling as always, rolling up the car windows and acting like there was nothing wrong with two people in their seventies planning to spend their weekend canoodling. With a baby, of course. What a dear she was.

Chapter 17

Sarah and Mr. Glenn went to check in while Mrs. Gordon sat in the car with Baby Owen. The proprietor offered them hot apple cider as they filled out their registration cards.

"Last week we had lemonade, but the weather didn't seem to call for that today. Jeepers, it's cold for July." He passed a cup to Sarah. He was wearing a wool sweater plus a corduroy jacket buttoned almost to the top.

"I had lemonade the last time I was here, in May," Sarah said, warming her hands on the cup.

"Well then, welcome back. We always appreciate repeat customers. Lemonade in May, hot cider in July. Go figure."

The steaming cider tasted delicious, and Sarah relaxed now that she was out of the car.

"Did you have to drive far in this soup?"

"All the way from San Francisco," said Mr. Glenn. "Thought we'd never get here. I haven't been down here in years. All those hairpin turns. It was farther than I remembered."

"Yes, a lot of people say that. And traffic. Sometimes that's a surprise, so much traffic these days," said the proprietor. "I see from your reservation that you need a crib in one of the rooms. How old is the child?" This he addressed to Sarah.

Sarah turned to Mr. Glenn. "I'm not sure. Mr. Glenn, do you know?"

"Darned if I know," he said.

The man looked from Sarah to Mr. Glenn. "Ahem," he said.

Sarah started to laugh. "The person who knows is in the car with him. He's a year and some months. Do you have to know exactly?"

"No, but we have two different cribs, and the older kids can climb out of the smaller crib. That age can be climbers. Better give you the big crib. His mother is in the car, then?"

"Not exactly his mother," said Mr. Glenn. The man glanced up from his writing.

"More like his grandmother." Sarah winked at Mr. Glenn.

"Ah, the grandmother. That's fine." He collected their cards and placed them on the counter. "Are you all related?"

"As much as a bunch of people who live together and see each other every day," said Mr. Glenn.

"We're not related, but we might as well be. I think of us as one big, extended family," said Sarah.

"You all live together, though?" The proprietor examined the cards again.

"We live in the same apartment building," said Sarah.

"Oh, I remember those days," he said with a smile. "I lived in the city for years, just after college, and I knew everything there was to know about my neighbors in my building. I lived in the Richmond district. How about you?"

"Pacific Heights," said Mr. Glenn. "I've lived there

forever. I've seen lots of people come and go."

"And you?" The man read from the card. "Sarah James? Have you been there long?"

"Just a year in San Francisco," Sarah said.

"Ah, a transplant," said the man. "I thought I detected a tiny accent. I'm from Virginia and I bet dollars to donuts you are too."

Sarah laughed. "You are the first person who's ever noticed. I thought I left it behind years ago. I can't hear your accent either."

"I've moved around. Haven't been back in years. I couldn't drawl if I tried."

"Me either," Sarah said. "Though I don't think I ever drawled to start with. I'm from the north, just outside DC."

"So am I! Arlington. It's a small world. What brought you to California?"

"My job," she said.

"She's a doctor." Mr. Glenn smiled at her and stood up taller.

Sarah set her empty cup on the counter. Mrs. Gordon must be wondering where they were all this time. "We'd better get going. They might be getting cold." She gestured to the driveway.

"Ah, yes, I'll let you settle in. The rooms are next door to each other. Dinner starts at five, but just let me or Marco, our chef, know if you're hungry before that, and we can fix you up. We've had some cancellations and we're not very busy this weekend." He handed them key cards and a pamphlet explaining the amenities.

"We strive to make this a pleasant trip for you," he said. "I am happy to try to accommodate any requests."

"Thank you," Mr. Glenn said. "Looks like Sarah was right about this place."

The proprietor beamed as he walked around the counter and opened the door for them.

Sarah breathed in the cool, foggy air. This would be a wonderful weekend, no matter what the weather.

They walked out to the car and found Baby Owen changed into a new outfit, the car somehow aired out, and Mrs. Gordon and Baby Owen both asleep.

Chapter 18

Enid Carmichael could tell the man was up to no good. She had a fine view of him from her apartment facing the street. She knew from experimenting herself that he could not see her standing in the dark apartment. The bright sunshine outside was in her favor as well. He would not be able to see her even if he stared directly into her window. Even if she turned on some lights. Which she did not intend to do.

She'd seen him earlier that morning and now he was back, ambling up and down the sidewalk, clearly staring at their apartment building. He had nowhere to hide on the cement sidewalk, this being San Francisco. No trees or other form of plant life blocked her view on their street. Which was just as well.

She might worry he was casing the joint, except he didn't look like a burglar. They usually wore dark clothes and knit caps. Maybe a mask. Ha! Burglars didn't wear masks. She knew that. Only on the covers of those detective magazines she used to read years ago. She had enjoyed those. Why had they stopped printing them? Why had they stopped printing everything she used to enjoy?

Anyway, this man wasn't a burglar. He wore a suit despite the warm day. His face was clearly visible, and his curly hair wasn't hidden under a cap, so she would be able to identify him if called upon.

The front door of the building opened with a squeak, and the man jumped. He stood so still she thought he might think he was invisible. But she could see him.

Not Jonathan Martin, the lawyer, though. Jonathan walked off without glancing the man's way.

Mrs. Carmichael surveyed the street, squinting in the sun. Oh, my God, what was that? A bear! An enormous black bear wandered down the street, heading for her bad guy. Bad Guy faced away, couldn't see the danger. The bear's back end rolled side to side as he picked up speed.

She fumbled with the window latch and got her window open. She had to warn him he was about to be eaten. She wanted some action, but she did not want body parts.

A whistle stopped the bear in its tracks. Bad Guy whipped around. The bear sat on its rump. Mrs. Carmichael squinted again. What kind of bear was this? A trained circus animal? Was there even such a thing anymore?

A young woman approached the bear from one direction and Bad Guy approached from the other. He was brave, she'd give him that.

With the window open and with her superior hearing, Mrs. Carmichael heard every word they said.

"Sorry. He got away from me there." The woman snapped a leash on the beast.

"First Newfoundland I've seen in the city," the man said.

"Such a hot day for him." The dog shook his head and drool and slobber flew.

Fancy Bad Guy Man looked at his suit.

"Sorry," the woman said.

"Good looking Newfie." He patted the dog's head and was rewarded with more slobber.

"Thanks." She pulled the giant animal in the other direction.

A dog. This creature was a dog. What if her Snowball encountered this brute? Better be on the lookout next time they went out for a poopie.

Fancy Bad Guy Man wiped his wet jacket with his clean hand and tried to shake off the viscous drool. He ended up rubbing his hands on the bricks of a building. Then he resumed his slow walk, eyes back on her building.

What was he up to?

Well, Mrs. Carmichael could stand there all day waiting to find out. She didn't have anything else to do, after all.

In fact, she needn't stand. She pulled over a chair that came in handy for this very purpose and settled in expectantly.

Chapter 19

Sarah sat in the resort's hot tub and felt her tense muscles soften. That drive was hard. She hadn't noticed the last time because the view was so exciting. All those hairpin turns in the fog left her nerves frazzled.

The pool was under a bubble-like covering and had huge windows. Stepping indoors was like stepping into a hot house. Sarah was blissfully warm, yet she could see the outdoors clearly, the gardens and the woods dripping from the cold mist. The air smelled of chemicals, but also of pine needles from a collection blown in near the door.

She was alone in the hot tub. Mrs. Gordon sat with Baby Owen on the steps at the shallow end of the pool. She wore a floral swimsuit with a skirt, and Baby Owen patted the skirt down when it floated up in the water. The little fellow was in heaven, splashing with both hands and laughing over and over when the water hit his face. Harold's turtle drifted nearby, at the ready if Owen ever tired of his game. Mr. Glenn sat in a deck chair with a crossword puzzle, shirt unbuttoned, sitting close enough to Owen that he and his puzzle got wet with the big splashes.

A man swam laps and his wife and daughter lay on lounge chairs. Otherwise they had the pool house to themselves. Sarah lazily watched the trees through the glass, swaying in the wind. She felt like ooze in the steamy water.

"Hot enough for you?"

Sarah started and almost cried out. She thought she was completely alone on her end of the bubble. Now a skinny young man in a white T-shirt and jeans crouched beside her. His name tag said "Dylan."

"Excuse me?" she said. He was so close she could see the faint peach fuzz on his cheek. He looked to be about eighteen or nineteen.

He didn't respond but he didn't move away, in fact, he leaned closer. The hot tub was very hot, and her brain was foggy. He was way too close, and she scooted farther away along the side of the hot tub.

The bubble door opened with a gust of cool air. The proprietor stepped in. The kid stood up without a word and wandered toward the pool. He picked up a mop and slowly pushed it around on the pool deck, soaking up puddles. The proprietor looked around the pool house, smiled and nodded at the guests, and left.

Sarah decided she was warm enough. She climbed out of the hot tub and wrapped herself in a large towel. She hurried over to Mr. Glenn in his deck chair, choosing the side of the pool opposite the pool boy.

"What's a six-letter word for 'job'?" he said.

"Career," Sarah said.

"Yep. That fits."

"How about 'mommy'?" said Mrs. Gordon from the pool.

"Doesn't fit," said Mr. Glenn.

"Hmph," said Mrs. Gordon. "What do they know? 'Mother,' then."

"Nope. I think they're looking for 'career.'"

"Double hmph," said Mrs. Gordon.

"See that pool boy?" Sarah said.

"Didn't even notice him until just now," Mr. Glenn said.

The boy mopped his way over to the mother and daughter across the pool from them. The daughter was about ten, splayed on her stomach with a book propped up on the end of the lounge chair. The mother leafed through a magazine and sipped a cold drink. The boy lingered behind them, ostensibly mopping up water, but it seemed to Sarah he was staring at her and not the deck.

"I think he's looking at you, dear," Mrs. Gordon confirmed.

"I'll go talk to him, if you like." Mr. Glenn puffed out his gray-haired chest and let his arms swagger for comic effect.

"No, I don't think that will be necessary, kind sir," Sarah said, smiling.

"He probably just thinks you're young and pretty, and he's screwing up his courage to talk to you," said Mrs. Gordon.

"We men can always hope," said Mr. Glenn. "Look what came my way." He leaned over and put a hand on Mrs. Gordon's shoulder. She blinked several times, her eyes shiny. Baby Owen gurgled contentedly. Sarah had to look away. The moment seemed too private.

Chapter 20

A housekeeping cart blocked Sarah's door when she returned to her room. A middle-aged couple was inside, both with the same light brown hair speckled with gray. The man was short and fit and carried a toolkit. He wiped his hands on a towel on his belt. The woman smoothed the down comforter on the bed. They turned toward Sarah in the doorway.

"Your faucet's fixed," the man said. His nametag said "George." The woman's said "Glenda."

"I didn't even know it was broken." Sarah sent up a silent "thank you" to Tommy, the handyman in their apartment building, because if she had a leaky faucet at home, she wouldn't have the faintest idea how to fix it.

"Come on in, honey, we've just finished. We'll be out of here right quick," Glenda said.

"Thank you," Sarah said.

"Funny to be here by yourself. Almost everybody has children." Glenda plumped the pillow and surveyed the room. "Makes our job easier, though, for the cleaning. No bits of cereal on the floor, no sticky counters."

"I'll bet," Sarah said.

"Not that we mind," Glenda continued. "We love children, George and I. We weren't blessed with them ourselves. That's why we love this job. We love having all these children around." She looked to her husband.

"Right," George grunted.

"Our days are filled with joy, working here. Children bring so much happiness. Seeing all these families with all these children, I feel like I have children myself," Glenda said.

"Well, we got Dylan, ain't we?" George said.

"Oh, Dylan." Glenda turned to Sarah. "He works here too. He's my brother's boy. He and my brother, well, they don't get on."

"We got Dylan now," George said again.

"Turned out all right for him," Glenda said. "He's got a job. And a place to live."

"He's got us," George said. He helped Glenda gather her cleaning supplies and they headed out.

So that was the pool boy, then, Sarah thought.

Sarah went with Alma Gordon, Mr. Glenn, and Baby Owen to the dining room right at five. They had finished off Mrs. Noonan's cookies on the drive down. Baby Owen snacked on rice cakes and cheese sticks all afternoon, but the grown-ups were starving.

At the door to the dining room, Sarah paused. She saw her table from the night she overheard the Blackwells argue. Where she waited for so long with little Ben. She remembered the intensity of the man's emotions. The tiredness in his wife's responses. What happened to them? How could things have turned out like this?

Tonight they sat on the other side of the room. The rain had stopped, and light poured in through the large windows. The trees looked silvery and sparkly.

She pointed out the other table to Mrs. Gordon and Mr. Glenn. She told them what she remembered about the argument.

"They might have been fighting about the very same things that led to the murder," Alma Gordon said.

"Only if he did it," Sarah said.

"Yes, of course. I didn't mean that," Mrs. Gordon said.

"But it does sound like they were an unhappy couple," said Mr. Glenn.

"Julia Blackwell said they were starting to patch things up," Mrs. Gordon said. "Paul called her to come down to take care of Ben so he and Andrea could have some time alone. After his mother came, they moved to their own room and spent a few days together, just the two of them. Apparently, it did wonders for them. That's what Julia said."

Sarah could believe it, wanted to believe it. She had seen the man's commitment.

"Time alone together is a wonderful thing." Mr. Glenn patted Mrs. Gordon's hand. "Even with the little guy, it's still like being alone." Baby Owen sat in a high chair next to him and munched on a cheese stick.

"Do you know, she decided to go with Spencer Tremaine," said Mrs. Gordon.

"What? When?" Sarah asked.

"She must have decided some time ago because he's already been on the case a week. I think she was too embarrassed to tell Frances."

"What was wrong with his old lawyer?" asked Mr. Glenn.

"Nothing, most likely. He was recommended by their family lawyer and I'm sure was doing a fine job," said Mrs. Gordon. "One thing Julia hopes for, and Spencer Tremaine apparently promised, is to get Paul out on bail. The judge thought he was too much of a flight risk and denied bail. Spencer Tremaine said this was inexperience on the lawyer's part, that a judge will always say this in a high profile case, and the trick is to find an angle, in this case Ben, to compel the court to think past a knee-jerk decision."

"What about Ben?"

"That Paul needs to be out of jail so he can be with Ben, and that he is not a flight risk because it is too hard to flee with a child. Or something to that effect. When Julia explained it, she had a lot of impressive phrases, but most of it's gone out of my head."

"Probably because it was just fluff," said Mr. Glenn. "Guy sounds like a shyster."

"But he *is* Spencer Tremaine," said Mrs. Gordon dreamily. "That might count for something."

"I hope so," said Sarah. "Ben must be lost without his parents. Poor kid."

"Milk, milk." Baby Owen had finished his cheese stick. He had a sippy cup in his fist, and he banged it on the high chair tray. "Milk, milk."

"Owen, Owen, dear, I'll get you milk." Mrs. Gordon took the cup and looked around the room. Baby Owen banged his hands on the tray. "Milk, milk," he demanded.

The waiter was across the room taking an order from another table. Mrs. Gordon fished in her purse and came up with another cheese stick. Baby Owen seemed satisfied and started to eat again.

The waiter came over. Sarah remembered him from before. Emanuel. His black hair was pressed back with a gel, and he had a trim moustache and one gold tooth. "Beverages?" he asked.

"Milk," said Mrs. Gordon. "For the baby. I'd like

hot tea."

"Hot tea for me too," said Sarah. The wind whistled outside, and the dining room was a little nippy.

"I'll have a beer," said Mr. Glenn.

"Sorry, sir, no beer. No alcohol at all," said Emanuel.

"No beer?" said Mr. Glenn. "Hmm. Just water, then."

"Could we order our food now too?" asked Mrs. Gordon. "I'm not sure how long Baby Owen will last."

"Of course," said Emanuel. "For the boy we have buttered noodles or spaghetti and meatball or pizza wheel."

"Buttered noodles," said Mrs. Gordon.

"And for the adults?"

The menu was written on a chalkboard by the wall. Linguini with clams, rosemary chicken, pizza with mozzarella slices and basil. Sarah and Mrs. Gordon ordered chicken and Mr. Glenn ordered pasta. The food arrived in less than ten minutes.

"This is delicious. And all included in the bill. You're right, Sarah, this place is a true find," said Mrs. Gordon.

"It's pretty neat to watch the chef." Mr. Glenn nodded toward the half wall where Marco worked away with two skillets. "Hopefully this place won't get too much publicity. If more people knew about it, I'm sure it would be packed."

"Well, I think it's pretty well known already. And not just locally. When I was here before, there was a family from Connecticut. Their kids were older and kept asking when they were moving on to Disneyland. Maybe there's not enough to keep the older ones interested."

"And it's just rustic enough to keep out the hip crowd." Mrs. Gordon pulled her sweater tighter around her shoulders.

"And no alcohol," said Mr. Glenn.

"Yes, no alcohol. I guess it's just the young families and us old folks," said Mrs. Gordon.

"The drive alone will keep us away," said Mr. Glenn.

"You're right. Maybe it won't be mobbed after all. Which is good for me," Sarah said.

The dining room was only half full, but far louder than when Sarah was there before. They saw the family from the pool and another with three young children, one of whom kept running around the table. The mother struggled with a screaming toddler and a baby while the father corralled the boy. When their food came, the boy sat still, and the toddler devoured her pizza without another word. Another couple had four children, and the family sang songs to keep their baby from crying. Sarah also recognized a couple from her first visit. She noticed them the last time because they seemed to be the only other ones besides Sarah without children. She had talked to them briefly, and they said they lived in San Jose and stopped at the resort sometimes if they took the scenic route back from her mother's in Los Angeles.

Baby Owen ate his noodles and had several loud outbursts. With all the other children, his shouts were no problem. At one point he called out "wing, wing," which meant he wanted to swing on Sarah's arm like he'd done with Harold. They'd started that afternoon, and Sarah's arm was sore. But she accommodated him, and after a while he wanted back in the high chair for more noodles.

Mr. Glenn spoke, but Sarah couldn't hear him over the dining room noise. She leaned in. He repeated, "When they say 'family resort,' I guess this is what they mean. This is not exactly a relaxing meal."

Sarah laughed. "I ate later last time. I think it quiets down a bit when the little kids go to bed."

Mrs. Gordon seemed completely at ease, sitting back in her chair with a smile on her face, perusing the room and sipping her tea.

"Sheer bliss," she said. "I don't have to worry about Baby Owen at all. He could yell all he wants in here and no one would care. This is the first meal out with him that I haven't been on tenterhooks the whole time. It's a parent's dream."

"This and those party places with pits full of balls to jump in," said Mr. Glenn. "A parent's dream and everyone else's nightmare."

Chapter 21

Sarah was relieved to see the weather clear as they drove up the coast. They got back to San Francisco on Sunday night. Baby Owen was asleep, and Mrs. Gordon carried him up to bed while Mr. Glenn dealt with the luggage. Sarah dropped them at the front door before she pulled into the small garage. She went upstairs to Mrs. Noonan's to return the car keys.

"How was the trip?" Mrs. Noonan asked.

Her voice sounded wistful, Sarah thought. Had she wanted to come? It had never occurred to Sarah to ask. At least she could be honest about the trip.

"Ah, a wonderful weekend. If you discount a little baby vomit, a lot of fog, not one glimmer of ocean seen the whole time, and some very frenetic mealtimes. Other than that, it was marvelous. Mr. Glenn might feel differently. He declined brunch today, said he'd rather read his Sunday paper in the peace of the pool, empty of children. Missed some very tasty cheese blintzes. There *were* a lot of kids in that place."

"Well, you always say it's a family resort." Mrs. Noonan's voice was back to normal, but she paced back and forth. It was not like her.

"Is something wrong?" Sarah asked.

"We've got a problem," Mrs. Noonan said at the same time. "Chantrelle is back."

Sarah sucked in her breath. Baby Owen's mother.

95

They knew she had to come back sometime, but the more time that went by, the more the baby became part of them. He'd been a little angel that weekend, aside from the vomit, a sweet, adorable, fun-loving angel. When he was with Chantrelle, he'd been totally different. Silent, sad.

"This is awful! What did she say? She just can't come back like this, can she? She's been gone forever!"

"Months and months. Four, five? I've lost track." Mrs. Noonan sighed loudly. "I didn't talk to her. Mrs. Carmichael saw her. She sees everything from that apartment of hers. She can look right down on the front door, and apparently she does that much of the time."

Sarah's apartment had the same view. She was directly above Mrs. Carmichael, but she very rarely looked straight down at the street.

"Anyway, she saw her at the door, ringing Alma's bell. Enid said she tried for a long time and even rang a few other bells, but no one answered. That was this morning. Mrs. Honeycut and I had taken Mrs. Flynn to church. I'm sure Chantrelle will be back. We have to figure out what to do."

"Good thing Mrs. Gordon doesn't have an answering machine. That would be a horrible message to come back to," Sarah said.

"Do you think Jonathan could help us? Would he know our rights?"

Jonathan Martin lived next door to Alma Gordon. He was a lawyer with a big firm downtown.

"It never hurts to ask. If he can't help us, he may know someone who can. Oh, what a mess. Mrs. Gordon's been so good for Baby Owen. She'll be devastated," Sarah said.

There was a soft knock at the door. Mrs. Gordon stood outside, and they could see by her face that she knew about Chantrelle. Mrs. Noonan reached out to hug her.

"Chantrelle," said Mrs. Gordon.

"I know," said Mrs. Noonan.

"I just got a call," said Mrs. Gordon.

"She called you?" Sarah wondered if she'd been calling all day, to have reached her so soon after they arrived home.

"No," said Mrs. Gordon. "It was Enid Carmichael. She saw me come in and called straight away."

Sarah and Mrs. Noonan exchanged looks. So typical. Mrs. Carmichael loved to be the bearer of news, any news.

"I was so upset I didn't even tell Mr. Glenn. Just left him with Baby Owen." She started to cry as she said his name. "What am I going to do without him?"

Mrs. Noonan hugged her tighter. "Don't worry, Alma. We won't let him go without a fight. We've got a plan to try to keep him." Though her words sounded soothing, Sarah could see the worry in her eyes.

Chapter 22

Frances Noonan spoke to Jonathan Martin the very next day. She didn't want to wake him, so she parked herself in the lobby first thing and waited.

And waited. She had plenty of time to think. Mostly about Chantrelle and Baby Owen. But also about little Ben and Julia and Paul Blackwell. And about her husband, Bill, and Alma Gordon and Mr. Glenn.

Why couldn't she be happy for Alma? Alma was certainly happy. She deserved this. She was so sweet and kind. She was perfect for Mr. Glenn.

But seeing Mr. Glenn with Alma's pill bottles was unnerving. Bill used to open Frances's pill bottles. Now Frances had to keep them in her medicine chest with the tops off because she couldn't manage them with her arthritis.

Bill used to do so many things for her. He did all the driving, and when he died, she had to learn the streets of San Francisco as if she hadn't lived in the city most of her life. She'd never paid attention to the roads, never had to. Bill paid all the bills, leaving her blissfully unaware that their car had been purchased with a high-interest loan, or that they paid a large sum for television cable each month. Frances had canceled that as soon as she saw the charge. The cable was for Bill, anyway, for his special sports channels. Bill had his favorite meals that she cooked with joy because he loved them so, pot roast and lamb stew. She hadn't made them in years. Well, truth to tell, she didn't really like pot roast. Or lamb stew. Still, it was nice to cook dinner for someone. Now she cooked for Sarah, and the two of them often sat side by side at her kitchen table enjoying the view of the San Francisco Bay just like she and Bill had.

She missed Bill every day, but the pain was less and less as time went on. Now, with a blossoming romance in the building between two people her own age, Bill came flooding back as if he were standing right there in the lobby next to her.

She was jealous of Alma. She might as well admit it to herself.

Jonathan finally stepped out of the elevator at nine. Mrs. Noonan got right to the point and told her story in just a few sentences.

"I wondered about that little fella." Jonathan adjusted his usual bow tie, yellow polka dot today, in the mirror by the mailboxes. "I actually do some adoption law myself. There are definitely angles we can work. Unfit mother. Abandonment. A court would not look favorably on Chantrelle as a parent, and it would be fairly easy to have her parental rights involuntarily terminated. Unfortunately, there's only a small chance that the state would grant placement to Mrs. Gordon. They will not like what she's been up to either. If Chantrelle would assent, we could consider a consensual arrangement, an independent adoption. Short of that, we may not have many options."

"A formal adoption? Oh, I don't think Chantrelle would go for that."

"The law is quite flexible about the arrangement," Jonathan said. "Chantrelle could have visitation rights, depending on how we set it up."

"Is there any kind of incentive we can offer her?"

"Do you mean money?" Jonathan asked.

"Well…" Mrs. Noonan shifted her weight. "Yes, money."

"No, I'm afraid the court is pretty strict about that. You can't buy a baby."

"No, no, of course not. This isn't a car we're talking about," Mrs. Noonan said sheepishly. "But…" she persisted, "what's in it for Chantrelle?"

"Well, first, you don't know exactly why she's back. She may have thought of something along these lines herself. In the best interest of the child."

Mrs. Noonan sighed. "No, I truly doubt it. But I suppose we have to face this. We have to meet her."

"If you'd like me to be there when you talk with her, I'd be happy to."

"No, Jonathan, thank you for all your advice. We'll meet her, then we'll talk to you again. We'll have to inquire about your fees as well."

"Oh, don't worry about that," Jonathan said. "We're neighbors. I'm happy I can help you with this."

"You haven't met Chantrelle," said Mrs. Noonan.

Chapter 23

Alma Gordon hadn't slept at all. The only part of the morning's newspaper she could concentrate on was her horoscope, and she read even that with trepidation. "A loss cannot be softened." She slammed the paper closed, then crumpled the entire section into a ball for the recycling, breathing so hard she had to hold on to the table.

As expected, Chantrelle returned a few hours later. She looked the same, messy blonde hair tousled in all directions, pretty face covered in too much and too many shades of makeup. Mrs. Gordon hadn't put on any makeup at all. Her eyes were puffy from crying, and her nose was red and raw.

Frances Noonan stood by her side, and Baby Owen napped in the bedroom. Mrs. Gordon had considered leaving him with Mr. Glenn or with her daughter, Sylvia, far away, so Chantrelle couldn't find him. But eventually Alma would have to give him up, and hiding him wouldn't help.

Her heart squeezed and her throat was tight. Could something like this cause a heart attack? She was seventy-five, after all. And she had high blood pressure. Why, oh why, did Chantrelle have to come back?

"I'm back," said Chantrelle, with barely a hello. "I want my kid."

So there it was. Mrs. Noonan had tried to comfort

Alma by saying they didn't know why Chantrelle had returned, that she may not be coming for Baby Owen. That she might just be checking on him. That she might even agree to a formal adoption.

But no. She wanted Baby Owen. Alma's precious Baby Owen. Just that morning, as he'd dropped his Cheerios one by one off his high chair, he'd looked at her with his impish grin and her heart melted. He sang his nonsense songs and dumped over his milk cup, and all she could do was cry. Even when he toppled over her lilac bubble bath and made a slick mess on the bathroom floor that caused her to slip and wrench her knee, her arms went out to cuddle him and hug him close. He had become her child.

"Chantrelle, dear, don't you look lovely," Mrs. Noonan said. And she did look lovely, aside from the face. She wore a low cut, silky white shirt and fitted black trousers, a very trim and different look for her.

"Yeah, this shirt cost me a fortune. But it'll pay off."

Mrs. Noonan gave Mrs. Gordon a quizzical look. To Chantrelle she continued, "And how have you been? How is Big Owen?"

Big Owen's whole being sprang into Mrs. Gordon's mind, his huge menacing presence, his surly attitude, and his threats. She shuddered and her heart squeezed again.

"Owen?" Chantrelle's face softened. Mrs. Gordon had never understood the attraction. "Owen's fine. Him and me's been seeing the state. Been in Los Angeles. I'm gonna make it there, I know I am."

Chantrelle had talked like this since they first met. They'd try to steer her back to school, and she'd keep on about her potential for stardom. They didn't want to quash her dreams, but they felt the responsibility of reality.

"We've got a nice room, lots of actors living in the house. They give me tons of help because they can see I've got what it takes. One girl, Inez, works at The Station, it's a real cool restaurant and bar, and she thinks she can get me a job."

Mrs. Gordon listened to this through a fog. She could not bring herself to say anything. She was grateful Mrs. Noonan was at her side, adding some semblance of normalcy and civility.

"That sounds just lovely," said Mrs. Noonan. "But maybe work in a bar isn't the best thing for a sixteen-year-old. Why don't you leave Baby Owen with us while you get yourselves situated? He'll be just fine here with Alma, and then when you're ready, we can talk again."

Chantrelle threw her a sideways look like a pouty challenge. "I'm seventeen now. And I'm ready. I miss the kid. He can be a pain, but he's mine and he loves me."

"Of course he does, dear," said Mrs. Noonan. "He will always love you. You're his mother. But is a room in a house full of others and a possible job in a bar, probably with night hours, is that the best for him right now?"

"Yeah, it won't be easy."

"I can't imagine you'd want to burden yourself with a baby just yet, what with your new life and all. He's been very happy here, and we'd be happy to keep him a while longer until your life settles out."

Chantrelle gave her the look again. "That'd be

nice, but, see, the state found out he's not with me, my mom turned me in, and they're going to stop my checks, so I have to get him back living with me or I lose my money."

"Ah…" said Mrs. Noonan.

"Oh, dear. Oh, dear," said Mrs. Gordon.

"Hiiiiiii," said Baby Owen.

"Is that him? Is that my baby?" Chantrelle rushed toward the bedroom but stopped short of opening the door. For a moment she looked uncertain, and Mrs. Gordon stepped forward.

"Here, dear, let's go in and see him." She could barely speak, could only manage a whisper.

The baby stood in his crib, hands on the rail, bouncing up and down. "Hi, hi, hi," he called.

Mrs. Gordon and Chantrelle approached him together. He slowed his bouncing and then came to a stop. He gaped at Chantrelle, his eyes large. Mrs. Gordon summoned her cheeriest voice. "Baby Owen, look who's here. It's your mamma. Your mamma is here."

He didn't cry. He let Chantrelle pull him out of the crib. He sat in her arms without squirming. But he didn't take his eyes off Mrs. Gordon.

"He's so big," Chantrelle said. "He's much heavier than I remember. And he's got hair now."

Mrs. Gordon nodded, watching the baby, *her* baby, in Chantrelle's arms. She couldn't get any words out.

She saw the problem well before Chantrelle realized what was happening. Though Alma had tears in her eyes, she could see a darkening ring start at the crotch of Baby Owen's blue pants. It spread quickly and within seconds Chantrelle yelped.

"He's wet, he's wet!" she cried. "Take him! It's getting on my shirt!"

Mrs. Gordon took the baby and deftly wrapped him in a towel hanging on the crib for just this purpose. "We've had some leakage problems," she explained lamely, imagining Owen's sodden diaper.

Chantrelle didn't hear her. She pulled the wet shirt away from her skin and searched wildly around for something to dry her off. The wet area was huge. How such a tiny child put out so much urine was a mystery. Mrs. Gordon was used to it. Of course, she didn't wear silk.

She had the baby changed and in a new pair of pants in no time, but Chantrelle did not want to hold him again.

"It's ruined," she said. "It'll have to be dry cleaned now. I can't believe it. I just got this shirt."

Mrs. Gordon regarded her own white cotton shirt and lavender sweater and thought how much urine and spit up and poo the outfit had seen. She hugged Baby Owen to her chest and said nothing. He clutched her arms so tight with his small fists it pinched and hurt, even through the sweater.

Mrs. Noonan talked some more with Chantrelle, trying to convince her that Baby Owen should stay where he was. Mrs. Gordon couldn't bear to listen. She could see by the hard set of Chantrelle's mouth that she had no intention of leaving Baby Owen behind. They had spoken to Jonathan just before Chantrelle arrived and decided their only hope was to get Chantrelle to agree to an adoption, an amicable independent adoption which would permit Chantrelle to visit whenever she wanted, but would free her from everyday childcare responsibilities. Mrs. Gordon had allowed herself to actually think Chantrelle might agree. If they could only offer Chantrelle something in return, some compensation…But Jonathan had been very clear. They would lose their chance at adoption if they even hinted at such a thing. So Mrs. Gordon clasped the baby in her arms, perhaps for the last time, and watched Mrs. Noonan struggle with a losing battle.

In the end, Chantrelle said she would be back the following day to pick up Baby Owen and take him to Los Angeles.

"You have a car seat?" Mrs. Noonan asked. "He's in a forward-facing seat now."

Chantrelle stared at them like they had asked if she had a chauffeur-driven limousine to drive them to LA.

Mrs. Gordon winced, wondering what else Chantrelle did not have.

"You can have ours, of course." She could barely get the words out but continued as best she could. "I'll get all his things together. He'll be ready. If you were thinking of a snack on the road, I recommend against apple juice. He has a tendency to vomit in the car."

Now Chantrelle winced. But she didn't back down. "I'll be here at noon," she said.

And that was that. Chantrelle was gone. Baby Owen was eerily quiet. Mrs. Noonan said she was very sorry. And then Mrs. Gordon was alone with the baby. Her baby. Her little fellow. Her pride and joy. She thought of him first thing in the morning and last thing at night. She thought of how much progress he'd made, how he never used to smile or laugh. Chantrelle wasn't a bad mother, she wasn't mean or violent. She was just inexperienced and uninterested. Which leaves a mark on a child. Her child. Baby Owen needed her. He loved her. And she loved him.

But Chantrelle was his mother. She loved him too. She could learn to be a good mother. Mrs. Gordon would see to it.

Chapter 24

When Chantrelle came to take Baby Owen, the Fog Ladies were there with Alma Gordon and so was much of the building. Frances Noonan, Mr. Glenn, Sarah, Jonathan the lawyer, Enid Carmichael, Harriet Flynn, and Olivia Honeycut, who didn't even live in their building. They sat or stood quietly in Mrs. Gordon's living room.

All these people to stand by her, and still Alma felt alone.

She'd fed Baby Owen his favorite oatmeal breakfast. He wore his best outfit, with a brown dog on his chest and little brown dog slippers on his feet. He sat on the floor with his bear. He was also quiet.

Mrs. Gordon had four grocery bags full of clothes and toys and supplies. She had three books on childrearing, and she had several pages of handwritten notes specific to Baby Owen's habits. She had a list of things Chantrelle needed to get as soon as they got to Los Angeles—more size three diapers, baby wipes, whole milk, Cheerios. She showed Chantrelle how to work the thermometer and gave her the bottle of liquid children's acetaminophen. Sarah gave Chantrelle a card with her telephone number and pager number in case Baby Owen got sick before she found a pediatrician.

Jonathan and Mr. Glenn carried the bags to the car. Mrs. Gordon carried Baby Owen and placed him in the car seat. She made Chantrelle strap him in to prove she could do it.

Chantrelle gave Alma a slip of paper with a telephone number on it, not hers, but one of the housemates. "I can't afford a phone just yet," she said.

Chantrelle looked twelve instead of seventeen as she stood by the car. Surely she didn't want to go through with this.

But the girl just said, "Well, that's that, then."

Mrs. Gordon hugged Chantrelle, so long she felt the girl squirm. Mrs. Gordon's chest squeezed as if she were hugging her heart tight instead of Chantrelle. "I'm happy to take him any time you need a break," she whispered in the girl's ear. "It's not always easy to be a mother, and I know you don't have many people you can turn to. You can turn to me."

Chantrelle nodded slowly, again looking so young. "Thanks. And thanks for keeping him. I wasn't sure he'd still be here. I can see you did well by him."

Mrs. Gordon reached through the door to grab hold of Baby Owen's little hand. She couldn't bear the bewilderment in his eyes. She held his gaze and smiled reassuringly. Her brain screamed at her to snatch him up and run.

"I love you, little man." She squeezed his hand and let it drop. He tried to hold on, but she withdrew quickly, her heart breaking. She closed the door and the car pulled away. Her Owen pulled away.

Chapter 25

In the months since Baby Owen left, Sarah went from gastroenterology to the oncology wards to rheumatology and then to the intensive care unit. Mrs. Gordon threw herself into helping with Ben Blackwell, and Sarah often saw her leaving in the morning on her way to take care of the little boy. Then Sarah started in the ICU, and she hardly saw anyone at all. The ICU was a hard rotation, and Sarah didn't know how Helen had done it with morning sickness. Helen was over her vomiting now, but she was nine months pregnant and, with the twins, she was enormous. Thank goodness Helen had the easier elective rotations now. She could sit most of the day, and she didn't take overnight call. Even so, Sarah didn't know how Helen managed any rotation at all. She thought for certain Helen would need bed rest, but the babies showed no sign of trouble, and Helen carried on as if anyone could do what she was doing.

On Halloween, Julia Blackwell brought Ben to their apartment building to trick or treat. She said her building had too many young people and no one stayed home. Ben was dressed as a lion. He tapped so softly on Sarah's door, she almost didn't hear him.

"Happy Halloween!" She dropped a chocolate bar into his pumpkin bucket. "Can you roar?"

He didn't answer her. He never raised his head. He

trudged away with only a quick thank-you. Julia Blackwell nodded sadly and followed him.

Sarah expected the boy to be different, but she was surprised by how much. Frances Noonan had prepared her and asked her to stay home until he came so he would have as many doors to knock on as possible. They wanted to make this holiday as normal as they could, a holiday which should be fun and exciting for a child. Frances Noonan and Alma Gordon decorated some of the doors and painted a pumpkin for the table in the lobby. Sarah's door sported a black cat cutout and an orange crescent moon.

"It's worse than you can imagine," Mrs. Noonan had told Sarah. "He's stopped talking. He doesn't smile. He has nightmares. He wakes screaming for Mommy. He barely eats. Julia is beside herself. She's been to the pediatrician, but he couldn't offer any suggestions except provide a stable, loving environment. She doesn't know what to do. She had her hopes pinned on Paul's coming home. Now that bail's been denied for a second time, she's losing faith. She's even starting to doubt Spencer Tremaine."

After seeing Ben, Sarah remembered how much she loved Halloween as a kid, the spooky costumes and the candy, and that made her all the more depressed about Ben. She planned to go out with Helen and Scott to a party given by a fellow medical resident, Karl. As she dressed, she debated calling Helen to cancel, but she had already asked them to start later because of Ben, so she couldn't bow out now.

She also wanted to support Helen. If Helen could trek to a party when she was out to here with twins, Sarah could go too. Helen was due, and her doctor told her walking might stimulate the birth process. Helen took it to heart, hoping to get those babies out. Plus, she said this might be her last adult Halloween party for years to come.

Karl lived near the Castro, so Sarah, Helen, and Scott started there, gawking at the parade of wild costumes. The Castro was notorious for its Halloween crowds, though nothing like in the past. The area was packed with noise and festivity. Sarah thought of the little boy who had no pleasure from Halloween.

They dressed up themselves. Sarah was Cleopatra, an obvious costume with her long black hair, and one she had gotten several years ago. If she'd had to think up and put together a new costume that year, she never could have done it. The ICU was so time consuming and intense, all she did that month was work and sleep. That week's mail lay in an unopened pile on the counter, and she hadn't looked at her e-mail in days. Even Sarah's Halloween candy had been supplied by Mrs. Noonan. Thank goodness the rotation was almost over.

Scott dressed as a devil, with red tights and a long pitchfork. Helen was a waddling white marshmallow, laughing and in a better mood than Sarah had seen in a while. Helen still had stamina, and they stood for half an hour watching the crowds pass on the sidewalk before they went to the party. Their costumes were tame compared with the revelers in the Castro. Sea creatures and mermaids cavorted in the streets, as well as men dressed as dogs on leashes and an occasional partier with no costume at all. Helen's outfit got a lot of attention, and some people tried to pat the babies through her padding.

Sarah couldn't figure out how they knew Helen was pregnant.

"It's her glow," Scott said, his hand on the front of the marshmallow too.

Sarah had never seen Scott so romantic. Helen told her that they had had a terrible row that week over where to move their desk. It used to sit in a huge San Francisco-sized closet they used as their study, but that study was now a nursery. The desk was in the living room along with the baby swings and playpen. The desktop was covered with stuffed animals and pacifiers. Scott saw every new toy as an assault on his PhD and said things he regretted. Helen said he was trying to make it up to her. And that he was doing a good job.

Sarah left the party early because she was on call the next night. She never got into the spirit of the party anyway. She couldn't stop thinking about Ben. When she left, Helen was still going strong, sprawled in her marshmallow costume on Karl's couch, her arm linked in Scott's.

The very next day, Helen delivered the babies. A boy and a girl, Aidan and Emily. Sarah saw them a few hours after they were born, nestled in Helen's arms on the maternity ward.

"You just missed Scott." Helen radiated tranquility, a tiny sleeping bundle in each arm. Her short hair stuck up on one side and her mascara ran down to her cheek, but she still looked like a superwoman to Sarah.

"Scott's gone home to rest. We were up most of the night. The contractions started as soon as we got home from the party. The doctor was sure right about stimulation. But these angels took their time coming out." Helen tilted her head. "Look at them, Sarah!

Aren't they perfect?"

All Sarah could see were their closed eyes and noses, swaddled as they were in blankets, a tiny hat on each head, one pink, one blue. But their little faces did look perfect.

"They are indeed. Perfect little angels."

A picture flashed in her mind of a trip she and her brother, Tim, had taken a few years before. They went to Mexico for El Dia de los Muertos, the Day of the Dead celebration, to honor and celebrate their parents. It had been cathartic and sad and happy and full of memories. They arrived on Halloween, and the Day of the Dead was two days later. Before that, however, was another celebration. Celebration was not the correct word, as Sarah and Tim did not see the same joy and spirit as on the Day of the Dead. They saw tears. Many tears.

That celebration, on the first day of November, was El Dia de los Angelitos. The Day of the Little Angels, to welcome back and remember dead children. Today, the day Helen's twins were born, was El Dia de los Angelitos.

Chapter 26

The first call came on Halloween night. Alma Gordon waited at her door for Ben to come, then almost cried when she saw him, small and morose, his lion costume hanging on his little body. He didn't say a word, didn't look at her, barely stuck out his pumpkin bucket for his licorice whips. Julia Blackwell smiled sadly, and they continued down the hall.

Mrs. Gordon untwirled a licorice whip to eat herself. Ben had changed so much since she last took care of him, just a month ago. At first she'd helped Julia several times a week, but Julia didn't need her now that Paul Blackwell's case had petered out. Ben had been somber but interactive when Alma last saw him, easily losing himself in the hide-and-seek game they played, even laughing when Alma tried to squeeze under the desk. What a dreadful change. Poor little boy.

The phone rang and she thought it might be Frances Noonan calling to compare notes about Ben. But it was not.

It was silly to think Frances would call anyway. Frances would come in person, knock on her door with a plate of pumpkin bread, and they'd sit together and talk. Or they would have. They hadn't done much sitting together lately. Or talking.

Part of the reason was Mr. Glenn. Alma did a lot of sitting and talking with Mr. Glenn. He was full of stories and interesting ideas about the world. Frances would knock on her door, see Mr. Glenn, and say she'd come back later. Alma actually thought she was being polite, allowing them their space. But those visits were a while ago. When she thought seriously about it, she realized she hadn't had a chat alone with Frances Noonan in a long time. Earlier that week, Frances had opened the lobby door while Alma and Mr. Glenn waited for the elevator, but she shut it again and turned back toward the street.

Alma saw Mrs. Noonan with the Fog Ladies, of course, but that wasn't the same. She jumped toward the phone, longing for her old friend.

At first she heard only a wailing girl. She couldn't make out any actual words. Then the wailing stopped, and the girl took a ragged breath.

Mrs. Gordon's heart pounded, forgetting all about Frances Noonan. Chantrelle! What was wrong?

Now Chantrelle was crying and saying Baby Owen vomited on his bear costume and cried every time the front doorbell rang. He refused to drink from a sippy cup and wanted to drink from a glass like she did, but he spilled when he tried it. He had a diaper rash that was oozing and screamed every time she changed him. Big Owen was no help and was never around when she needed him. Her housemate Inez could get her a job at the restaurant where she worked, but she couldn't start yet because there was no one to watch the baby. His supplies cost almost as much as her monthly check, and how could anyone think you could live on that, and who knew diapers were so expensive?

Mrs. Gordon heard Baby Owen crying in the background, a whining cry that changed to a shriek when the doorbell rang. She heard adult trick-or-treaters at the door and imagined the type of scary costumes they might wear. She listened to Chantrelle without saying much. Her heart ached for her little boy, ached to hold him and comfort him and love him.

"I feel better after talking to you," said Chantrelle.

"Please call any time," Mrs. Gordon said. She reminded Chantrelle about the diaper rash cream. She told her Baby Owen liked to have his back rubbed and that might help to calm him down.

"Oh, yeah, you wrote that on the papers."

Mrs. Gordon was happy to hear the girl had at least read them. The doorbell rang again and Baby Owen shrieked, and Chantrelle said she had to go.

Mrs. Gordon lay in bed that night worrying about Baby Owen and worrying about Frances Noonan. She could talk to Frances about Baby Owen, soothing both her worries at once.

She took the elevator up to see Frances Noonan first thing the next morning. She felt so formal, not like she'd been doing this day in, day out for years. She stood in front of Frances's door, hands at her sides, not able to knock.

The door flew open and Frances Noonan almost bowled her over.

"Alma! Good heavens, what in the world are you doing lurking out here?"

"I wanted to talk to you," Alma squeaked.

"Not now, not now, dear. Sorry. I'm in a rush. Perhaps later." Mrs. Noonan headed for the elevator and was whisked away before Alma could think what more to say.

Alma returned to her apartment and retrieved the

phone number Chantrelle had given her before she left. She dialed with shaking fingers, ready to tell Chantrelle to bring the baby back, to come home, both of them.

The number was disconnected without a forwarding number. Mrs. Gordon set down the telephone and cried.

Chapter 27

That man was out there again. Enid Carmichael knew faces, but even if she hadn't recognized the guy's face, she'd still remember him. Not a lot of people dressed this way, decked out in a suit and shiny shoes. It had been a few months, but she hadn't forgotten.

She was about to eat lunch, had her turkey sandwich almost to her lips when she spied him. She took a quick gulp of sherry and deposited the sandwich in the refrigerator in case Fancy Bad Guy Man stayed a while. She took her place by the window.

Hmm. She might need to intervene this time, march right out to him and demand to know what he was up to. No good. He was up to no good. That much she knew.

She peered closer. Her eyes weren't as good as her ears. Were his lips moving? Was he talking to himself?

She turned the latch and carefully, silently, swung wide the window so she could hear. Her tiny dog, Snowball, took that moment to skitter across the floor chasing a shadow. He slid into the table leg, knocking over her glass of sherry, which rained down on him like the Newfoundland drooling on that hot summer day. Snowball barked and barked, his high-pitched Bichon Frise yip, as if he'd been hit with a frigid dog shower instead of a tiny dollop of liquor.

Mrs. Carmichael recoiled from the window as the

man looked up. He couldn't see her, she knew that, but reflexes were reflexes.

She retrieved the turkey sandwich from the refrigerator and plopped it on the floor by the frantic dog. He set on it at once, and she returned to the window.

If he had been talking to himself, he wasn't now. Darn. He might have spilled a secret. Let slip his mission. Loose lips sink ships. She'd be ready if he did decide to speak. Her ears were ready.

Last time, he'd just ambled up and down the sidewalk, slowly back and forth, eyes locked on their building.

It reminded her of when she used to saunter past her husband's apartment building before he was her husband. Hoping he'd come out and she could say, "What a coincidence, I was just visiting my friend Lois who lives on this street, I didn't know you lived here too."

She needn't have bothered with all that pretending. All that time wasted. He never came out. Her friend Lois had to come right out and tell him Enid was interested, and he called her immediately and the rest was history.

Oh, they had some fun times. That was before Clarice was born, before all the fights about who should stay home from work when she had an ear infection, who should go out in the night to get the milk when they ran out, who should get her to and from her ballet lessons. They never figured out the logistical part of parenting. Well, that's not true. They never figured out anything about parenting at all. When Clarice turned twelve, she painted her face with lipstick and eye shadow and hemmed her skirt up above her knee and expected them to just accept it. Stanley never said a word. Mrs. Carmichael thought he might actually have been scared of their own daughter. Understandable. The girl was a force.

That left Enid to deal with her all by herself. No help from the man of the house. The man of the house wasn't home much by then. He was "at the office" or "out with clients." She knew where he was. He didn't fool her. He was with some young thing whose skirt was as short as Clarice's.

Their teenager turned on them, and her husband turned tail and ran.

Good riddance, that's what she said. What was the point of it all? She made the decisions about Clarice alone anyway, whether he lived in the house or not. She confiscated the pill bottles, took away the cigarettes, paced the floor at night waiting for Clarice to return. "Just wait 'til you have children of your own! Then you'll see," Enid shouted. But Clarice would never know these traumas of parenthood. Clarice didn't have children, wasn't even married. Go figure.

Stanley never knew either. He never helped Enid before or after he left. They were not a team.

Not like Mr. Glenn and Bessie. Now there was a team, dealing with drug-addled Lionel together, dealing with Bessie's cancer together, a rock-solid marriage right up until Bessie died. Now look at him with Alma Gordon. They looked like a team as well, the way they took care of that baby, taking weekend trips together, bowling. Alma even got him to go to yoga.

Like the murderer.

Mrs. Carmichael frowned at the man across the

street. What did he want with them?

There were murderers in this city, and they looked just like you and me, Mrs. Carmichael thought. This man could be a murderer for all she knew.

Chapter 28

One of the hardest things for Sarah about the ICU was seeing people her own age or even younger, people who never in their short lives imagined they could get sick, now fighting to live. Meningitis, brain aneurysms, carbon monoxide poisoning from a faulty heater—these were problems any unlucky person could get. Some people went home. Some people did not. When the patients were young, it was easy for Sarah to imagine herself or her brother or her friends in the same situation. It made it hard to be objective, which was an important part of medicine. But maybe not the most important part.

One of Sarah's patients was a newlywed who mixed ammonia and bleach while cleaning the bathroom to surprise his new bride, who arrived home to find him unconscious and barely breathing. She had to do mouth-to-mouth herself until the ambulance came, and he was in full arrest when he arrived at the hospital. He had been on a ventilator for weeks now, and neurology tests showed he had suffered severe brain injury from not enough blood flow. He had never regained consciousness. There was little hope he would recover. Despite multiple conversations with Sarah and the attending physician, his wife and his parents couldn't bring themselves to make the decision to turn off the ventilator, couldn't even decide to make him

"DNR" or "Do Not Resuscitate." If he died, if his heart stopped, the doctors would be obligated to bring him back to life. To the life of the machines.

His family was frozen.

Sarah sat with them every day. She held his mother's hand. She brought his father coffee.

Sarah was almost done with her ICU rotation. She would turn this man and his family over to the next team. She was alone with his wife at his bedside, maybe for the last time. Sarah brushed away a lock of the man's hair that was caught under the tubing on his face. He was so young. His wife was so young.

The man's kidneys had shut down, and he couldn't get rid of his fluids. His face was swollen, and the tubing left an imprint as Sarah shifted it. His wedding band was long gone, removed before his fingers turned into sausages. The skin on his edematous arms was pale and stretched and weepy in some areas. He had catheters and tubes and patches and lines everywhere.

"His bachelor apartment was such a mess." His wife said this out of the blue. Sarah smiled at her from across the bed.

"He always said we were meant to be together, and I'd joke that the state of his bathroom was keeping us apart. I never liked staying at his place."

For the umpteenth time, Sarah studied the photo pinned to the bulletin board of the young couple. Their heads were tossed back, laughing, and their arms were linked. Sarah imagined them together, carefree.

The woman touched her husband's swollen hand lightly with her fingertips. "He proposed to me with a diamond ring and a toilet brush. He said the ring was for me and the brush was for him. Our bathroom would never come between us." She bent and brushed her lips on his cheek.

Sarah busied herself adjusting a ventilator setting.

"He promised to make our bathroom sparkle because I was the sparkle in his life. That's what he said. That's how he is."

Sarah's hand dropped. Her eyes smarted. She tried hard, but she couldn't help herself. She'd been up most of the night with her last call night of the ICU. The fatigue and the stress magnified every emotion. She started to cry, thankful her back was turned. An alarm sounded and she spun back to him, but it was just the IV.

His wife stared at Sarah and her tears. The young woman's lips pressed together and her face turned red. She took a few short breaths, then let out a soft howl as tears flowed down her cheeks. Sarah hurried around the bed and put her arm around her shoulder. They leaned into each other and sobbed. Then the room was silent except for the ventilator as they stood side by side.

The cardiac monitor broke the silence. Sarah's head flew up and she read the rhythm on the monitor. V-fib. He was coding. The harsh alarm brought the nurses into the room pushing the code cart. The respiratory tech ran in behind them.

"He's in V-fib." Sarah pointed to the first nurse into the room. "Lianne, start chest compressions."

Sarah tore open the defibrillator pads and placed them on the man's chest. She cranked the knob on the defibrillator. She turned her head back and nodded at the man's wife. "You should wait outside. I'll come as soon as I can."

"Everybody clear!" Sarah shouted, making sure the

team stepped away from the bed. She hit the button and the pads delivered the shock. The man's body jumped.

"Resume CPR," Sarah said, and Lianne started compressions again.

"Two minutes, doctor."

"Hold CPR." The monitor showed a sinus rhythm. Sarah checked his pulse. She felt it, faint but growing stronger. The code was over. The man had been brought back to life.

As the nurse checked his blood pressure, footsteps rushed into the room. Sarah's ICU attending stopped short of the bed, glancing from the monitor to Sarah. "Excellent work, Dr. James. I see I'm not needed here at all."

Sarah smiled despite the sad surroundings. "If it's all right with you, I'd like to let his wife know."

"Of course. Yes. I'll finish here."

Sarah found his wife just outside the door, crying. Sarah reached out and touched her arm. "He came through," Sarah said. The woman cried harder.

The team filed out of the room. Sarah's attending nodded at the man's wife. "You can go back in now."

"Come with me?" The woman pulled Sarah back in. They stood again next to the bed. The man looked exactly the same, as if the code had not happened.

His wife whispered, "In the hall, I wished you couldn't save him. Then it would be over. Then I wouldn't have to make the choice. But I know what the right choice is. You've been telling me all along. I can see how much you care about him. So I know this decision is best."

She waved her hand over the bed. "This not my husband, my darling, the man who lived for me and me for him. I know he's not here."

Sarah couldn't get any words out. Her throat was tight, her eyes full of tears.

His wife knelt down next to the bed. "I love you, my sweet." She turned her face up to Sarah. "It's time," she said.

So on the last day of her ICU rotation, after the man coded and they brought him back to life, they turned off the ventilator. Sarah dug her fingernails into the palms of her hands to keep from becoming a bawling mess. She barely held herself together. All the emotion, all the sleepless nights, all the highs and lows of the month in the ICU culminated in this family's story.

She hugged the man's wife, his parents. She left them in the room to say their final good-byes.

Her attending waited outside the door. "Tough case," he said.

Sarah could only nod.

He leaned against the nurses' desk, arms crossed. "The only reason they changed their mind was you. You helped them find their way. You got emotionally involved, you let yourself be vulnerable. Yet you could still conduct yourself calmly during the code. Strong work." He pushed himself up and walked down the hall.

Sarah had hoped to go forward as a doctor with objectivity and without emotion. It was impossible. She couldn't change who she was. Not yet, anyway. She was a resident, and residency was three years. She'd get better at this. But today she was happy to be where she was.

Chapter 29

Sarah visited Helen and the babies before she left the hospital. The babies were sleeping and so was Helen. Sarah crept in and left a note. They looked so peaceful. Far from what Sarah was feeling, after her last call day in the ICU.

Sarah felt wide awake when she got off the bus and climbed the hill for home. Her whole life had been on hold while she was in the ICU. Mail, e-mail, texts. Her phone had to be off in the unit, and sometimes she was so tired, she just kept it off. Now she could catch up. She felt full of energy, exhilarated. She could read her newspaper through for the first time in a month. And eat a real dinner instead of another bowl of Cheerios. She wanted to talk to Frances Noonan about the ICU. She wanted to tell her about Helen and the twins, and she wanted to hear about Ben. She hoped he'd perked up after he left her on Halloween. If she visited Mrs. Noonan early enough, she'd get invited to dinner. Which was always delicious. She stopped and bought some flowers.

She went right up to see Mrs. Noonan, who greeted her with a huge smile.

"Have you been home yet, Sarah?"

"No. I brought you these." Sarah handed over the flowers. She tried to think how to invite herself to dinner. Usually Mrs. Noonan assumed she would stay and mentioned it right off the bat, and Sarah never had to ask. She could smell something delectable cooking right now. "Helen had her babies! I have a picture," she said. Invite me to dinner, she thought.

"What beautiful little angels," Mrs. Noonan said, taking a quick look at the photo. She seemed distracted.

Sarah again remembered about El Dia de los Angelitos. Mrs. Noonan lost her child, Isabelle, when she was little. Did she remember and mourn on the first of November?

Today was El Dia de los Muertos. The day for Sarah to remember her parents. For all the people who'd lost loved ones and parents. Like Mrs. Noonan and her husband, Bill. Like Ben.

Before Sarah could ask about Ben, Mrs. Noonan said, "Ah, you have your paper. Did you read this?" She passed a section of the paper to Sarah, folded back to an article on page A7.

"Jail Fire Injures One," the headline read. "Wife killer Joseph Stalk was injured Friday in a kitchen fire at the Philadelphia Industrial Correctional Center. He sustained second-degree burns on his arms and chest in a grease fire while on kitchen duty. Stalk is awaiting trial on charges in the strangling death of his wife, Shelley Stalk, last October. Shelley was found in the back of the family car. Their infant son is now living with relatives in Petaluma, CA. Stalk stood to gain one million dollars from his wife's life insurance policy."

"What do you think of that?" Mrs. Noonan asked.

"Just like Paul," Sarah said. "This happened over a year ago. The guy's still in jail, still awaiting trial. These things drag on forever."

"Spencer Tremaine told Julia that if he couldn't get

Paul out on bail, it might be six to eight months before the trial date. You have a right to a speedy trial, but somehow lots of things get in the way. Mostly motions filed by your own lawyer, motions to dismiss the case, motions to suppress evidence. All very important, apparently, but they delay things. Ben will be a different boy by then, a scared, sad, haunted little boy."

"This man's son is all the way across the country. That must be worse for the child. The little fella couldn't have known these relatives very well. Not like Ben and his grandmother."

"That's just what I was thinking," said Mrs. Noonan. "But I bet they have some ideas about what a child might be going through. They're a year farther into the process than we are. Maybe we could learn from them, learn something to help poor little Ben."

"Whoever they are," said Sarah.

"Yes, well…" said Mrs. Noonan.

Sarah could tell Mrs. Noonan wanted something. She waited.

"It's about Andy." Mrs. Noonan smiled, her mouth wide and her eyes crinkling.

"Andy?!" Her Andy? Sarah's heart skipped a few beats, like it was dancing in her chest. She could see from Mrs. Noonan's expression that this was good news. The last she knew, Andy was in northern India. He sent her a photo of a baby elephant standing backwards underneath the mother, both silhouetted in sunshine through a golden haze. That was a whole month ago. She hadn't heard from him since.

"He's back." Mrs. Noonan could hardly contain herself and told the news all in a rush. "He arrived yesterday and went straight to see you, then raced up here to find out where you were. Said it's over six months, long enough already. He'd seen his elephants and now he wanted to see you. He couldn't believe you weren't here, he said he e-mailed you twice with his itinerary. He's down there right now waiting for you."

"Andy's back? Look at me, I've been on call all night. I didn't have time to take a shower today. I'm a mess."

"No, no, dear, you look fine. Just go on down."

"Andy's back!" Sarah jumped up to go, but Mrs. Noonan put a hand on her arm.

"When he's back to work at the newspaper, could you ask him to do something for me?"

Sarah nodded and started for the door.

"Could he find out more about this little boy? Where he is in Petaluma? I'd like to visit and talk to the family."

"Andy's a photographer. I don't think he can find out information like this," Sarah said over her shoulder.

"We'll see. We'll see what he can do for you."

Chapter 30

Sarah raced down from Mrs. Noonan's and pounded on Andy's door. It opened immediately and she was pounding so hard, she fell in, right into Andy. He was there, in the flesh. He was back.

He held her up and she didn't let go. She leaned back, eyes riveted on his, biting her lip to keep from crying.

He cocked his head to the side, his lopsided grin hesitant. "I thought you'd be there to greet me after my long journey." His tone was light, but he stared at her intently.

She held his gaze, mesmerized by his red hair, much longer than when he left, his green eyes, the same color as hers, and that lopsided grin.

"I thought you might be at the airport," he said a second time.

She had no idea what he was talking about. "How would I meet you? I didn't know you were coming."

He dropped his arms and turned his head.

Then Sarah remembered the ICU rotation and her unread e-mail and even texts, and she told him in a gush about her month.

She saw the relief on his face. He took her back into his arms and they stood there. Together.

She had tried not to think too much about Andy while he was gone. Being busy at work certainly helped. When she did think about him, she told herself she was remembering wrong, that her view was distorted by distance, that no one could be that thoughtful, that kind.

But he was. As the days went by, Sarah remembered everything she loved about him. He was sweet, laid back, gentle, and handsome to boot. He was tall and broad and newly freckled from his time in Thailand and India and wherever else he'd been.

They met the day Andy moved into the building, on a rainy, gray day when his dresser tumbled off the moving truck and his prize possession, his grandmother's piano, got soaked. His calm reaction was quintessential Andy. When she found out he would only be there a few months, she tried to keep her feelings in check. Which was hard, especially when he was so darn nice.

Now it was like he'd never left, except every so often he said words in another language, and he liked his food much spicier, and he drove slower in case a cow roamed into the street. Being with him was easy and comfortable and exciting.

As Frances Noonan predicted, Andy was able to find exactly what she wanted. Even before he formally started back to work, he combed the archives of the Philadelphia Inquirer and came up with an immense amount of information. Sarah relayed the information to the Fog Ladies as they gathered in Alma Gordon's apartment for their weekly card game.

Joseph and Shelley Stalk had been married four years. Joseph Stalk had been arrested early in the marriage for domestic abuse, but Shelley wouldn't press charges and the matter was dropped. They were shopping the day of the murder, and the clerk in the department store heard several sharp words from Mr. Stalk. Nine-month-old Joey Stalk was found alone in the lobby of the building by a neighbor returning from walking her dog. She took the child up to the Stalk's apartment where she stated Mr. Stalk appeared surprised and angry. Mr. Stalk did not appear concerned about Shelley, said she was likely in the building somewhere and he had a ball game to watch. The neighbor, Mrs. Barbara Burkheimer, initiated a search on her own, telling the police later that she knew Shelley would never leave little Joey alone even for a moment. She found her easily in the back of her unlocked car, covered with a blue baby blanket. She had been strangled with her own scarf after being hit on the head with a blunt object. The police think Mr. Stalk had not yet had time to dispose of the body and had left the child in the lobby to be able to carry down the tools to do the job. A shovel and a pair of work gloves were in the apartment in the front hall next to the door. Mr. Stalk insisted he had planned to dig a sandpit for his child.

Shelley Stalk had a half-a-million-dollar life insurance policy through work and a second half-a-million policy that each spouse carried on their own. They had purchased the supplemental policies a year before, soon after Mr. Stalk began an affair with a client he met at his job as a Mercedes salesman. The woman, Ms. Theresa Sinclair, was cooperating with police and told them Mr. Stalk promised many times to leave his wife and even alluded to "never having to work again."

The boy, Joey, was now almost two, and living with his mother's sister, Evelyn Ringley, in Petaluma.

Andy had an address for them but could not come up with a telephone number.

"I think that's about everything." Sarah smiled in spite of the seriousness of the conversation. She was like a kid at Christmas, always grinning, always happy, now that Andy was home. She looked around the room. The Fog Ladies were not silent for long.

"What kind of a father could do such a thing, possibly right in front of the child? What a sad and sordid story," said Olivia Honeycut in her low voice.

"I knew Andy could help us," said Frances Noonan.

"All men are vile," said Harriet Flynn.

"A coldhearted killer," Mrs. Honeycut agreed.

"No worse than our own killer, stabbing his wife over and over with the kitchen shears," said Enid Carmichael.

"Oh, dear. Oh, dear," said Alma Gordon, who stood apart from the others, perhaps because she was hosting.

"We do not know that!" said Mrs. Noonan from the other side of the room.

"You are grasping at air," rasped Mrs. Honeycut. "These men are killers, blinded by money."

"And sex," said Mrs. Carmichael.

"Human flesh..." said Mrs. Flynn.

"Oh, dear. Oh, dear," said Mrs. Gordon.

"Ladies, ladies," said Mrs. Noonan. "We are here for the child. To see if this sister can help us at all with Ben."

"Well, we have an address," said Mrs. Carmichael. "What are we waiting for?"

Chapter 31

Frances Noonan recommended that only two should go for the visit. Didn't want a whole cadre of five old ladies descending on the poor woman. Since she had a car, it was understood that she would go. All the ladies were interested, but Enid Carmichael was desperate in her desire to meet the sister, Evelyn Ringley.

"Anything I can do to help the kid," she said, but Frances didn't think she even remembered Ben's name. Be in on the action, first to meet this woman, hear the juicy details, that was what Enid was after.

Enid was her usual forceful self, complaining they always left her out of the loop and that she had as much right to go as anyone else, more so, since it was her idea. Mrs. Noonan couldn't dispute this, and it was easier to say yes than continue to come up with excuses. Plus, in the back of her mind was a small thought that driving with Enid Carmichael might be preferable at the moment than driving with Alma Gordon and hearing happy stories about Mr. Glenn.

Mrs. Noonan had seen them standing hand in hand by the elevator, and then Mr. Glenn leaned in and gave Alma a peck on her cheek. It was so romantic, but so hard to watch. Bill had never been one to hold hands, but he did love those pecks.

So, against her better judgment, Mrs. Noonan set

off with Mrs. Carmichael. Her misgivings were born out even before they were out of San Francisco. As they approached the Golden Gate Bridge, not ten minutes from home, Enid shifted her tall frame uncomfortably. She yanked the lever to shove the seat farther back, but it was at its limit. She blurted, "She better have something to say. I hope I'm not making this trip all the way up there for nothing."

Mrs. Noonan bit her tongue. Bill would say she got what she deserved, avoiding Alma Gordon this way.

"She's the sister, after all," Mrs. Carmichael continued. "She must know more about this than she's telling."

"Yes, I certainly hope she can help us with Ben," Mrs. Noonan managed.

They found the address without difficulty, thanks to directions provided by Andy's cellular telephone map. He offered to let her take the phone with her, but even turning it on was tricky, especially with her arthritic, misshapen fingers. She copied the directions down instead.

The house was a one-story ranch, well kept, with a tricycle on the front porch and flowers along the front path. As they got out of the car, Mrs. Noonan wanted to tell Mrs. Carmichael to "be nice" and "contain yourself," but you couldn't say that to a grown woman, an eighty-year-old woman at that.

They waited a long time on the porch after ringing the bell. Mrs. Carmichael put her bony finger up to push the bell again, but Mrs. Noonan gently held her back. She sensed someone on the other side of the door, probably peeping through the peephole trying to decide whether to open the door or not. Mrs. Noonan stood up straight and put a pleasant smile on her face. She looked at Enid, who was scowling and picking her teeth with her fingernail.

They heard a commotion and a child's cry and a hush, all from the other side of the door. Soon after, it opened.

Evelyn Ringley was petite, blonde, and about thirty years old. A towheaded boy held her legs, his face buried in her jeans. Her hand rested on his head.

"Yes?" she said.

"Hello," said Mrs. Noonan. "I am Frances Noonan, and this is Enid Carmichael. We came from San Francisco hoping to talk to you. We don't want to bother you, but we think you can help us. We are in a situation similar to yours, helping out with a little boy," she dropped her voice to a whisper, "who lost a parent. We would like to learn from you, if possible, anything you can tell us to help the boy through this."

Evelyn Ringley considered them, then glanced down at the boy by her side. "Is this about that man in San Francisco? That man who k-i-l-l-e-d his wife?" She spelled the word out.

"Yes," said Mrs. Noonan. "The little boy is staying with his grandmother, a friend of ours. The boy is in trouble. We thought you might know something that could guide us."

"Come in," Evelyn Ringley said.

"Or know something more about anything else," said Mrs. Carmichael hopefully as they followed Evelyn into the living room. Mrs. Noonan elbowed her in the arm and shook her head.

The house smelled wonderful, but almost immediately Mrs. Noonan's throat tightened as she inhaled another delicious breath.

"We made cookies today. Molasses," Evelyn Ringley said. "Would you like one?"

"No, no thank you," Mrs. Noonan said quickly. Bill's favorite cookies. That molasses smell brought him back, but he wasn't there.

Enid Carmichael was quicker and louder. "Yes. Fantastic. I'm starved."

Evelyn offered Mrs. Carmichael the plate, and she took two of the large cookies. "None for you, Frances? You always like baked goods."

Enid grabbed a third cookie before Evelyn could set the plate back on the counter. Mrs. Noonan's throat was so tight she couldn't swallow a cookie if she wanted. She hadn't been this way in years, so melancholy about Bill. All this romance between Alma Gordon and Mr. Glenn was just too much.

"It's nap time." Evelyn motioned them through to a child's room. She lifted little Joey into the crib, and he lay on his back with a tiger under his arm. She bent over him, stroking his hair. Mrs. Noonan took some deep breaths, trying to ignore the molasses smell from Mrs. Carmichael's cookies. In minutes, the little boy fell asleep. Mrs. Noonan composed herself as well.

"It's been very hard," Evelyn said, settling them in the living room. "I'm thankful that Joey's so young. I think that makes him more adaptable. What a tragedy. Losing his mother, which he can't understand. His father in jail. Moving all the way across the country. My husband thinks it's good that I look like my sister. Joey knows I'm not Shelley, but sometimes he calls me 'Mama.' He actually seems to be doing all right, considering."

"Well, that's a tribute, I'm sure, to you and your husband," said Mrs. Noonan. "I hope you can give us some pointers."

"My husband and I have tried our best with him." Evelyn's eyes suddenly filled with tears. "I don't know if a child can truly get past something like this. We think he was there, you know."

Enid Carmichael perked right up. She dropped half a cookie on the rug in her excitement. "He was? He was there to see his father kill his mother?"

Mrs. Noonan shot her a look. But Evelyn seemed unperturbed, sitting quietly, her eyes closed now. Which was just as well because Mrs. Carmichael was attempting to retrieve her cookie piece with her foot but only succeeding in grinding it into the carpet.

Evelyn continued speaking. "Joey sometimes has nightmares. Not nearly as often as before, thank heavens. He wakes up shrieking, crying out for her. I can't imagine what he's dreaming, what horrors are in his memory. He never asks for his father. He actually doesn't say much at all. We went to a child psychologist to find out what to do, but all he could say was consistency and love, which is obvious. He said children are resilient, that Joey can be a normal little boy. And, for the most part, he seems happy. He plays with the other children on the street, he smiles, he laughs."

"He's very lucky to have you," Mrs. Noonan said. "I'm sure you've done everything you can."

Evelyn stared at the cookies on the table. Her face crumpled. "He's not lucky. I didn't do nearly enough."

"Oh, there, dear…" Mrs. Noonan said.

"I knew about the affair," Evelyn said.

"You knew?" Mrs. Carmichael jumped right in. "You knew? What did you do?"

"Nothing," Evelyn whispered. "I did nothing."

Mrs. Noonan kicked Mrs. Carmichael in the ankles. Mrs. Carmichael glared back but kept silent.

"I overheard him on the telephone. I'll never forgive myself for not saying something, for not warning her. I didn't know what would happen." Tears welled again in her eyes. "Poor Shelley, my poor, poor Shelley. Poor Joey. They seemed so happy. I didn't know." The tears rolled down her face. Her shoulders shook and she clenched her arms around her body.

Mrs. Noonan reached out to pat her knee. In a moment Evelyn could speak again, her voice still soft. Mrs. Carmichael leaned so far forward, Frances was afraid she would keel over.

"When they were first married, he had an affair then too. Shelley knew about that one. She thought it was her punishment because she started going with him while he was still living with his previous girlfriend. The affair devastated her. She truly thought she was the one for him, the one he had been looking for. She was heartbroken to find out he was just plain looking.

"They had a huge argument and Shelley slapped him and he slapped her back. A neighbor woman overheard and called the police. It was actually the same neighbor who found Joey in the lobby after Shelley was killed. The police arrested Joe because Shelley had a split lip. But she wouldn't let them charge him. And she swore that was the one and only time he hit her. I believed her about that. What a fool I was.

"He did end that affair, and they really did seem happy. When little Joey came, Joe seemed so proud, I thought he had actually changed. I thought they had a chance. Joe talked about Joey nonstop, all the things they would do together. Joe played the lottery and was convinced he would win one day. That he wouldn't have to work, and he and Joey would go fishing and play football and camp out. Shelley seemed so happy.

"But Joey was a hard baby. Joe didn't have the patience for all the crying, all the diapers. Shelley did it all and worked too. She didn't complain, just kept trudging along. When she was with us that last summer, she made excuses for Joe, for why he wasn't helping more."

Little Joey called out from the other room. Evelyn paused. Mrs. Carmichael noisily swallowed the last of her cookie. The boy didn't call again, and Evelyn went on. "Joe had the gall to call his girlfriend right from this house. I heard him and I didn't say anything, not to him, not to Shelley. I know I should have talked to her, told her right then about Joe. But I couldn't bring myself to. She still loved him. I didn't want to be the one to break her heart again."

Mrs. Noonan could see Enid perched on the edge of her chair, barely able to contain herself. She tried to catch her eye, to motion her to keep silent, but to no avail.

"You probably could have stopped the whole thing, then," said Mrs. Carmichael, "if you'd just said something."

"Oh, no, dear, I'm sure that's not true," said Mrs. Noonan quickly.

Tears stained Evelyn's face, but her voice was clear. "Yes, yes, she's right. If I'd told Shelley about the affair, she would have left him. I know she would have. She might even have stayed in California with us. She was only in Philadelphia because of Joe. She loved it out here. And if Joe knew we all knew about the affair, he would never have thought he could kill her and get away with it, get the money."

"It certainly is a lot of money," said Mrs. Carmichael. "A million dollars."

"Yes, a million dollars. My husband was astounded when Shelley told us about their insurance policies. We were on vacation at a place without internet and Joe was mad because he couldn't look up the numbers for his lottery ticket. Shelley said if she ever died, he would never need a lottery ticket again. The irony is, the policy was so high because of Shelley. When she was pregnant with Joey, she made them get the extra policies. She had to hunt around to find a company to issue them. She had this idea that if a family loses a parent, it's so devastating that the least you can do to soften the pain is to be rich. And the money would allow the living parent to stay home with Joey. Well, now look."

"She sweetened the pot just too much," said Mrs. Carmichael. "To think he could have his paramour and a million dollars. What a temptation for an unscrupulous man."

"Yes, and now the money will probably come to Joey," Evelyn said. "To us, if Joe gets convicted. Joe can't collect, of course. Joey's the contingent beneficiary on the life insurance, and we're the guardians in their wills. Shelley made them get wills too. Joe must be furious."

"It's his own making. He's a murderer, after all," Mrs. Carmichael said.

"Oh, I know. Believe me, I know. When I think of what he did…to my sister…" Evelyn fought to control herself. "Shelley loved little Joey so much. She'll never get to see him grow. He can toss a ball now. He can climb up on a chair. She'll never see this. When they were here, we all went down to Big Sur. Joey was only six or seven months old then, and he had this game where he bounced up and down holding onto her knees, and he was so strong he could almost pull her over. They both loved it and laughed hysterically. Now he does it with us, bouncing up and down and pulling on our legs. He still laughs and laughs, but it's all I can do not to cry."

"Crying won't help the tot," said Mrs. Carmichael.

"You went down to Big Sur?" said Mrs. Noonan.

"Yes. It was the last vacation Shelley ever took. She and Joe came to visit us for two weeks, and we spent a week at a resort in Big Sur. A beautiful place."

"Do you remember the name?" asked Mrs. Noonan.

"No, but I have the brochure right here. I saved it because it was such a nice place." Evelyn stood slowly, as if she had aged with all this talking and was as old as Mrs. Noonan. She crossed to a desk in the corner and opened a drawer.

"Here." She passed the brochure to Mrs. Noonan. "Paradise Cove."

Chapter 32

"No, it couldn't be." Sarah stared at Frances Noonan incredulously. "It's too much of a coincidence."

"I know, I know." Mrs. Noonan passed her another berry tart. "I was dumbfounded. But she gave me the brochure. It's the same place. Look."

Sarah took the brochure gingerly. Paradise Cove. She turned it over. On the back was the proprietor's familiar face and his name, Allen Werble. She opened it and saw the incredible Big Sur coastline. It was the same place.

"Is this possible?" Sarah asked. "Two women, two unhappy marriages, two little boys, two insurance policies, two families who went to Big Sur? This seems unbelievable."

"I know. I want you to tell me everything you remember about the place. Stay to dinner?"

"Not tonight. I'm going out with Andy at seven."

"Of course, dear." Mrs. Noonan's voice was too bright. Before Sarah could think about it, Mrs. Noonan immediately added, "Maybe you can get Andy to do some digging as well."

Andy had pitched right in to help the Fog Ladies find Evelyn Ringley. Sarah was sure he would willingly gather more information if they needed it. He was such a sweetie.

She broke into a huge smile and nodded. "I'll ask him. We're going out for Indian food. I've never had some of the dishes he orders now, cauliflower and potato in tomato sauce, dosa."

"Dosa?"

"Huge, flat rice crepe affairs stuffed with potatoes and onions and spice. Andy said he ate the cauliflower dish and dosa for breakfast in India. Dosa cost fifty-five cents there."

"My, my." Frances Noonan took a bite of her tart. "Well, then, tell me everything you know."

Sarah told Mrs. Noonan what she remembered about the Paradise Cove Resort and the people she met there, the beautiful setting in the woods, the large shingled buildings, the pool and its bubble, the broad area of green grass and the gardens, the secluded beach, the families, the children, the proprietor, Glenda and George the housekeeper and maintenance man, their nephew, Dylan, Emanuel the waiter, and Marco the chef.

Sarah suggested they ask Alma Gordon and Mr. Glenn. "They might remember something else."

Mrs. Noonan waved her hand vaguely and said she'd meet Sarah down there.

Mrs. Gordon and Mr. Glenn were as shocked as Sarah to hear the coincidence.

"Try to remember anything that might be important," Sarah said.

They both commented on how cool and foggy the weather was for July and how cozy it was indoors. Mr. Glenn dwelled on the noise in the dining room. Mrs. Gordon's eyes teared up and Sarah knew she was thinking about Baby Owen.

Mr. Glenn fidgeted with his belt buckle.

"Anything else?" Sarah asked.

"Well, I did have a somewhat embarrassing conversation with the maintenance man, George," Mr. Glenn said.

"I never met him," Alma said.

"I know. This was when I skipped brunch. I took a walk and he and I got to talking. He's a Phillies man, if you can believe it. All the way out here. He grew up there, has been a fan for life. Still catches the occasional game there. Anyway, I was complaining about my bum knee, but it turned out he'd had a serious health issue. I felt a little silly for mentioning my knee. He said he had a heart attack and almost died. It scared him, and he didn't want to go to an early grave like his dad. His doctor told him he needed to make some changes, eat right, exercise more, cut down on stress. And he did. He said it was the resort, the beauty of the scenery. He said the place had done wonders for Dylan, his nephew, too, that the kid had a troubled past and that his whole outlook had changed."

"A troubled past?" Sarah asked.

"Yes. He said he had difficulty with his dad, and he was into drugs and all kinds of things, but now he'd sobered up and since working at the resort, he was a new person."

"Drugs? Difficulty with his dad? I bet those two things are related," said Sarah. She was immediately sorry, remembering about Mr. Glenn's son, Lionel, and his problems with drugs.

Mr. Glenn continued right on. "Dylan's clean and sober now. George stressed this. Has been for years, before he started working there."

Mr. Glenn paused, and Sarah thought he was done.

Mrs. Gordon piped up. "There's nothing embarrassing about this story, dear."

"Yes, yes, I'm getting to that." Mr. Glenn sighed. "George said he really got into diet and exercise after his heart attack. Said he felt better now than ever in his entire life. In three and a half years, he lost *eighty* pounds."

"Wow," Sarah said.

"Yes. Turned his whole life around." Mr. Glenn took a breath. "Then the guy looked me up and down, and said, 'If you don't mind my saying so, you might consider it too.'"

Mr. Glenn looked sheepish. "I told him I'd made it to age seventy-five, so I thought I was doing pretty well."

Mrs. Gordon chuckled and patted his knee. "That you are, Albert. That you are."

Sarah only then noticed she'd interrupted their dinner. Mr. Glenn's uneaten plate had a large pork chop and a hefty scoop of potatoes and gravy. Mrs. Gordon's plate had mostly green beans and a tiny slice of pork chop. No potatoes.

"I'll let you get back to your dinner," Sarah said. "Thanks for the story, Mr. Glenn."

Mrs. Noonan had never materialized, and Sarah walked back up to her apartment. She told her about Dylan and his drugs.

"He's so young," Mrs. Noonan said. "I don't see how he could be involved."

"I know," Sarah said. "But he is a little creepy."

"Sarah, this whole thing is creepy. It's too much of a coincidence," Mrs. Noonan said. "Bill did not believe in coincidences."

Could there be a connection between the resort and the murders? If there was, Sarah couldn't see how.

Chapter 33

Frances Noonan accompanied Julia Blackwell to her next meeting with Spencer Tremaine. The meetings were infrequent now. Alma Gordon stayed with little Ben. He didn't acknowledge that Julia was leaving. She had to stoop down until her face was even with his and gently lift his chin. Julia kissed his cheek and said good-bye, and he nodded without meeting her eyes. Frances hoped Alma Gordon could work some magic while they were gone.

Spencer Tremaine sat behind his desk and they sat in front of it, the huge glass desk that enamored Alma Gordon so. One file only graced its surface again, though not so thin anymore.

He got right to the point. "This is the endless middle of the case, with no resolution in sight and when victories, however small, are elusive. This is when loved ones can lose hope. But we mustn't do that. That is of no use to anyone. My uncle, a great lover of opera, always said, 'It's not over until the fat lady sings.' This case is far from over. These small setbacks are nothing more than that, mere small setbacks. Nothing has happened that is insurmountable. We are not yet to intermission, let alone the final curtain."

He was smooth, Frances would give him that. Though she might have said "final act" instead of "final curtain," considering the circumstances.

He spread his arms wide. "We must all support one another"—here he opened his arms wider as if to include Frances—"and dispel any thought of failure, any doubts that we will not succeed, that justice will not prevail."

He dropped his arms and opened the cover of the file on the desk. As if he had guessed that Julia doubted even him, he demurred, "Trial dates can seem distant. We have a strong team in place. I do not intend to make any changes from this point forward, as changes simply delay the process further. I would advise against changes of any sort."

He leaned toward them over the great expanse of glass. He lowered his voice. "These are the times we need to shore up the accused. To make certain he understands that freedom will be his, but that victory takes time. We do not want any harm to come to him. I will use my influence to make certain the jail is aware of the danger of despair. I have saved more than one from self-injury."

Frances watched Julia Blackwell's face take in Spencer Tremaine's words. The threat of suicide which only he could prevent. That sneaky devil had sealed his continued involvement in the case. How could Julia possibly contemplate replacing Spencer Tremaine after this performance?

Chapter 34

Andy had more information in no time. Sarah could see he was bursting. He could hardly keep the words from spilling out, and he was talking so fast there was spittle at the corner of his mouth. She was a little embarrassed for him, then she decided that was silly. She glanced around to see if the Fog Ladies had noticed, but they just seemed interested in his tale. It was actually endearing how excited Andy was. They sat in Mrs. Noonan's apartment, eating chocolate chip cookies, of course, gathered at Andy's request because he had some "big news."

Andy started his story by telling them about Paradise Cove, which at one time had been a camp for wayward boys, then a girls' boarding school, and for the past ten years, a family resort. The current owner's name was Allen Werble and, on the website, he was quoted as saying he wanted to create an affordable vacation destination in a peaceful setting. The chef of one year was Marco White, and he had previously worked for many years in an upscale restaurant in Los Angeles. Emanuel Garcia, along with Glenda and George Parkman, had worked at the resort for several years. No complaints were listed with the county or state boards, and the police had never been called to Paradise Cove.

Andy had found something else, something even

more coincidental than two dead women vacationing at the same resort. He had searched the archives for domestic murders going back five years. There were more than he could imagine, he said, more than fifteen hundred a year for women victims recently and about half that for men. But two stood out because of the motive. The same million-dollar life insurance policies.

A mother in San Antonio, Maria Romero, was shot by her husband five years earlier. For the million-dollar insurance money. He tried to make it look like a burglary. He was a businessman who traveled frequently and said he returned home to the murder scene. They had two children who now lived with her parents. He was serving a life term.

Sarah could see Andy still hadn't told them his "big news." His face was flushed, and he talked nonstop, but he had saved the best for last. He had found one more case.

"This was the day after Christmas, four years ago," Andy said, drawing out the suspense.

Sarah smiled and watched Andy savor the moment. He was adorable. A far cry from Christmas four years ago for her. The first big love of her life dumped her on Christmas Day her second year of medical school. They met her senior year of college, and she thought at the time they would be together forever. So dumb. She'd chosen her medical school solely because of him, his city, his job. They hadn't known each other long enough for that big a life change, which became more and more apparent as time went on. But to dump her on Christmas. That hurt. She hadn't thought about him in a long time and never without a slew of emotions. Not today, though, not with Andy here, winking at her and holding court, perfectly comfortable among this group of older ladies.

He continued his story. Serena and David Evans both had million-dollar insurance policies through their mutual business. They lived in Chicago and by all accounts had a passionate but volatile marriage, with loud arguments and accusations from both spouses for years. She had previously filed for divorce but later withdrew the papers. Then one spouse was killed, hacked up by the other on the day after Christmas with a machete-like blade they used to trim the bushes. But it wasn't the wife who was killed. It was the husband.

"On the day after the Lord's birth." Harriet Flynn crossed herself.

"*She* hacked *him* up? With a machete?" said Olivia Honeycut.

"Oh, dear. Oh, dear," said Alma Gordon.

"Sin is not confined to men," said Harriet Flynn. "Eve was the one to take the bite, after all."

"Statistics show this is extremely rare," said Frances Noonan.

"What a woman," said Enid Carmichael.

"But not a lady," said Olivia Honeycut in her low voice.

"I haven't told you the best part," said Andy.

"Don't tell me they had just visited Big Sur," said Sarah.

"Nope, it's better than that. Guess who her lawyer was," said Andy.

They all looked at him, but Frances Noonan understood first.

"You've got to be kidding," she said. "It can't be."

"But it is," said Andy.

"What? What? Tell us," said Olivia Honeycut.

"No, no, it's not possible," said Alma Gordon.

"I'm with Mrs. Honeycut," said Sarah. "Tell us, those of us who are slow."

"It's Spencer Tremaine, isn't it?" said Enid Carmichael with a flourish, cookie pieces flying around as she waved her hand.

"Yep, none other," said Andy.

The ladies all broke out talking at once. Mrs. Gordon looked miserable, but Mrs. Noonan was absolutely delighted.

"Does this really mean something?" asked Sarah. "That they had the same lawyer? The same famous lawyer?"

"He certainly didn't mention this case to Julia when he was tooting his horn. I just saw the man," said Mrs. Noonan. "And these cases are pretty similar."

"Million-dollar life insurance policies. Sharp instruments of death," said Mrs. Carmichael.

"Oh, dear. Oh, dear," said Mrs. Gordon.

"But there's more," said Andy. "She's right here."

"Who's here?" said Sarah.

"The woman, Serena Evans."

"Oh, for heaven's sake, you've got to be kidding. Don't we have enough of our own murderers in this state? We have to import others?" said Mrs. Flynn.

"Her kids are here. She has twin ten-year-old girls and her brother is raising them. He lives in Modesto and she got transferred to Central California Women's Facility in Chowchilla to be closer to them. They would have been six when this happened," Andy said.

"Oh, what a shame. More children. Such heartache for them, losing two parents at once," said Mrs.

Gordon.

"And such horrific circumstances," said Mrs. Noonan. "One parent killing another."

"It happens all the time, unfortunately," Andy said. "Domestic violence turns out to be very common. I had no idea, but I turned up thousands of cases across the nation in the past five years. The thing that's different about these cases is the money."

"A million dollars!" said Mrs. Carmichael.

"Right," said Andy. "Serena Evans told the police that there had been an uptick in crime in their neighborhood, and that she thought she was being followed. The police agreed there had been an increase in crime, and they said she used that as a pretext for her murder plot."

"I bet there are more cases we don't know about, where the man got away with it, killed his wife and got the insurance and no one was the wiser," said Mrs. Honeycut.

"Ladies, ladies, you're forgetting something," said Mrs. Noonan. "Paul did not kill Andrea. His case is not like the rest of these. He didn't do it."

"No!" Sarah agreed, too loudly. "I met him. He's not a murderer!"

No one else spoke. The silence continued awkwardly and Sarah tried to think of something more to say. As she scanned the faces of the Fog Ladies, she could see they thought Paul was guilty, as guilty as Joseph Stalk in Philadelphia or the businessman in San Antonio who shot his wife.

Finally, Mrs. Gordon said gently, "Too bad he has no alibi."

"Yoga!" Mrs. Carmichael snorted.

"And even that was a lie," said Mrs. Flynn.

"But none of you know him. How can you condemn someone you don't even know?" Sarah said.

"Do any of us know anybody?" said Mrs. Honeycut.

"Speaking of getting to know people, any chance of meeting this Serena Evans, this man-hacker-upper?" asked Mrs. Carmichael.

"Enid!" said Mrs. Gordon, her cookie stopped in midair.

"Associating with the devil," said Mrs. Flynn.

"She says she didn't do it," said Andy.

"It actually could be quite worthwhile," said Mrs. Noonan.

"Oh, dear. Oh, dear." Mrs. Gordon clenched her fist so tightly, her cookie snapped in two.

Chapter 35

On Thanksgiving Day, Chantrelle called again. Alma Gordon waited for her daughter, Sylvia, and Harold to pick her up for dinner at their house. She covered her cranberry jelly with a cheese cloth and set it on the counter by her handbag. She thought the call might be from Sylvia, and she answered cheerily.

Her horoscope that morning had read, "Patience and kindness take the day." She thought of all the families at Thanksgiving dinner avoiding conversation about religion, money, and politics. She was thankful to be eating with Sylvia and Harold.

"It's me." This was the unmistakable voice of Chantrelle.

"Chantrelle! How are you?" Mrs. Gordon almost knocked over the cranberry jelly in her excitement.

"Owen's gone."

"Oh, my God, oh, my Lord, oh, heavens, Chantrelle, he's just a baby, where is he?" Mrs. Gordon cried.

"Geez, not him," said Chantrelle. "Baby Owen's right here. Well, in the other room. Watching TV." Mrs. Gordon heard her yell, "You okay in there Owen?" Then she was back. "Big Owen. He left. Him and Inez both."

"Your housemate Inez? Who works at the bar?" said Mrs. Gordon.

"Yeah, well, the bimbo was sleeping with Owen. So I threw his stuff out the window and told him to never come back. *I* found this place. She said if he was going, she was going, too, and I said, 'Damn right you're going.' Him and her can just go to hell."

What was it these girls found attractive about Big Owen anyway? Mrs. Gordon had never understood what Chantrelle saw in him, and now here apparently was another girl changing her life for him. The man was an uncouth oaf. And mean. He frightened Alma. She was happy to hear Big Owen was gone for now. Even if he was Baby Owen's father, he was not a good influence.

"Two guys next door liked our place better, Zach and Zeke, and they moved in, so the rent's covered at least," Chantrelle said.

Mrs. Gordon shuddered, thinking about all the comings and goings. "How is Baby Owen?" she asked.

"Aw, he's okay. He's having a lot of trouble sleeping, though. Hey, did you know he sucks his thumb when he sleeps? It's the cutest thing."

Mrs. Gordon smiled, remembering Owen's thumb sucking. It was good to hear Chantrelle sounding so besotted.

"What the—Owen what are you doing? No, that's not yours. Put that down. Owen!" Mrs. Gordon could tell by the tone of her voice that she was talking to the toddler and not a returning Big Owen. "Just a minute," Chantrelle said and put down the phone. Mrs. Gordon heard Baby Owen start to cry. She sighed.

Chantrelle came back. "Anyway, I just wanted to ask you if you ever tried this thing called diphenhydramine to get him to go to sleep. Zach, he's one of the guys who moved in, he says a kid should sleep better than Owen does, and this medicine would help. Did you ever use that?"

Mrs. Gordon gasped. She remembered her own experience with diphenhydramine when she'd gotten hives from penicillin a few years earlier. Put her to sleep for hours. She'd missed a quilting get-together with the ladies. And she'd only taken a small dose.

"No, dear, I don't think that would be good for him," she said. "I don't remember him having problems sleeping. He usually went right to bed after his story. Usually around seven."

"Yeah, well, now he's still wide awake when we all go to bed at eleven or so, and he cries when I put him down, and he wakes up as soon as he falls asleep."

"Oh, dear," said Mrs. Gordon. "Maybe he's overtired from being up so late."

"Well, I only let him stay up because when I try to put him down earlier, he screams bloody murder. He's just not tired."

"That's so unusual," said Mrs. Gordon. Then she had a thought. "Chantrelle, remember when you used to give him Pepsi?"

"Yeah, so?"

"Are you still giving him that? Because Pepsi has caffeine in it and that could make him not sleep."

From the other end of the phone came silence.

Mrs. Gordon couldn't believe it. She had written out an entire page of food that Baby Owen liked, all nutritious, healthy food for a child. She had written amounts and how to prepare them for a child his age. When she first met Chantrelle, Baby Owen was eating chips! A baby less than a year old! What was happening now?

"Okay, gotta go," said Chantrelle.

"Please call again soon," said Mrs. Gordon. "And Chantrelle, Happy Thanksgiving."

"Yeah, you too."

Mrs. Gordon sent up a silent prayer that Baby Owen would eat a lot of turkey and sleep well that night.

Chapter 36

By mid-December, Frances Noonan had the Fog Ladies set up for their first visit to the prison. They would teach the incarcerates a skill. That's how they put it to the warden. It had been far easier than she anticipated to get authorization for their project, partly because the prison was chronically short of funds and always open to educational activities and partly because the warden's mother had been a quilter.

The prison was three hours away. Enid Carmichael complained the entire way, though she sat up front next to Mrs. Noonan where there was more room. Alma Gordon, Olivia Honeycut, and Harriet Flynn were smooshed into the small back seat, quiet, uncomplaining. The big woman complained about the dust that came in through the window when she put it down and the heat from the sun when she had it closed. She complained about the endless brown view and the smell of the cows. She even complained about the road, with few cars and therefore few people to spy on. "Give me the city any day," she said.

They made good time on the empty central California roads, and it took them less than three hours, including a stop at a barren rest area for the bathroom and a snack. Mrs. Noonan had an entire quiche packed into a plastic tub, minus one piece, because she'd expected Sarah to dinner the night before. They hadn't talked about it. Mrs. Noonan just assumed. She enjoyed having Sarah to eat with. Had grown used to her at the kitchen table. But the girl had gone out to dinner with Andy. Of course.

Not just dinner. Ice-skating, too, down at the rink at Union Square. Mrs. Noonan had heard all about it from Sarah that morning. The big open area was set up for the season and Andy suggested they skate, even though he'd never done it. Sarah said she held him up the whole time, and they fell so many times she thought they'd end up in the emergency department. Sarah showed Frances pictures of the gigantic Christmas tree, taller than the Macy's building, lighted with so many lights you couldn't see the tree underneath. One of the hotels had a gingerbread house display, and Sarah and Andy enjoyed that as well. Sarah regaled her with endless details of the date, so Frances felt she'd been a witness.

Frances was glad Andy was back. The two were obviously smitten. But Frances also missed Sarah's company.

The Fog Ladies arrived at the prison, which sat in a vast sea of brown—brown dirt, brown grass. Mrs. Noonan had arranged for three sessions with the inmates, and the Fog Ladies brought all the supplies with them as a donation to the prison. They would break into groups so they could teach as many women as possible. The warden suggested ten inmates to a group, each group getting two hours of instruction and two groups each visit. Sixty inmates total.

The Fog Ladies brought a lot of supplies, though they left the quilting frames home on this first visit and just brought embroidery hoops. They had precut all the squares from a variety of different cloths. They planned on simple patchwork quilts with a one-patch design. They estimated six quilts could eventually be made if each group of ten was able to complete a quilt.

The prison was fairly new but looked worn. They waited in a lobby with magazines without covers, all out of date. The Fog Ladies clustered at the water fountain after their long journey, but it was broken.

Mrs. Noonan had already filled out pages of paperwork, and each of the Fog Ladies had been through a background check, but the first visit started with more paperwork still. They had their photographs taken for identity badges, and they went through a pat-down search.

"We've already been through the metal detector," Harriet Flynn complained.

"And I had to go through without my walker," Olivia Honeycut added.

"Shh," said Frances Noonan as the guard approached.

"I hope you don't expect me to take off my shoes again." Enid Carmichael peered down from her high heels. The woman guard glared and motioned for the shoes to come off.

Even Alma Gordon, always so cooperative, let out a yelp when the guard did her search.

They then met personally with the warden. Mrs. Noonan stressed the calming effects of quilting, as she had in her application, and that finished products could be auctioned, "especially if, for instance, the quilter had some notoriety."

"Oh, we don't have anybody like that," the warden said. She was a tall woman with her hair pulled severely back in a bun. "This isn't San Quentin."

"Well, their families would certainly enjoy the thoughtful present of a well-crafted quilt," Mrs. Noonan added.

"Any quilts made will be the property of the state," the warden said.

"Oh, you must have some famous prisoners," Mrs. Honeycut said.

"We wouldn't want to capitalize on one in our charge," said the warden.

"Quilting would be helpful for everybody," Mrs. Gordon said meekly. "Especially those with problem pasts."

"We want your worst ones," said Mrs. Carmichael. "The rapists, the ax murderers."

"This is a women's prison. We don't have any of those," the warden said. "There aren't that many true female murderers. Just women trying to get out of abusive relationships the only way left to them. Most of our women are in for nonviolent crimes. You'll have to settle for ordinary criminals, drugs, forgery. But I'm sure they can benefit from quilting." The warden showed a hint of a smile for the first time.

"Don't you have even one murderer?" Mrs. Noonan persisted. If she hadn't already gotten the go-ahead, she would not be so pushy. How unfortunate to spend all this time and effort and not get to talk with Serena Evans. The thought of driving out here two more times with Enid Carmichael next to her, all for nothing, was downright depressing. How selfish, she told herself. Quilting would benefit the other inmates, too, even if they couldn't speak to the lady killer.

"Like I said, we have women who killed their

husbands or boyfriends, but for the most part, they were trying to protect themselves or their children. Those of us who haven't been in their shoes cannot judge what we might do in similar circumstances. But there is one woman who did it for money. A million dollars."

"Oh, my, really?" Frances Noonan tried to hide her excitement.

"Yes, horrible crime." The warden winced. "Hacked up her husband with a machete."

"Oh, dear." Alma Gordon put her hand to her mouth.

"She's been a model prisoner, though. I did intend for her be part of this, if you have no objection," the warden said.

"Oh, no, none at all," said Mrs. Noonan, elated.

"Yes, we'd better include her. Her soul needs cleansing too," Harriet Flynn piped in. "Quilting can be quite good for the soul."

Chapter 37

Serena Evans was in Frances Noonan and Harriet Flynn's second group of quilters. Mrs. Noonan saw to that. For all they knew, though, they might have already met some murderers in the first group. It was impossible to tell. All the women looked the same in their jumpsuits, with similar hair, either long and flat or short and flat. And they all had the same demeanors, polite, downcast. They didn't wear signs around their necks announcing their crimes.

A scuffle broke out over needles in the first group. Mrs. Noonan thought that might be the end of the quilting. Two women wanted the red corduroy patch and one woman, a surprisingly small and gentle looking woman named Maya, intentionally pricked the other woman in the arm. At least that's how it looked to Mrs. Noonan. And to the injured woman, a stout middle-aged woman who cussed nonstop throughout the session. Before Frances Noonan could explain that she had plenty more red corduroy patches, the cussing woman elbowed Maya in the side, and Maya jabbed again with her needle but missed. Mrs. Flynn stood with her eyes squeezed shut, but Mrs. Noonan stepped between the two.

"Here's another piece of red." She guided Maya to the other side of the table. "We can't have two red patches next to each other, that won't look right. Let's have you sit over here."

A guard leaned against the wall. Enid Carmichael and Alma Gordon's group was between him and Mrs. Noonan's table, and he didn't budge. Several cameras fixed on them from the ceiling, but no one ever said anything to Mrs. Noonan, so she assumed this sort of thing must happen from time to time.

Frances Noonan watched the other table. Enid Carmichael towered over tiny Alma Gordon. When they divided into their groups, Alma had naturally moved next to Frances, but Frances asked her to work with Enid.

"Just in case she says something untoward, you can step in and smooth things over," Mrs. Noonan said. It was a smart idea, but Mrs. Noonan wasn't fooling herself that this was the real reason. Alma Gordon's stricken face told her Alma did not believe the fib either.

At the end of the first session, a needle was missing from Olivia Honeycut's group. It was found quickly on the floor, and the next group started right on time. The warden had been very strict with Mrs. Noonan. All the needles must be counted ahead and accounted for after.

The husband killer stood out immediately. Serena Evans was a beauty, even with her unwashed, no-style hair and lack of makeup. She was dark and tall and had marvelous posture, unlike most of the women in the room. Including us Fog Ladies, thought Mrs. Noonan, straightening her back.

Serena had some experience with quilting as a girl, she said, and she helped the women on either side with their stitch. Mrs. Noonan moved to her side, using her sewn pieces as an example for the group of the correct amount of seam allowance. Once she stood next to her, Mrs. Noonan pounced on Serena's sewing experience as an excuse to start a conversation.

"How did you learn such an even running stitch?"

"I made a quilt each summer with my cousins and granny." Serena concentrated on her cloth pieces.

"Oh, how lovely. Is your grandmother still alive, dear?" Mrs. Noonan continued.

"No, she died while I was in college."

"Oh, I am sorry. Where did you go to college?"

"Northwestern. Close to home. I'm one of their more infamous graduates. They don't talk about me on the prospective student tours." Serena forcefully bit off her thread with her teeth.

"Oh. Well." Mrs. Noonan paused, then plunged right in. "You're from the Midwest. What are you doing out here?"

Mrs. Noonan learned Serena's whole story, from her marriage to a man who was domineering but seductive, to the birth of their twins, and on to his death, in which Serena was straightforward about having had no part. She wasn't adamant, she didn't go into explanations of why, she just stated it as a matter of fact. After starting her sentence in a prison in Illinois, she was able to transfer to California, where she saw her daughters every weekend.

"You should see them. They can swim. They take piano lessons." Serena's face opened, glowing with pride. She lowered her voice. "Most of the women have children, but they can't see them nearly as often as I see my girls."

"Oh?" Mrs. Noonan said.

"This prison isn't exactly centrally located," Serena

answered. "These women are from the cities, San Francisco, Los Angeles, San Jose. We're hours from there. And most families can't afford to come that often. I'm lucky, my brother lives pretty close, and he brings my babies every week. He's been great. With the insurance money, he was able to cut way back on work. He's like a dad to them. The three of them are the only thing that keeps me going."

Serena squeezed her eyes shut, but Mrs. Noonan could see the tears. She put her hand out and held her arm. The woman on Serena's other side, a large woman with curly black hair, rolled her eyes. "I ain't seen mine in a year," she said. "And I'm still going. We all gotta get by."

Chapter 38

The Fog Ladies sat that night in Alma Gordon's living room. After the long day plus the long ride home, Alma wanted to put her feet up and think pleasant thoughts, but Frances Noonan, at least, still wanted to talk murder.

"Serena said her brother essentially got the insurance money after she was convicted because it went to the girls and he is their guardian. He can't use it for anything obvious like a sports car, but she mentioned a vacation to Mexico. Evelyn Ringley will control the money that Joey gets. Do you think these guardians could be the killers?"

Alma shuddered. "Evelyn Ringley killed her own sister? No. I cannot believe that."

"Not Evelyn," Frances Noonan said. "Her husband. Evelyn told us her husband was amazed to hear how much insurance Shelley had. Shelley told them that summer she was there. Serena's brother may have known about David Evans's insurance as well."

"Oh, yes, yes, I like this," Enid Carmichael said. "Evelyn Ringley's husband killed Shelley and then reaped the money from the kid. The brother-in-law did it."

"'Thou shalt not hate thy brother in thine heart,'" said Harriet Flynn. "Or brother-in-law. No, this is too much. Two different killers concoct the same plan, such horrific crimes, all for money. Greed. No, I don't believe it."

"What about 'Thou shalt not kill?'" asked Olivia Honeycut. "Seems someone out there forgot that one."

"I don't believe it either," Alma said. "Because that would mean Julia Blackwell killed Andrea. She is watching Ben now. She is the guardian." She could feel her blood pressure rise, all this talk of family killing family.

"Okay, not Julia," Frances Noonan said. "But maybe the others? Oh, I don't know. This idea is a little outlandish. Bill always said find a pattern. A simple pattern. Things are usually just what they appear."

"Which means we met a killer today," said Enid Carmichael with relish.

"She sure didn't seem like a killer," said Mrs. Noonan. "And that brother is coming next week for Christmas. Better hope he's not the one."

Alma felt she had to change the subject. "Speaking of Christmas, Julia Blackwell told me Ben will get to see his father for two hours, that's it," she said. "But two hours is longer than any other visit he's had. Ben actually drew a picture for a present, and Julia was thrilled because it was the first time Ben wanted to do anything. Then she saw what he had drawn. She doesn't know what to do now. Ben drew a picture of their family and a Christmas tree. Their whole family. Andrea too."

"Oh, my, that is very sad," said Frances.

"That man should hang it in his cell and reflect on what he's done," huffed Olivia Honeycut.

"Olivia!" Alma and Frances shouted together. Olivia Honeycut just wagged her finger.

Harriet Flynn, bless her, broke in to change the subject once more. "Serena Evans and Paul Blackwell may be the only ones with visitors for the Lord's birthday. No one else told me today they were expecting anyone."

The Fog Ladies realized this might be true. Christmas was a week away, yet many of the women in the groups did not think they would see family or friends for the holiday. The prison was so far, and the families didn't have the means to go.

Alma Gordon could see by Frances Noonan's expression that her mind was churning. Alma looked around the room. It was clear the other Fog Ladies could see it too.

Olivia Honeycut was already shaking her head. "The women in my group were all quite civilized, but they are in prison to pay a debt to society. It is not our place to change the system."

"I don't intend to change the system," said Frances Noonan.

Alma Gordon agreed with Frances. "A woman in my group learned to read and write while in prison and is dying to show her boy she can read to him. But he can't be there. Wouldn't that be a wonderful Christmas present?"

"That woman's boy is thirteen," said Enid Carmichael. "What's she going to read to him that he can't read himself?"

Enid Carmichael had been right next to Alma at the table, but she still didn't get it. She could be so thick. "That's just it," Mrs. Gordon explained. "He's thirteen, he's almost a man. And now his mother can read. That's something anyone can be proud of. He can be

173

proud of her, instead of embarrassed. That's why she did it."

She thought of Baby Owen. Would he be proud of Chantrelle? Would he ever see his father again?

"We had a woman whose little girl is two, and she only sees her every few months." Harriet Flynn's voice was urgent. She looked different to Alma, with a spark in her eyes that made her look younger, less severe.

Harriet Flynn continued, sitting up straight on her hard chair. "Remember her, Frances? They grow so fast, she said she sometimes isn't sure which girl is hers and which girl is her niece when they visit. They live here in San Francisco."

Two years old. Owen wasn't even two. How much was he growing? How much was he changing?

"Lots of them are in this city." Mrs. Noonan nodded vigorously. Mrs. Gordon knew exactly what was coming. She had known her friend a long time, and she knew how her active mind worked. She felt a pang. She missed Frances Noonan even though they were right here in the same room together. Something had changed about their friendship, and Alma did not know why or what.

Mrs. Noonan was on her feet now. "It's Christmas. We have to try to get them together. We can organize a group of cars and take as many family members as we can fit."

"I can't stand the thought of riding in that car one day longer than I agreed to," said Mrs. Carmichael.

"You wouldn't be coming, Enid," said Mrs. Noonan. "We need all the space for the families."

"Mr. Glenn and I were going to Sylvia and Harold's on Christmas Day," said Mrs. Gordon. "I suppose we could make other arrangements."

"No, we don't need you," Mrs. Noonan said, a little dismissively perhaps, Mrs. Gordon thought. Mrs. Noonan continued, "We need cars. We need all the cars and drivers we can get."

"Mr. Glenn can drive." Mrs. Gordon was pleased to have something to contribute. "I'm sure he'd be happy to help."

"Frances, we always spend Christmas together." Mrs. Carmichael sounded crestfallen. "You always cook for us. Who's going to make the dinner if you're at the prison?"

Mrs. Gordon was lucky to have Sylvia so close. Enid Carmichael's daughter was in Los Angeles. Like Baby Owen. Frances Noonan and Harriet Flynn didn't have children. Olivia Honeycut's family lived far enough that she saw them only a few times a year, not usually at Christmas. The Fog Ladies, minus Alma, had had Christmas together for years. No wonder Enid looked so lost.

"I'll be here," said Mrs. Flynn. "You can have Christmas with me and the Lord."

"Oh, goody," said Mrs. Carmichael.

"Me too. I'm not going." Mrs. Honeycut thumped her hand on her walker. "We can manage to make dinner ourselves. Or order it from the grocery store. We'll survive."

Mrs. Flynn had that spark in her eye again. "Actually, Frances, I can't drive, but I would like to come. This is a good idea. A very good idea."

Mrs. Gordon had never seen her like this, positive, passionate.

Mrs. Carmichael let out a wail. "You too? Who

will be here with me?"

Mrs. Honeycut's low voice cut in. "You, me, and the supermarket."

A knock on the door interrupted Mrs. Carmichael's protest. Mrs. Gordon came back with Sarah.

"I thought you all might be here. I came to show you this picture from Helen." Sarah held out a photo of two tiny babies sitting on Santa's lap. Both faces were screwed up, both mouths open, howling. "Helen said this is the best picture of the lot, not one without the tears."

"Babies!" Mrs. Gordon clapped her hands in delight. "Aren't they adorable. I do miss volunteering in the nursery. Even when they cry." Again she thought of Baby Owen and how she heard him crying on the telephone. Would he get to sit on Santa's lap? He was certainly on her mind today.

"There's a photo studio in the same building in Embarcadero Center as Spencer Tremaine's office, and it's the same studio Bill and I used all those years ago with Isabelle, just a different location. It was on Market then. They did such good work with babies," Frances Noonan said.

How she was able to talk about Isabelle, her daughter who died young, without bursting into tears, Alma did not know. If something had happened to Sylvia at that age, Alma Gordon was not certain she could have recovered.

"I'm glad you stopped by," Mrs. Noonan said to Sarah.

"Here it goes," said Mrs. Honeycut.

"I hope you like prisons," said Mrs. Carmichael.

Sarah smiled slightly and tilted her head. Mrs.

Gordon chuckled. Sarah would go along with the plan because she was a good sport. She almost never said no to Frances Noonan. None of them did.

"We need Andy's car," said Mrs. Noonan. "And a driver."

"Oh, I'm sure that's no problem. He or I would be happy to drive you somewhere. Is yours broken?"

"On Christmas Day. You have to drive three hours to the middle of nowhere and breathe dust," said Mrs. Carmichael.

"And visit criminals," said Mrs. Honeycut.

"She doesn't have to visit criminals. She just has to drive their families. Mostly children. And those women didn't look like criminals to me," said Mrs. Noonan.

"Well, most of them," said Mrs. Gordon, remembering the cussing woman in Mrs. Noonan's group.

"Won't you do it, Sarah?" Mrs. Flynn said. "The Lord will smile on you."

Sarah stood there smiling herself. "I'm all yours. Andy and his brother are flying home for Christmas. Helen and Scott have the babies' first Christmas. All the medical residents I know have to work. I've been wondering what I would do. This sounds just fine."

"It's God's will," said Mrs. Flynn.

"If it's God's will, then what about me?" Enid Carmichael whined.

In the end they had four cars. Mrs. Noonan drove, as did Mr. Glenn. Sarah drove Andy's car with Mrs. Flynn riding shotgun, and Mrs. Gordon's son-in-law, Harold, shuttled a group from San Jose in a minivan borrowed from a friend. All told they took eighteen family members, husbands and children plus one mother of an inmate who hadn't seen her daughter since she went to prison.

Mrs. Gordon heard from Harold later that it was the best Christmas present he'd ever given anyone.

Chapter 39

Baby Owen arrived on the day after New Year's. Alma Gordon had spoken with Chantrelle on Christmas Eve, and there was no hint they were coming. Her horoscope that morning read, "A new year brings new challenges." She felt tired just reading it.

Her buzzer rang, and Chantrelle's voice came over the intercom. "We're here. Let us up."

Mrs. Gordon walked as fast as she could to the door. Her heart pounded. Had she remembered to take her blood pressure pill that morning? The elevator whirred and creaked going down, and she waited impatiently for it to return.

And then there he was. Her little angel. Baby Owen.

Only, he didn't look like much of an angel. His hair stuck out on one side and his nose was running. His shirt was dirty and he wore no shoes. But he broke into a huge smile when he saw her and ran over with both arms held straight out. He could run! Look at her boy run!

Mrs. Gordon squatted, and he grabbed her around the neck and held on tight. He pulled her hair, and she gently tried to loosen his hands. He wouldn't let go. He was hurting her, but that wasn't why she was crying. She had thought she wouldn't see him again, and here he was, five months later, her Baby Owen.

Chantrelle twisted one hand in the other and darted her eyes around. Mrs. Gordon had never seen the girl nervous, but Alma knew nerves when she saw them. She bustled them all inside. Baby Owen finally let go and seized onto Alma's skirt instead.

"It's too much." Chantrelle sat on Mrs. Gordon's squishy couch with an untouched cup of tea in front of her. "I can't be his mom. He constantly needs something or wants something or cries. He never lets up. I can't do it." She was on the verge of tears.

"There, there, now," said Mrs. Gordon, but inside she was turning cartwheels.

"At first it was fun. He's so cute and everybody likes him, and we get lots of attention. But you can't have a moment to yourself, you can't do anything, and there's no one else to take care of him but me."

"There, there, now," said Mrs. Gordon. Baby Owen was still attached to her skirt.

"And Zach, he doesn't like kids much. He can't even see how cute Owen is. He just says he's in the way."

Ah. Zach. The new roommate. He was the one. Mrs. Gordon could kiss him.

"Anyway, I came…I came all the way from Los Angeles so I could ask you in person. I came to ask you about what you said."

"What I said?" Mrs. Gordon couldn't believe it. It was really going to happen. She was really going to get Baby Owen back.

"What you said about adoption." Chantrelle was crying now, her shoulders heaving up and down and her pretty face smeared with mascara.

Mrs. Gordon tried to rein in her happiness and help

this poor girl who might feel as bad as she did about losing the little fellow. She went to the couch and sat next to her, hoisting Baby Owen onto her lap facing away from his mom so he wouldn't be upset by her tears.

"You said we could have an open adoption and I could visit," Chantrelle said.

"Absolutely! Absolutely! That would be good for Baby Owen too."

"I can't believe I'm doing this," Chantrelle said. "But it's too hard to be a mom. I don't know how you do it."

"You're just young," Mrs. Gordon said. "Too young to have this kind of responsibility. Some day you'll see. The time will be right for you."

Chantrelle leaned in against Mrs. Gordon's shoulder. She was a child herself. Baby Owen slumped on Mrs. Gordon's other side, warm and soft against her hip. Mrs. Gordon felt like she couldn't breathe for all the joy she felt in her heart.

Chapter 40

Alma Gordon's lawyer neighbor, Jonathan Martin, explained the adoption process. Mrs. Gordon had screwed up her courage and asked Frances Noonan to come down to be with her. Why she should feel so insecure around her old friend, she did not know. But she was glad Frances was there.

Jonathan had a blue-striped bow tie today. The process sounded straightforward. Chantrelle agrees to relinquish her rights to the child. Baby Owen stays with Mrs. Gordon for a trial period. Mrs. Gordon petitions the court for adoption. A private agency does a home study to make sure the placement is appropriate. The court gives a final adoption order.

Jonathan looked from Mrs. Gordon to Mrs. Noonan and shifted in his chair. He coughed. He twisted his bow tie with his fingers.

"There's something you're not telling us," Frances Noonan said.

"There are some potential problems. I thought a lot about this since we last talked, and I think I may have misled you in my advice."

"Oh, dear. Oh, dear," said Mrs. Gordon.

"Jonathan, please, tell us everything," said Mrs. Noonan. "Few problems are insurmountable."

"There is the matter of the father. He has been a part of the child's life, and he will have to sign the papers as well."

"Oh, dear. Oh, dear," said Mrs. Gordon.

"Oh, that is bad," said Mrs. Noonan. "We don't even know where he is. And the last time I saw him, he was threatening me. I don't think he cares for us."

"And he may not be so eager to give up his son. He could make this difficult if he chose to. He might do that just to spite the mother," Jonathan said.

"Oh, dear. Oh, dear," said Mrs. Gordon.

"But there's one other thing," said Jonathan.

"Something else?" said Mrs. Noonan.

"Yes. And I can't see any easy way around this," said Jonathan.

Mrs. Gordon sat back, ready, but Jonathan didn't say anything.

"Perhaps you'd just better say it," said Mrs. Noonan.

"It's the home study," said Jonathan. "They have to decide if your situation is suitable."

"Why wouldn't my situation be suitable?" said Mrs. Gordon. "I watched him for months."

"And he blossomed when he was with her," Mrs. Noonan said. "Alma was the best thing that happened to him." Mrs. Noonan nodded at her and patted her hand.

"I know that, and you know that, but they might see it differently. They have to think about the future," said Jonathan.

"I'm too old," said Mrs. Gordon.

"No," said Jonathan. "Yes. You're too old. You're seventy-five. And you're a single woman. This child needs a parent to look after him until he reaches the age of majority. You will be over ninety then. Over ninety when he graduates from high school. I don't think they'll agree. I'm sorry."

Mrs. Gordon was stunned. She had never considered this. Baby Owen would grow older, and she would grow older too. When he graduated from high school, she would be older than anyone she knew.

Even Mrs. Noonan was silent. Mrs. Gordon started to cry.

"I'm sorry," Jonathan said. He stood and slowly walked out.

Chapter 41

Frances Noonan watched Jonathan Martin leave. Alma sat next to her on the couch, crying, her face hidden in her handkerchief. How could this be, that Alma would be denied the very thing she was so perfect for, just because she was old? How did they know she wouldn't live until ninety? How did they know anything about the situation? Look at Alma, kind, loving, nurturing Alma. Look at how she transformed Baby Owen.

And look at how she transformed Mr. Glenn. The truth of the matter was, Mr. Glenn had been a sad, wallowing widower before Alma Gordon. Look at him now. Spritely and cheerful. Giving Alma pecks on the cheek. Humming all the time. This was Alma's doing. Alma was good for him.

Alma was good for all of them. Frances herself had missed her sweet, gentle nature, her listening ear, her encouragement.

Mrs. Noonan tried to sit up taller on Mrs. Gordon's squishy couch, but it provided no support. She had to content herself with awkwardly turning her body.

"Alma," she started.

Alma was still crying. Mrs. Noonan reached for her hands, smelling the lilac bubble bath Mrs. Gordon loved so much. Mrs. Noonan inhaled deeply. What had she been thinking all these months?

She had allowed herself to be consumed by green-eyed jealousy, as green as one of Bill's favorite wintergreen breath mints. What a fool. What a waste.

Missing Bill was not a reason to avoid Alma Gordon and Mr. Glenn. They were happy together. Mrs. Noonan inhaled the lilacs again. She was happy for them. There. She really meant it. She was happy they were happy.

She could be sad about Bill and happy about Alma and Mr. Glenn all at the same time. Her heart was big enough for that.

Alma Gordon had been her good friend for so many years. She was there when they were all young couples, living in the city and seeing their husbands off to work every day. She was there when those husbands retired and suddenly sat around the house all day with nothing to do. She was there when Frances needed her most, when Bill died. She was there to help when Frances broke her hip and wrist. She was a fellow Fog Lady, first to volunteer for anything Frances might propose.

They were old, old friends. Nothing could change that.

Frances missed Bill. But that was an entirely different issue, an issue that had zero to do with Alma Gordon. Alma was her friend and she needed to be there for her.

Chapter 42

The next visit to the prison was a few days later, a cold, gray January day. Frances Noonan had given up driving at night, and now she wondered if she should give up driving in gloomy, dark weather too. Hopefully the drive home would be brighter. At least she had Alma Gordon, chattering gently away in the back seat, brightening her mood. The dreary weather didn't penetrate inside the prison, either, where it might be summer or it might be winter in the artificial light.

The Fog Ladies were eager to watch the progress of the quilts, which were a motley collection of multiple squares sewn together by each woman according to the pattern shown the time before. They had brought the quilting frames and the batting today to add inspiration. Mrs. Noonan demonstrated how to link the pieces into one giant quilt. She placed the squares together to show how it would look.

Maya-the-pricker and the cussing woman were across from each other but realized they would have to sew their squares together. The cussing grew louder, and Maya raised her needle threateningly. Mrs. Noonan said they probably didn't want so many red squares in one area, and why didn't Maya slide down the table and sew her red squares to blue.

The cussing stopped abruptly, and the stout woman leaned over to inspect Maya's work. "You frickin' copied me. I got these same five red bits."

Both women had five red squares, two corduroy, two plaid, and one deep red velvet.

"I didn't copy you, moron," Maya said. "I just liked the look of these ones."

"They're frickin' beautiful. Did you feel this velvet? I could frickin' touch it all day."

"Hey, what if we made this side of the quilt red? Look at our pieces. They look pretty good together."

"Frickin' brilliant. Turn yours this way, put the velvet next to my plaid. Look at that. Our side's bitching."

Frances Noonan and Harriet Flynn examined the layout, one side shades of red, the rest a patchwork of colors and textures. They shifted a few women and a few squares until the red was in the middle, surrounded by color.

"Frickin' bitching," said the stout woman.

"Yes, it is attractive," said Mrs. Flynn.

As the next group shuffled in, Mrs. Noonan positioned herself next to Serena Evans. Serena looked as if she expected it, tilting her head toward Mrs. Noonan and nodding as they sat down together. They'd spent most of the first visit talking, branching out from Serena and her past to current events, which Serena knew from the radio and television, but her information was fragmented. They discussed books and plays they had seen years ago, places Serena had traveled, and all their favorite foods. Serena confided that she hadn't made friends, and that she didn't have anyone to talk to except her brother.

Here was Mrs. Noonan's chance. "Did your brother know about your insurance policies, dear?"

Serena answered without hesitation. "Yes, he was actually the one who recommended we get them. He's an insurance agent. It's one small comfort, to know my girls are well taken care of."

"Yes. One small comfort." Mrs. Noonan couldn't bring herself to say anything else. Hoo boy, she thought, wait until I tell the ladies.

"I'm glad you got to meet him at Christmas." Serena paused and took a deep breath. "What you did for Christmas, that was lovely. The women here can't stop talking about it."

Mrs. Noonan smiled. "It was our pleasure."

Serena's face changed. Mrs. Noonan thought she might cry.

"Christmas," Serena said. "That Christmas in Chicago was the last normal day of my life. I didn't know it. I didn't know anything. I didn't treat it like it was anything special. Like our life was anything special."

Serena's hand was stopped midair, her thread dangling from the needle, the cloth forgotten on the table.

"David died the next day. My life died with him. If not for my girls…"

Mrs. Noonan gently placed her hand on Serena's and lowered it to the table.

Serena shook her head. "I shouldn't complain. Look around. Everyone here had a life that died somewhere along the way."

Mrs. Noonan studied the room. The women in their orange jumpsuits were just women, women whose lives might hopefully change again, as Serena said, "somewhere along the way."

From where she sat, Mrs. Noonan could supervise the entire table. A scrawny woman with a tattoo of a flower on her neck hunched on Mrs. Noonan's other side. "That is quite a lovely design. What kind of flower is it?" Mrs. Noonan asked her.

"Eh, I can never remember. Some kind. This tattoo hurt like the devil. Lady said it wouldn't be any worse than any other place. What did she know?"

"You have others, then?"

"This one." She hoisted up her jumpsuit arm and showed Mrs. Noonan a black tree on her wrist. "Did this myself. Bunch of us. We all gave ourselves tattoos. And hepatitis C."

"Oh, my," Mrs. Noonan said. The woman bent into her sewing, and Mrs. Noonan showed her a new stitch.

She turned back to Serena Evans whose face looked perfectly composed now as she focused on her cloth. Mrs. Noonan wanted to ask about Spencer Tremaine. She had seen him just the day before, an unsatisfactory meeting where Julia Blackwell tried in vain to get a timeline estimate for the coming months, and Spencer Tremaine repeated back to them that the "fat lady was a long way from singing," and that Julia's job was to support her son. And not ask questions, Mrs. Noonan concluded after half an hour of this.

He walked them out of the office and into the elevator to the lobby. Mrs. Noonan realized he had not counted on them taking up so much time, and he was late for another engagement elsewhere. He'd made it seem as if he were doing them a favor, said he'd "see them safely to the street," but this flimsy excuse did not escape Mrs. Noonan or Julia Blackwell.

The lobby door was blocked by a large stroller and

a quarreling couple, so Spencer Tremaine was unable to make his getaway. They heard how the woman caused the couple to be late for the babies' photo shoot by mistiming their feeding and how the man forgot the second outfits for when the babies vomited on their clothes.

Imagine Frances Noonan's surprise when she recognized the woman was Helen. This brought an immediate halt to the argument. Mrs. Noonan introduced Helen and Scott to Julia Blackwell and Spencer Tremaine, babbling on in her embarrassment about Helen being a doctor and knowing Sarah and how Frances had used the same photography company all those years ago.

Spencer Tremaine smiled his celebrity smile and repeated their names as if he cared deeply, gushed about the adorable tots, and commented on the tough job of working parents, all the while sliding the stroller aside so he could exit first. He waved back to Julia as if he were the queen and said he'd be in touch.

What an unsavory character. Mrs. Noonan wanted to know everything Serena Evans knew about him without necessarily telling her why. She wasn't sure how to start the conversation, but all she needed to say was, "I saw Spencer Tremaine on television recently. Isn't he your lawyer?" From this she got almost thirty minutes of conversation.

"He approached me," Serena said. "I didn't even know who he was. Why would I? He said I'd get life in prison and would have gotten the death penalty if Illinois still had it. Said I needed the best and he was the best. Said the men on the jury would be out for blood."

Mrs. Noonan nodded. This sounded familiar.

"His fees were exorbitant, but every time I questioned something, he told me talent was expensive and did I want to end up rotting in a cell. My husband and I had a lot of savings. It's all gone now. Tremaine used to tell me he'd get me off and I'd be rich again with the insurance money. He was the one getting rich."

Serena told her about Spencer Tremaine's first marriage with a sniping wife who was never satisfied. Then two additional wives and multiple children he rarely saw. About his alimony and child support and expensive lifestyle. About his penchant for Las Vegas and showgirls and gambling. About how he showed up once with a black eye and split lip and said he'd been hit by the boom on his sailboat.

"He's not my lawyer anymore," Serena finished. "I fired him right after he told me I reminded him of his first wife. You have to spend so much time with your lawyer, and for a long time he was the only person I talked to, and each time he'd leave I'd feel slimy. I just couldn't work with him anymore. I don't know if he helped me or not. I didn't get life. But I'm not out free with my girls."

Chapter 43

"All men are vile." Frances Noonan could have predicted Harriet Flynn would utter this very phrase. Frances had finished her tale about Serena and her brother and Spencer Tremaine. The Fog Ladies, including Sarah, were in Alma Gordon's apartment. Baby Owen had run from one lady to another as they filed in, almost tripping tall Enid Carmichael. Owen was staying there while Chantrelle was in town. Mr. Glenn had watched him all day and made a hasty departure as soon as the ladies arrived, saying he was going home to nap and that toddlers were energetic little tikes.

"Remember, don't steal third with less than two outs," he had said to Owen as he left.

"Two outs," Baby Owen repeated.

"Bedtime," Mrs. Gordon said and shooed him into the bedroom. She was back in no time, setting out tea and packages of cookies as Mrs. Noonan spoke.

Frances Noonan sank back into Alma Gordon's cushy couch and sipped her tea, pleased to be in this apartment with no extra emotion, no envy, no unkind thoughts.

"So...the brother, huh?" rasped Olivia Honeycut. "Killed his sister's husband for insurance he recommended himself."

"The perfect crime," said Enid Carmichael.

"Except that now he's saddled with two small children. Seems like too much trouble to me."

"But it is suspicious, don't you think?" said Mrs. Noonan.

"Not nearly as suspicious as this Tremaine character," said Harriet Flynn.

Mrs. Gordon put her hands to her ears. "I can't believe *the* Spencer Tremaine is so unseemly. On television he makes it seem like he cares."

"Believe it," said Mrs. Noonan. "It's pretty much the same spiel Julia Blackwell got, just toned down. I think there's more here than meets the eye."

"Women, gambling, fights. Not to mention his association with murderers. He is not leading the life of the Lord," said Harriet Flynn.

"He does know his way around killers," said Enid Carmichael.

"Paul Blackwell is not a killer," said Mrs. Noonan. "And Serena says she didn't do it either."

"That's what they all say," said Olivia Honeycut. "We know for certain the Baker Beach killer did it."

Mrs. Noonan surveyed the room. She had pondered something the whole drive back. "I know this is far-fetched, but do you think there could be a connection between Spencer Tremaine and all these killings?"

"I was wondering the same thing myself," said Mrs. Honeycut.

Of course she would agree, Mrs. Noonan thought. She was always on the lookout for a conspiracy theory.

Sarah, who sat in the corner looking as dreamy as Alma Gordon these days, sat up and shook her head. "Come on. How could he possibly be involved?"

"He deals with killers all day long. Maybe he has a

killer's mind," said Mrs. Carmichael.

"Maybe he wants business," Mrs. Honeycut said slowly. "Maybe he's *creating* business."

"By killing married people?" asked Sarah. "Too bad you ran into Helen and Scott, then. I'm sorry I told Helen about that photo studio."

"You told her because I told you, so I'm sorry too," said Mrs. Noonan.

"You think Spencer Tremaine is a killer?" said Mrs. Gordon. "Oh, dear. Oh, dear."

"It would actually be pretty clever," said Mrs. Noonan. "He could kill one spouse and incriminate the other but leave some crack in the case so he could save the day and get the accused off the hook."

"And get some of the million dollars for himself," said Mrs. Honeycut.

"A brilliant scheme!" said Mrs. Carmichael.

"Except he hasn't gotten anybody off," said Sarah. "Paul Blackwell and Serena Evans are still in jail."

"Yes, that's a problem," said Mrs. Noonan.

"You ladies are too much," said Sarah.

"But you have to admit, it's a pretty good idea," said Mrs. Noonan.

"No one would do that just for money," said Mrs. Gordon. "Not Spencer Tremaine. Not Serena Evans's brother."

"Paul Blackwell and Serena Evans herself supposedly did it for money," said Mrs. Noonan.

"And Joseph Stalk, the adulterer," said Mrs. Flynn.

"And for Spencer Tremaine, it's not just money," said Mrs. Carmichael. "It's money *and* fame."

"Maybe it's time we found out who Joseph Stalk's lawyer was," Mrs. Noonan said.

"No!" Mrs. Gordon protested. "Spencer Tremaine is not involved. You might as well find out more about Joseph's Stalk's brother-in-law, then. He and Evelyn have little Joey's insurance money. Anyway, it can't be Spencer Tremaine. He's already famous. He's a celebrity. He doesn't need more."

"There's never too much 'more,' too much fame," said Mrs. Honeycut.

"And we don't know how desperate he is for money," said Mrs. Carmichael. "Remember, he gambles. There may not be that many cases of rich murderers to support that kind of lifestyle."

"But these are real people he has to deal with. He would have to work with them and see the destruction he's caused," said Sarah. "No one would do that. Or if you did, you'd choose couples without children."

"Good point," said Mrs. Honeycut.

"They don't have life insurance," said Mrs. Noonan. "Remember, the Stalks only got theirs because they were going to have a baby. Most people don't need life insurance like this."

"Another good point," said Mrs. Honeycut.

That was the beauty of the Fog Ladies, Mrs. Noonan thought. So many points, so many ideas.

"No." Mrs. Gordon mindlessly stroked Baby Owen's bear. "It's impossible. The man has children himself. Think of little Joey Stalk. And Ben. And these two girls of Serena's. No one would do that to a child, for money, for fame." Her voice rose. "Children are delicate creatures. You can't yank them from place to place, not knowing who's going to take care of them, who's going to love them. No one would do that."

"And yet we are supposed to believe that their very

own parents did just that," said Mrs. Noonan.

"Only because they got caught," said Mrs. Carmichael. "Otherwise they would be sitting pretty, money rolling in, children intact. And rid of their pesky spouse. Why didn't I think of this?"

"Because it involves murder," said Mrs. Honeycut.

"That didn't stop someone out there," said Mrs. Noonan.

Chapter 44

"I'm not actually for sure Big Owen is the daddy."

Sarah jerked her head toward Chantrelle. She and Alma Gordon and Frances Noonan sat with Chantrelle to tell her what Jonathan had said.

"What?" All three women spoke at once. Mrs. Gordon's teacup stopped midway to her mouth. Mrs. Noonan choked on her cookie and grabbed her milk to wash it down.

"What do you mean Big Owen's not the daddy?" asked Sarah.

"I'm not saying he's not the daddy. I'm saying I'm not for sure." Chantrelle bounced Baby Owen on her knee a little too hard and he bit his tongue. He began to scream, and she handed him to Mrs. Gordon for comfort.

"Good thing Zach left. He can't stand to hear this crying," Chantrelle said. She and Zach were staying with his brother in Dogpatch, a wonderfully named neighborhood on the east side of the city. Zach dropped her off before heading on to a sports bar.

"There, there. Shh." Mrs. Gordon gently rubbed Owen's cheek.

"Then who is the daddy?" asked Mrs. Noonan.

"Oh, I don't know. Jordan. Mick. I can't remember everybody. Big Owen was around when I found out, so I said it was him."

"Oh, dear. Oh, dear," said Mrs. Gordon.

"No, Alma, don't you see? This is good. If Big Owen isn't the daddy, then he doesn't have to agree to the adoption," said Mrs. Noonan.

"Yeah, well, he doesn't have to agree anyway," said Chantrelle.

"Why not?" asked Sarah.

"'Cause he's not on the birth certificate. That's how I got my money from the state. No daddy," Chantrelle said.

"Hmm. I wonder if that counts. If he thought he was the daddy and says he's the daddy, though not to the state, of course, I wonder if he could claim parental rights now?" said Mrs. Noonan.

"Well, for one thing, he'd never do that. If he's the daddy, then he should have been supporting the baby and he wasn't, and he doesn't want to be found out. Second, the more I look at Baby Owen, the more I see Mick. See these feet? Mick couldn't spread his toes apart and neither could his brother and neither could his dad. No muscles between the toes. Defective feet. Well, look, Baby Owen's got them."

They all inspected Baby Owen's feet. They did look a little strange, Sarah had to admit.

"You mean this is Baby Mick?" said Mrs. Noonan.

"That's what I think," said Chantrelle. "Anyway, that's what I told Big Owen the last time I saw him, before he took off with that floozy. I told him about the feet. I don't think he'll be back."

Sarah felt a pang for poor Big Owen. He was an unlikable character, but he always seemed so proud of Baby Owen. How awful to find out he might not be the father after all that time.

"So, Zach wants to know if you can watch Owen this week? We have to get back, and it would be nice to be on our own for a while. I could drive up next weekend and get him." Chantrelle peered out from under her hair.

"Oh, yes. Yes. That would be fine." Mrs. Gordon clapped her hands in excitement.

"Even if you're too old to adopt him, you're still good for this."

Sarah thought Chantrelle meant it as a compliment. Mrs. Noonan winked at her. Mrs. Gordon just smiled.

Sarah went from seeing Baby Owen to seeing Helen's twins, just a few months old. On her way out of the building, she met Harriet Flynn in the lobby. Mrs. Flynn stood before the mirror by the mailboxes fluffing her hair. Sarah had never seen Mrs. Flynn look in a mirror at all, let alone this interest in her hair. Sarah did a double take. Mrs. Flynn's steel wool hair was darker, salt and pepper, brown and gray, not just gray.

Mrs. Flynn must have noticed her because she whipped around with a guilty look.

"Hi, Mrs. Flynn. You look lovely today. You have a new hairdo," Sarah said cautiously.

Mrs. Flynn's hand touched her hair again. She actually giggled. "I made a change. You might think this is nonsense. An old lady like me."

"I think it suits you," Sarah said.

"You do? I like it too." Mrs. Flynn ducked her head, but Sarah saw the smile.

Sarah started for the door. Mrs. Flynn spoke again, her voice serious.

"You don't know what it's like, Sarah, getting old. I assumed the next best thing that would happen in my

200

life would be my passing into heaven. I welcome that. But right here on earth, right in this building, is the next best thing. Look at Alma and that baby. Look at Alma and Mr. Glenn. She found love a second time around. Look at Frances Noonan with her crusade to free a murderer and make things right for these innocent children. Look what we did at Christmas with those ladies in prison, bringing in their families. Look how much they enjoy the quilting. I didn't think I could be of use to anyone anymore. But I can. I am."

Mrs. Flynn's head was still down. Now she lifted it and stared into the mirror, catching Sarah's eye.

"You are absolutely right," Sarah said, smiling back at her.

"I'm not headed for death and salvation yet. I can make a difference. I looked in the mirror for the first time in years. I don't know when I got so old. St. Peter won't mind a little hair color."

"He certainly will not."

Mrs. Flynn grinned at her reflection in the mirror. Sarah wondered if she'd ever seen her smile.

"You think it suits me?"

"Most definitely. It suits the new you."

Sarah smiled all the way to Helen's. Harriet Flynn was so right. The Fog Ladies made such a difference. Sarah would have been lost without them last year. And Baby Owen. Because of the Fog Ladies, he was a confident, sturdy toddler.

Helen's twins were tiny compared to strapping Baby Owen. A boy and a girl, Aidan and Emily, one in a blue onesie, one in pink. They looked pretty similar to Sarah, apart from the onesies, but Helen and Scott knew exactly who was who.

Helen looked exhausted. And sad. Scott hid in the kitchen, taking an awfully long time to fix them a snack.

"I can't do it," said Helen. "I can't do this breastfeeding. I can't believe I'm such a total failure."

"What are you talking about?" said Sarah.

"I can't do it. They eat all the time. They're not on the same schedule, so I never get a break. Emily took forever to learn to latch on correctly and I'm so sore and I've got mastitis for the second time and I have to take antibiotics again and the doctor says it's safe to continue breastfeeding while I'm on them, but I don't know for certain that it's safe and they're so little that I couldn't stand it if the antibiotics made them sick and it's so hard to keep breastfeeding and it hurts so much and I can't do it and I feel awful because I wish the doctor had said I had to stop."

"Oh," said Sarah.

"And Scott wants me to keep trying because breastfeeding is so good for them, but he's not the one who has to do it, and I haven't been out of the house all week and I never get off the sofa because there's always a baby attached to me."

"Oh," said Sarah.

"And look at them, they haven't gained enough weight and I might not be making enough milk and I have to go back to work soon, and then I'll have to pump and I'm sure I won't make enough milk then and I can't do it."

"They're beautiful babies," said Sarah. "Would you like me to watch them for an hour so you and Scott can go for a walk or something? Get out of the house? It's a sunny day today, just a little cold."

Helen started to cry. "I can't. I can't. Aidan's ready to eat and then it will be Emily's turn and she takes so long, by the time she's done Aidan will be hungry again."

Scott came into the room then with a tray of fruit and pretzels. A vase sat to one side with a single red rose. In the center of the tray were two baby bottles and a small can of formula.

"Maybe I could see if I can get them to drink from these," he said.

Helen kept crying and he took her in his arms. "Why don't you and Sarah go for that walk. I'll try the bottles."

They exchanged places and Scott sat on the couch with a baby on each side. "Hurry back just in case," he called as they left. "I'm sure we'll be fine, but hurry back just in case."

Chapter 45

Frances Noonan drove to the last prison visit feeling bittersweet. Even Enid Carmichael made it the whole three hours in the car without a word of complaint.

The women at the prison were clearly pleased by the results of the quilts. They thanked the Fog Ladies and said the quilting was one of the highlights of the year.

The women who had visitors on Christmas were especially grateful, and several brought cards they made themselves. The Fog Ladies passed out photographs they had taken of the families together at Christmas. Some of the women cried.

As Frances Noonan took her place next to Serena, she could see the young woman was down.

"I look forward to this, to you coming. You treat me like a real person. I get to talk like an adult, about adult topics like world news and books and theater. I'll miss you."

Mrs. Noonan put her hand on Serena's. Mrs. Noonan's skin was dry and wrinkled and had several large brown splotches. Serena's was smooth and supple. Mrs. Noonan couldn't remember when her skin had changed. In sixteen years, would Serena's hand look like Mrs. Noonan's? No, certainly not.

"I'll be back to just talking to my girls and my

brother. Which is fine. I know I'm lucky to have them," Serena said.

"Yes," said Mrs. Noonan, screwing up her courage to ask about the insurance money as a motive. How could she ask this woman if her brother, her one and only lifeline, could be a murderer? "About that, about your brother..."

Serena looked at her expectantly.

"He recommended that you and your husband get your high insurance policies? He was an insurance man himself? And he now controls your girls' money? Do you think there could be a connection?" There. She just said it.

Serena looked at her blankly. Then she started to laugh. "My brother? You think my brother killed David?"

Mrs. Noonan sat silently.

Serena moved her hand out from under Mrs. Noonan's and wiped a tear from her eye, she was laughing so hard.

"Thank goodness I never had to even remotely wonder about that. He was the first call I made after I was arrested, to his home phone here in California. He was in California, not Illinois. So don't be getting any ideas."

Mrs. Noonan inhaled and exhaled, more relieved than she realized. She remembered the affable man she'd met at Christmas. He looked so much like his sister. The twins clung to him as they left, and he had kissed Serena and said, "See you next week, Sis. Hold in there. I love you. We'll be back."

"I don't have any ideas," Mrs. Noonan said truthfully. "I very much enjoyed meeting him at

Christmas." Thankfully, Serena didn't seem offended by the whole idea. More like amused.

On that last day, they discussed widowhood. Serena's smile faded. She said one of the hardest things was grieving the loss of her husband while in jail for his murder.

Mrs. Noonan contemplated this. Losing a husband was bad enough. Grieving was bad enough.

She didn't answer Serena directly. She still didn't know what was true and what was hopeful memory regarding David Evans's death. The mind could play tricks over time. If Serena's brother hadn't killed David, the pool of suspects was shrinking. And Serena was at the top of the list. Murderess or not, Mrs. Noonan had to admit, she enjoyed talking to Serena. The woman had charisma.

Serena didn't look charismatic now. She was near tears.

"The last words I said to him were, 'Go to hell.' We were fighting. I don't even remember what about. Such a waste. I loved him. And the last thing I said before he died was, 'Go to hell.'"

Mrs. Noonan hugged her. Without thinking, she said, "He knows you love him." She wondered if she meant it, if she knew in her heart of hearts that Serena hadn't killed him.

The two hours were nearly over. Mrs. Noonan had asked before, but she needed to make absolutely sure. As they gathered the materials, she asked about Spencer Tremaine and anything else Serena could remember. Serena said the only other thing was that he was the one who had arranged for the transfer to California.

"For that, even though I never liked the man, I will

always be grateful. It seemed like he felt guilty and was trying to make it up to me."

"Guilty?" Mrs. Noonan perked up.

"I guess he felt bad about not getting me off," Serena said.

"Hmm," said Mrs. Noonan. The women lined up to go and she still had more questions. She wanted to sound casual, but she couldn't think of a segue, so she just asked.

"Have you ever been to Big Sur? It's a beautiful part of our state."

"Yes, I've heard," said Serena. "I had never been to California before this. Hard to believe, I know, especially with my brother here. I've been all over the world, but somehow never made it out west. What a shame. Now I may never see it."

"Oh, dear, that can't be. In sixteen years, you'll still be a spring chicken. With a full life in front of you. When I was in my fifties, I was in my prime. Dear, you'll see. And it may not be sixteen years. The warden told us you're a model prisoner. You may get out early, for good behavior or something."

"Or something. I keep trying to tell myself this. I keep trying. Four years has seemed an eternity. I can't imagine sixteen more."

They were silent. Mrs. Noonan looked at the beautiful woman next to her and thought of the girls she'd met at Christmas. Serena was right. Such a waste.

Before they parted, Mrs. Noonan rattled off the names of everyone who worked at Paradise Cove Resort. She had Mrs. Gordon describe the men as best she could. Serena shook her head and laughed. "What an inquisition. I thought I was done with inquisitions."

"I'm sorry, dear. I have a good reason for asking. A friend's son is in trouble. Trouble like you. I'm trying to help."

"I understand," said Serena. "I thought you must be here for something other than good works. Though I thank you for coming. Anything to have something to look forward to."

"I'll write to you," said Mrs. Noonan.

"And I'll write back. I write a lot of letters in here. We don't have access to anything electronic."

Mrs. Noonan placed a photo into Serena's hand of Serena and her brother and her girls from the Christmas visit. The girls wore matching red satin dresses and their first pairs of stockings instead of socks. Her brother had a green sweater. Serena was in her orange jumpsuit, but her smile lit up the picture.

"God bless," said Mrs. Noonan.

Serena didn't say anything. She pressed the photo to her chest and joined the line of women filing out.

Chapter 46

Alma Gordon lay back on the sofa gasping for breath. Owen tugged her hand.

"Chase, chase," he said.

They'd been "chase, chasing" for the entire morning. Mrs. Gordon looked at the old clock on her desk and saw she was mistaken. Less than ten minutes.

"Story," she said between breaths. "Choose a book and I'll read to you."

"Chase, chase," Owen persisted.

Much as I'd like to, I can't, she thought. I'd like to explain it to you, little man, but I'm breathing too hard.

She lay there like a fish out of water, sucking in air and willing her heart to slow. Owen climbed on top of her and bounced on her belly.

"Horsey," he said.

Harold had taught him this, bouncing Owen on his tummy as if the boy were a feather. Mrs. Gordon had never tried herself. She certainly couldn't do it now. She could barely breathe under Owen's sturdy weight.

This parenting thing might kill her yet.

Owen climbed off and wandered into the kitchen, jumping with his arms in the air.

"Water," he said.

She tried to heave herself off the couch, which enveloped her like a soft pillow. She pushed and rolled and, in the end, vowed to never lie on the couch again.

It was too hard to extricate herself. Her knee hurt and she limped toward Owen and his sippy cup.

She was seventy-five years old. Owen was no longer a baby. He was a true toddler. An active, exuberant toddler. What was she thinking?

Forget about ninety. Was she able to take care of a toddler now?

Her horoscope read, "Accept your limitations. Your limitations are limitless." What a lame horoscope. How was that in any way helpful?

Chantrelle would be back soon. What should she tell her?

She went to see her doctor the very next day. Mr. Glenn, bless his heart, took Owen for the afternoon, telling her he had a recording of a doubleheader Owen should see and take her time coming home.

The doctor listened intently. She took Alma's blood pressure and ran an EKG and did a chest x-ray. She recommended some blood tests and a heart stress test to make sure the chest squeezing and pounding heart were nothing worrisome.

What if she did have a heart condition? Giving up Baby Owen would be best for her heart. But her heart would break if she didn't have Baby Owen.

"Assuming the tests are normal," the doctor said, facing Alma and looking her right in the eyes, "there is absolutely no medical reason you cannot take care of this little boy. Even if the courts won't believe it. I see grandparents in my practice all the time who take in grandchildren while the parents sort things out. Sometimes forever. Sometimes it's better for the grandchildren. Experience, stability, unwavering love. There is no reason you cannot do the same."

Mrs. Gordon knew it was true. For now, at least, Owen was better off with her than with Chantrelle and Big Owen or Zach or whomever the current man might be.

She didn't think she could do it. Her heart squeezed again. Even if her heart was healthy, she was not. She loved Owen. But toddlers were exhausting.

She was gone less than two hours. Mr. Glenn handed Owen over immediately.

"He likes baseball all right," Mr. Glenn said. "Only he didn't want to watch. He wanted to play. Roll the ball back and forth, back and forth, back and forth forever. Don't babies get bored?"

He handed her a baseball. "I found it. The one Lionel and I caught back at Candlestick Park. You play with him now."

Chapter 47

"What was the name of that resort you went to?"

Sarah and Helen were shopping for baby clothes. Helen was due back to work in a week. Her maternity leave had flown by.

Sarah laughed. "I don't know if I should tell you. Everyone who goes there ends up dead."

"I'll be dead if I don't get some kind of vacation. I can't believe I have to start right in on medicine wards."

"Couldn't they put you on something else?" Sarah asked.

"Unfortunately not. I used all my elective time while I was pregnant. I'm lucky I didn't need to go on bed rest. Then I would have had to go back sooner. Or extend my residency. But it's back to the wards for me. I think a vacation before I start would be good for Scott too. He's about to be a solo dad."

Helen pushed her double stroller between the racks, holding up pink and blue outfits and putting them back. "Too small. Too small," she kept saying.

As she took out an enormous size eighteen-month outfit, Sarah gently put her hand on her arm and guided her to a chair.

"They're not even three months old." She took the dress from Helen's hand. "They won't wear this size for a year."

Helen's mouth twisted as she tried not to cry. "Look at them. They're growing so much. I'm going off to work and they'll get bigger and I'll miss it all." She wiped her teary eyes on a yellow bib with a duck. The twins were sleeping, leaning backward and tucked into blankets.

Sarah sat with her arm on Helen's. Helen gave her eyes a final swipe.

"Look at me. I'm a mess. How am I going to function at work? My hormones are raging, my emotions are a roller coaster, I cry at commercials, I'm not getting any sleep. Look at these babies. I wish I had a stroller to sleep in like this. All I think about is sleep."

Sarah laughed. She remembered feeling so tired once as an intern that she envied a sick patient lying in a hospital bed. "When do they start on a routine? Is there any semblance of a schedule yet?"

"Oh, yes, they have a schedule. They *each* have a schedule, and the two have no bearing on each other. They each sleep four hours straight at night, just not the same four hours."

"How's Scott doing?" asked Sarah.

"Now that he got them to take a bottle, Scott does almost as much at night as I do, so we're both walking around like zombies this week. It's hard to be pleasant on so little sleep. We just snap at each other. I think a change of scene would do us good."

"I have an idea," said Sarah. "I have a weekend between rotations. Why don't I come with you and I can take the twins at nighttime, and you and Scott can sleep."

At first Sarah thought Helen hadn't heard. Then she started to cry again, and Sarah could see these were tears of joy.

They drove down together with Helen in the back between the two baby car seats. Scott was absolutely jubilant and had actually brought a newspaper to read in bed in the morning like he used to. Helen looked serene and said she was going to do absolutely nothing. Sarah was armed with chocolate-covered espresso beans to help her stay awake.

The day was bright and sunny but cold, typical for January. They heard the surf crashing as they got out of the car. Sarah smelled the familiar pine and salt. Helen inhaled deeply and said this was just what she needed.

The proprietor recognized Sarah immediately. "Welcome, Doctor. Who have you brought this time?"

Sarah laughed in spite of herself. Three visits in eight months. It did seem like a lot. And she didn't even have children. She introduced Helen and Scott.

"Sarah's spoken so well of this place, we had to come before I go back to work and my life is over," Helen said dramatically.

"What adorable babies," the proprietor said. "What a shame you have to go back to work. You can't put it off any longer?"

"No, I'm a doctor like Sarah," Helen said. "But I've lined up very reliable day care."

Scott groaned.

They filled out the registration cards. The man read off Helen's employer and asked Scott for his.

"None," Scott replied tersely.

"Right, then." The proprietor moved on quickly. "Emergency number?"

Scott looked at Helen who looked at Sarah. "We would probably put you, but you're here. Who did you put?"

"It's just in case of emergency, someone to notify," said the proprietor. "People often put down a relative, parents or a sibling."

"Nope," said Scott. "No parents. No siblings."

"What?" said the proprietor. "Neither one of you?"

Helen explained about how they had met.

"Jeepers, what a coincidence," the proprietor said.

"That's why I married him," Helen said. Scott rolled his eyes.

"I meant it's a coincidence because I'm an orphan too," the proprietor said.

"Oh, wow. I'm sorry," Helen said.

"Yes, well…" said the proprietor.

"Maybe put Frances Noonan on the card, like I did," Sarah said, realizing that not one of the four of them had living parents. At least she had her brother, Tim.

Scott settled into the room with two sleeping babies, his feet propped on the windowsill, newspaper in his hands. Sarah and Helen set out for a walk. When they looked back through the large window from outside, they could see he had already fallen asleep in his chair.

"This will be good for us." Helen sighed. "Also bittersweet. I can't believe I have to go back to work. I even thought about an extension, but that would mean not finishing my residency on time. Aidan and Emily are so little. They need me. I need them. I want them."

They walked slowly down the steep stairs to the beach. Gulls swooped into the sea, crying and chasing each other. The few rocks were crowded with sea lions, and they sat on two towels to watch their antics.

"Look at that one. He reminds me of Karl," Helen said.

Sarah squinted into the sun. Helen was right. Same sloping tall forehead as their fellow resident, same underhanded manner as the sea lion tried to get the best spot in the sun. He'd start out innocently on the edge of the rock, but each time the ones toward the center shifted slightly or lifted their heads to look around, the "Karl" sea lion would nudge his large mass closer in, closer in, until the sea lions in the middle fell off the other edge of the rock.

"Look! They're actually going after him. Not like us," Sarah said. At the hospital, Karl broke the rules but continued to barrel along without redress. The sea lion community wasn't so nurturing. They banded together and jumped back onto the rock and used their combined weight to push Karl off. Kerplunk. He slithered through the water, found another rock with another group of sea lions, and the process started over.

"We should take a lesson from them. Did you know that he was supposed to work New Year's Eve? He called in sick with a migraine headache. I think he started his celebration early. They even called me by accident to see if I could work," Helen said.

"Yep, I know. Guess who ended up working New Year's."

"No, not you?"

"Yes, me. It was actually okay because Andy was still out of town, so I didn't have any plans. I'll get repaid at some point."

"How is Andy? I haven't seen him in ages. I haven't seen anyone in ages. That will be one thing about going back to work. I'll get out of the apartment and back among real people, adults."

"Andy's fine." Sarah's heart skipped a beat, a happy skip, like it did when she first saw him every day. "He's trying to put together his elephant book and work full-time at the newspaper, so he's busy, but so am I, so I guess it evens out. He's in New York this week talking to the publisher, showing them his initial layout idea."

"Good for him. I hope Scott's PhD goes as smoothly. If he somehow doesn't get his thesis finished in time, I don't know what will happen. Until we can afford some kind of child care, he's all we've got."

"Hey, speaking of finishing things, Mrs. Noonan told me Paul Blackwell finished his book, and his agent found a publisher. I guess that's what happens when you have a lot of time on your hands. She says it's really good, they got a pretty big advance for it. Not that he gets the money."

"It's so eerie. You met them right here," Helen said.

"I know. I'm looking around to see what it could be about this place that might cause something like that. Twice. Remember about the Philadelphia case. Maybe there's something in the water."

"I remember now that you mention it. I'd actually forgotten," Helen said. "Baby brain."

They looked out at the ocean, blue today under the bright blue sky. The beach was in a small cove with high cliffs curved behind them. Waves lapped innocently on the protected beach but were monstrous against the cliffs on either side. A tiny rainbow danced in the spray. It was a powerful sight from this vantage point. They hiked back up to the top and stood gazing out again. From above, looking down from the craggy cliff, the crashing surf was frightening.

"I think the tide's coming in," Sarah said.

"Oh, my gosh, what time is it? I forgot to take my antibiotics for the mastitis. I've forgotten half the pills already. No wonder it's not healing. Baby brain," Helen said again.

"You'd better lose that baby brain soon," Sarah said. "You have to go back to work this week."

"I know, I know. I'm hoping it's gone by tomorrow after my first full night's sleep in weeks."

"Good luck," Sarah said. "But that means I might be the zombie tomorrow."

"Maybe it's lack of sleep that caused those killings. Maybe that's the common thread." Helen seemed dead serious. "You should see Scott and me going at it. Sleeplessness could make a parent snap."

Chapter 48

Sarah and Helen could hear the babies screaming as they came along the path in the garden. Everyone else could hear them too. The few people they passed all gaped at Helen's room. Two small babies could make an awful lot of noise, but Scott's voice was added to the ruckus, loud and profane.

"Uh, oh." Helen broke into a run.

Sarah jogged behind her. She had never heard Scott swear.

They opened the door and saw the mess. Two naked babies lying on the bed, screaming and red, eight arms and legs kicking, with lots of poo spread on them and the bedspread. Scott had his share on him too.

"Where the hell have you been? It's been over two hours," Scott shouted.

"We were—"

"It came shooting out. Tried to change a simple diaper and now look. Hers came loose, too, and she somehow worked it off. The crap's everywhere. And they won't shut up." He was still shouting.

Sarah went to close the door. A young couple with a baby strapped to their chest stood on the grass and gawked outright. George the maintenance man pushed a cart along the sidewalk. He caught Sarah's eye and shook his head sadly.

"What a mess," said Helen. "You always try to do

too much at once. You have to have everything set up ahead and work with one baby at a time. Otherwise stuff like this will happen."

"Don't tell me what to do. You weren't here. And you're not going to be here either," Scott yelled. "You're going back to work."

Sarah saw the window was open. She closed that too.

"You know what?" Sarah said. "Why don't I take care of this. I have to practice sometime anyway. Why don't you go to my room to clean up, and then you two can have some time for yourselves. Consider me on duty. We can meet for dinner."

Scott was out the door before she finished. Helen didn't want to go, but Sarah pushed her gently out too. She turned to the screaming babies and started to sing, every lullaby and children's song she could remember. They finally started to quiet, after she'd been through her entire repertoire and was starting over. She scooped them up in one big towel and took them to the sink. The sink was large and they were small. They both fit in together. They liked the water and were quiet and placid during the whole bath. Sarah hadn't seen them smile yet, but during the bath she thought she saw Emily's mouth crinkle. Not gas, like people always said about babies, but a real smile.

She got them dressed and fed them a bottle and put them in their crib, both in one crib lying foot to foot with their heads at opposite ends. God, they were tiny. How could Helen stand it, going back to work when they were so small?

Sarah exchanged the dirty bedspread for a new one. Glenda said not to worry, it happened all the time.

The twins fell asleep again in their stroller on the way to dinner. Helen and Scott were already seated at a table near the kitchen. Sarah parked the stroller near the half wall and nodded at the chef who nodded back. Emanuel, the waiter, handed her a menu as she slid into her seat.

"It will be a miracle if they sleep through dinner," Scott said. "We haven't had a quiet dinner with both of us sitting down through the entire meal since before they were born." He was in a much better mood, though he and Helen put Sarah in between them at the table.

"I'll take a picture to remember it by," Sarah said.

"Better wait half an hour to see if it's true," said Scott.

"Oh, just take the picture," said Helen. Sarah took a picture of the twins and then one with the adults crouched by the stroller. Helen's smile looked strained.

"Oh, wait." Helen fished in her diaper bag. "I brought something to celebrate with. It'll cheer us up." She brought out a bottle of champagne and set it on the table. "I hope they can uncork it for us."

Before Sarah could explain about the alcohol, the proprietor himself came to take their order. Helen asked him about the corkage fee, and he gave a little cough.

"I'm afraid this is an alcohol-free resort. In any case, do you think it's safe to drink while you're breastfeeding?" he said.

Helen's small chin dropped as she opened her mouth and closed it again. "Well, I'm not breastfeeding," she said.

"Jeepers, miss, I'm sorry. I just assumed," he said.

"I think we need more time to decide," Sarah said, and he went away.

"Nosy little man," Helen said. "What business is it of his? I can't believe I answered." She put the bottle back in the bag. "Oh, here are my pills. I've missed so many doses, I'd better take one now while I'm thinking of it."

"Does that mean we can't have the champagne? Darn. It looks so tempting," Scott said.

"We can have it tonight," Helen said. "After dinner we can have it in our room."

"Shh," said Sarah. "He's coming back."

The proprietor took their order. The babies woke as the dinners arrived, wailing and flailing. A man chuckled behind them, and Sarah swiveled to see the chef watching from the half wall. He put his hand to his forehead and gave a salute.

The babies seemed to have only one volume. Loud. Scott groaned. Helen looked like she was about to cry herself.

"You two go ahead and eat. I'll take them for a spin and join you in a little bit." Sarah wanted them to eat in peace. They needed this.

"Sarah, that's too much. You already bailed us out once today," Helen said.

"Exactly. That's why I'm here. This is your last bit of time before you go back to work. I have quiet time every day of my life. Please let me do this for you." She was already maneuvering the stroller around the table.

The stroller was long and unwieldy, and a wheel caught on Scott's chair.

"Here, allow me." The proprietor was back, lifting the front end of the stroller free and then guiding it through the tables.

He held the door as Sarah pushed the stroller

through. The angle was all wrong, and he had to help her again. How did Helen manage this thing?

Sarah thanked him and walked out into the cold night with the babies. She tucked a blanket around each one and zipped her own sweater. The babies were quiet and still now that they were in motion. The night was cold but windless, so she thought they would be all right outside. Stars filled the sky, more stars than she'd ever seen. It was dark and the path wasn't well lighted. She decided to sit on a bench and wait.

She rocked the stroller back and forth, back and forth. Emily made a little noise and smiled again. Sarah was certain. Helen hadn't said anything about the babies smiling. She'd told Sarah about each other milestone. Was Sarah the only one who had seen it? Should she tell Helen? She didn't think so.

Sarah leaned back to see the stars shining bright in the black sky. The city had so many lights. The stars never looked like this. She immediately saw a shooting star.

"Did you see that?"

She jumped. She thought she was alone. Now she saw someone sitting on a bench nearby. The chef, Marco. He still wore his white chef hat. He pointed to the sky.

"I saw it," she said. "It's incredible."

"My uncle was an amateur astronomer. Knew everything there was about the sky. If he ever lived in a place as dark as this, he'd be in heaven." Marco pulled out a pack of cigarettes and offered one to Sarah.

She shook her head and he lit one. The tip glowed in the dark night as he drew in the smoke. She thought of asking him not to smoke around the babies, but that seemed overly rude. She turned the stroller away from him, trying to be subtle.

"These kids yours or theirs?" he asked.

"Oh, they're not mine. I'm helping my friends."

"Crying babies, screaming kids, the place is full of them. I don't even notice," he said.

Sarah nodded.

"I got two kids myself," he said.

"Oh, that's wonderful. How old are they?"

"Five and seven, a boy and a girl."

"What great ages," Sarah said.

"Yeah, well, I wouldn't know." His voice turned bitter. "My wife took them. Packed 'em up and moved back to France where she was from. She got a fancy lawyer who said there was nothing I could do about it. It could be Mars, it's so far away."

"France?" Sarah asked.

"Yeah. We met when I was traveling in Europe after high school. Took a cooking class in France and she was there. She seemed so exotic with her accent and her rose perfume. That smell used to drive me crazy. Now I can't stand it. It drives me crazy in another way."

Sarah knew someone who used rosewater perfume, but she couldn't remember who it was. They'd better steer clear of this guy.

He threw his cigarette down and ground it under his shoe. "She never liked it here. And then she said she didn't like me either. Bitch."

"Oh," said Sarah.

"They left when the littlest one was in diapers. Now I see them once a year, tops."

"Oh," said Sarah. "That's too bad."

"Your friends had some fight today," he said.

"Oh, you know…" Sarah tried to sound offhand.

"Believe me, I know. I know what's coming," he said. "I know how women are."

Sarah started to feel uncomfortable. "Well," she said, "I should be getting back."

"Yeah. Me too. Break's over." He stood. "You tell them to watch it. Those kids deserve better."

As he strolled past, Sarah drew the babies close to her, feeling more and more uneasy as she did.

Chapter 49

Helen and Scott had finished dessert when Sarah rolled the twins back into the dining room. Sarah's dinner was still there, and a white box sat next to her plate to put the meal in to take with her. She scooped the chicken and roasted potatoes and green beans into the box, inhaling the delicious herby smell. She involuntarily turned to look at the chef, who again gave her a little salute. She nodded back.

Emanuel came over with a brownie wrapped in a napkin. "Don't want to forget dessert."

Sarah thanked him and they walked out of the dining room, now about half full and noisy.

Helen and Scott didn't speak on the way out and they seemed tense, so there wasn't much discussion on the short walk. Sarah pointed out the sky, and both of them glanced up briefly without comment. They paused at their door, and Helen went in to get supplies for the twins for the night. A crib was already set up in Sarah's room. They left Scott alone, and Helen and Sarah went to put the babies to bed.

"Thank you so much for doing this. I think a full night's sleep will do Scott and me a world of good. I don't think I'm thinking straight. I'm so irritable and he's so irritable. It's got to be lack of sleep."

"Yes, I'm sure. You guys sleep as late as you want. Come over when you're ready."

They changed the babies and fed them and put them to bed. Helen leaned over the crib and patted their backs and hummed a lullaby. They drifted right off, but Helen warned that they'd be up again in a few hours.

"Just like being on call," Sarah said.

"Without the pager," Helen said.

"Have a good night's sleep," Sarah said. Helen looked again at the twins, tucked a blanket tighter around Emily, and waved good-bye.

As Helen promised, the twins woke an hour after Sarah fell asleep, first Aidan, then, as soon as she'd gotten him fed and back in the crib, Emily. She wouldn't go back to sleep, and Sarah had to walk her around as she whimpered and flailed. Helen had told Sarah about this, so she wasn't worried, but it took almost an hour before Emily was sleepy enough to go back in the crib with her brother. Then, an hour later, Aidan was awake and hungry again. Then Emily. The whole night went like that. Sarah lost count. When morning came and Helen and Scott knocked on her door, she was asleep and so were the twins. It was after nine. Sarah felt like it was the middle of the night.

"They were fine," she said. Helen and Scott were smiling, and Scott had a paper cup of coffee for Sarah.

The babies stirred and Emily started to cry.

"We'll take them off your hands, and you can get more sleep if you want," Helen said.

Sarah looked out at the day, bright and sunny and cold again. "No, I think I'll get up. Maybe I'll go swimming. That should wake me up."

Helen and Scott took a baby each and had them diapered and changed into new outfits in no time. "We'll come back and get you for lunch," Scott said.

"How about noon?"

"Fine," said Sarah.

Scott wheeled the babies away. Helen clasped Sarah's hand. "Thank you, again. What a wonderful night."

Sarah splashed cold water on her face and drank her coffee. She opened the door and squinted at the light. The housekeeping cart was parked outside. There was no sign of Glenda and George. She met them sitting on a bench on her way to the pool.

"Oh, dear, you're up now. We'll get to your room right quick," Glenda said. "We wanted to let you sleep. We saw you had the watch last night. Twins. Can't be easy."

How did they know Sarah had the watch? How close were they watching *her*?

Dylan appeared out of nowhere and joined Glenda and George on the bench. He had a small doll in his hand with a yellow dress dirty from mud.

"Found it," Dylan said. He brushed at the dress with his hand. George handed him the towel from his belt, and Dylan brushed the mud away, then rubbed the towel over the doll's face to clean that too. He handed the towel back to George and started off, the doll tucked into his elbow.

"Little girl got that doll for Christmas," Glenda said. "Dylan found her crying and screaming and got it out of her that she'd lost the doll. He's been searching for it ever since."

"Good for him," said Sarah, thinking she'd misjudged the boy.

"Dylan has a soft spot for Christmas. I don't like Christmas myself." Glenda turned toward George sitting silently next to her. "Not George, neither. Too many memories."

"Oh?" said Sarah.

"George almost died on Christmas."

"But I didn't, did I?" This was from George.

"No, but you could've." Glenda turned to Sarah again. "George had a heart attack a few years ago on Christmas Eve. They told me he had a good chance of not making it. Spent Christmas in the ICU."

"Oh, no," Sarah said.

Glenda continued. "Dylan had just come to live with us, his dad threw him out and he didn't have anywhere to go. Took a bus from Pennsylvania, that's where we all grew up, my brother and I, and George. My brother's still there. Dylan turned up on our doorstep one day. He was in a state then, just a teenager but doing all kinds of things we didn't understand. It was very stressful."

"Dylan didn't cause the heart attack. You know that," George said.

"I know. I'm just explaining," Glenda said. "My brother, Dylan's dad, he didn't know much about raising a boy."

"He knew about his belt," said George.

Sarah shuddered.

"Yes, you should have seen Dylan when he first came to live with us. Now look. Anyway, that Christmas, I didn't think I could do it, take care of George, plus take care of Dylan and all of his problems. I didn't even know if George would live or die. He almost died. That's why I don't like Christmas."

"Me, neither," said George. "Like New Year's, though."

"Yes, you like New Year's. And you should." Glenda smiled proudly at Sarah. "After his heart attack, George made a New Year's resolution. Get fit. Look at him now. Eighty pounds lighter, off all his blood pressure medicine, doctor says his heart is A-okay."

"That's wonderful," Sarah said. "Very few people can do what you did."

"I wasn't ready to die," George said. "Plus, we had Dylan."

"Yes. And the next year, they made a New Year's pact," Glenda said. "Dylan saw George keep his promise to get fit, he saw how much better George felt. He'd lost thirty pounds by then. Dylan had cleaned up his act, but he was still struggling. They made a pact to get fit together, George would keep losing weight, and Dylan would keep off the drugs and alcohol. George held up his end and Dylan held up his."

"Yep," George said.

"That's amazing," Sarah said.

Glenda and George headed toward her room. Sarah continued on to the pool, chastising herself for her unkind thoughts about Dylan. As she pulled her sweatshirt off, Dylan himself came in, loping along silently despite a chain with keys dangling from his blue jeans. He and Sarah were the only ones in the pool area. She hesitated, feeling self-conscious and vulnerable. This is ridiculous, she thought. He is Glenda and George's nephew, he had a tough childhood, he turned himself around, he just did a nice turn for a girl who lost her doll. You are being silly.

Without looking at her, Dylan bent to get a sample of the water. He dipped a strip into the water, shook it out and waited. Sarah dove into the water. When she

230

came up, he still squatted by the edge of the pool with the strip in his hand, but his eyes were on her.

What else was there to look at in here? Of course he'd be looking at her, Sarah told herself. She started her laps. When she was finished, several families had joined her, a mom with young ones splashing in the shallow end and a dad with a girl on each arm, whirling them this way and that in the water. Dylan was stocking fresh towels in the cart. Sarah was happy to have one already, so she didn't need to pass by him.

Sarah left the pool feeling foolish, until she looked back and saw him standing in the doorway watching her.

Helen and Scott were still in good spirits at lunch. They rolled the sleeping babies over to the half wall, and Helen held up crossed fingers.

They all ordered chicken Caesar salad and sat munching contentedly in peace. The dining room again was not full, and the twins were the only children.

"Sarah, we want to ask you something," Helen said.

"You might have to think about it, and we'll understand if you say no," Scott said.

Sarah looked from one to the other. She steeled herself. She wasn't sure what was coming.

"Would you consider being their guardian?" Helen asked.

"You know we don't have any family, and so it would be a big responsibility, taking them on if something happened to us," Scott said.

Sarah looked at the babies, Aidan sucking on his lips and Emily tucked into her pink blanket. She looked at Scott and Helen, their faces expectant. She thought of herself with only her brother as family.

"Of course I will," she said.

Scott let out his breath loudly. Helen put her hand over his.

"We've been wanting to ask you," Helen said.

"Thank you so much," said Scott.

The babies slept through the entire meal. They wheeled them out and walked in the garden. There wasn't much to it now that it was winter, but the plants were well tended, and one confused bush even had pink flowers.

They sat on one of the benches, the babies still quiet but awake. All of a sudden, Scott let out a yell.

"She smiled! She smiled! Did you see that? Emily smiled."

They all crowded around, and Emily obliged by smiling up at them, a large toothless smile. Scott took Helen in his arms and lifted her off the ground.

"This place is magic," Helen said.

They sat there a long time, staring at the babies, smiling themselves.

Sarah looked around lazily. She started suddenly. The pool boy, Dylan, skulked behind the flowery bush. He stood watering the plants, but the water flowed along the sidewalk because he faced toward their group.

"Look, look," Sarah whispered, motioning with her head.

She looked back. The hose was properly aimed at the shrubbery, and Dylan's eyes were on the job.

Chapter 50

"There are some interesting characters out there."
Sarah sat next to Frances Noonan at the older woman's
kitchen table, gazing out at the San Francisco Bay and
the beginnings of the sunset. Camouflage rested on the
floor between her feet and Mrs. Noonan's. Sarah took a
cookie from the plate in front of them.

"Well," said Mrs. Noonan, "where in life aren't
there?"

"Oh, my gosh, this cookie is the best thing I've
ever tasted." Sarah chewed and swallowed. "What are
they?"

"Molasses," Mrs. Noonan said.

"Molasses. Of course." Sarah took another bite,
savoring the chewiness and the spices. She hadn't had a
molasses cookie in years. Maybe since her childhood. It
reminded her of her mother. She felt no sadness
thinking of her. How could she when she sat next to
Mrs. Noonan, with her gentle manner and her twinkly
blue eyes just like Sarah's mother's.

"Is this a new recipe? They're fabulous."

"No." Mrs. Noonan spoke softly. "No, this is an
old recipe."

"Well, I love them," Sarah told her.

"So did Bill," Mrs. Noonan said. "I haven't made
them in a long time."

She didn't say anything else. Sarah leaned over in

her chair so their shoulders touched.

After a moment, Mrs. Noonan said, "I hope you brought me pictures of the babies. It's a little lonely around here because Alma agreed to let Baby Owen go with Chantrelle for the weekend to her sisters'. Chantrelle and her sister apparently patched things up."

"Poor Mrs. Gordon."

"Poor Mrs. Gordon is right. I hope she's having a well-deserved rest."

"Well, I'll show you Helen's babies. They're tiny compared to Owen."

"Is this the resort? What a pretty spot." Mrs. Noonan nodded at a picture of Sarah and Helen in the garden of the resort.

"Yes, these were all taken there."

"And is this one of those men? He doesn't look very pleasant." Mrs. Noonan had moved on to a picture of Scott looking back over his shoulder, a nasty scowl on his face.

"Oops, no, that's Scott. Helen's husband. You've met him. That's not a very flattering picture. Maybe I should delete it," Sarah said.

"Oh, yes, of course, I remember him now. I think he's put on a little weight. He certainly doesn't look like a man on vacation."

"He looked better by the end. That was the first day." Sarah told her about the incident with the diapers, laughing despite herself as she remembered him covered in baby poo. She told Mrs. Noonan about Scott being a stay-at-home dad and about his Japanese history PhD.

"Hmm." Mrs. Noonan took a bite of cookie.

"They really had a good time. I think it was exactly

what they needed. Although getting the babies into the car was a problem. I don't think anyone wanted to leave. The babies thrashed around, and Scott and Helen couldn't get them buckled in. Scott hit his head on the trunk of the car and swore up a storm. The proprietor had to tell him to keep his voice down, with all the families present."

"Hmm," Mrs. Noonan said again.

"I think it will be all right. Scott's really very good with the babies. He's just worried…"

"Yes, I'm sure you're right. Babies have a way of growing on you and making other things less important." Mrs. Noonan looked at the next picture. "How about this one? Is this one of the men?" The picture showed the babies in their stroller in the dining room in front of the half wall. The chef stood above, and in the picture, he stared straight down at them.

"Yep, that's the chef, Marco. He's the one with the kids he never sees." Sarah told Mrs. Noonan how angry he'd seemed.

"That must be hard, never getting to see his young children," Mrs. Noonan said.

"Wait, I just remembered who wears rose perfume!" Sarah exclaimed. "It was Andrea Blackwell! You don't think her perfume could have set this man off, do you?"

"Andrea Blackwell? Oh, my. Who knows what could set off an angry man? I've heard of stranger things. Bill once told me about a case where a man attacked anyone wearing a baseball cap with another teams' logo. Though that may be different. You know how worked up men get about their sporting teams."

"This is really far-fetched. But do you think

Shelley Stalk wore rose-scented perfume?"

"Or Serena Evans, for that matter. I'll see what I can find out. You know, maybe we should also think about this man's wife and children."

Sarah put her cookie down and stared at Mrs. Noonan. "You mean they might not be safe in France awaiting his visits?"

"We'd just better make sure," Mrs. Noonan said.

"I'll ask Andy. He may be able to find out."

Mrs. Noonan nodded and turned back to the pictures. "This must be the housekeepers."

Sarah had taken a picture of the pink flowering bush, and Glenda and George were somehow standing in the background, passing by with their cart.

"That's them," she said.

"And this wouldn't be the pool boy, would it?" Mrs. Noonan pointed to a picture with Sarah and Helen.

Sarah leaned in and squinted over the picture. In the left corner, behind an empty flowerbed, Dylan hovered, hose in hand. Perfectly innocent.

"Yes, that's him. And this one has Emanuel."

"You don't have one of the proprietor, do you?"

Sarah quickly flipped through the pictures. "No, he's not in any of them. Wait, I think I still have the brochure. He's on the back."

"That's right. I have one, too, from Evelyn Ringley." Mrs. Noonan went to her desk and came back instantly with the Paradise Cove Resort brochure. "Here he is." She tapped the back.

"That's him," Sarah said.

"Can I make print copies of your pictures?" Mrs. Noonan asked. "I think I'll mail these to Serena Evans and make certain she doesn't know these people. I'll find out about her perfume. I wanted to write to ask her more about Spencer Tremaine anyway. The more I remember about him, the stranger it seems. He contacted Serena. And he contacted Julia, after all, not the other way around. Why did he single out Paul Blackwell's crime?"

"Gosh, I hope we're wrong. I truly hope that these crimes are just what they appear," Sarah said. "It would be even more tragic if there were two victims each time, the dead and the accused."

"Yes, well I hope we're right. It's the accused that we can still salvage. That's why I want to know more about Spencer Tremaine. I just don't like the man."

"Remember what a hard sell he had?" Sarah said. "Mrs. Blackwell felt like she had no choice but to change to him after the claims he made."

"It was the same with Serena. Not that he seems to have helped either one of them."

"Did he ever explain why he never told Julia Blackwell about Serena Evans and her case?" Sarah asked.

"Julia did ask him," Mrs. Noonan said. "He said he didn't like to advertise that case since he didn't get her off. Julia was pretty peeved since the circumstances are so similar."

"So similar," said Sarah.

"How many people out there have million-dollar life insurance policies, after all?"

"Well, we do," said Sarah.

"What?" said Mrs. Noonan.

"Well, not me exactly. But the hospital covers a five hundred-thousand-dollar life insurance policy as one of our benefits, and we can all increase to one million dollars if we pay more. Helen told me. She increased hers this year because of the babies."

"She told you?"

Sarah told her about being the guardian. Mrs. Noonan beamed. Then her smile vanished.

"If Olivia Honeycut were here, she'd say Helen and Scott had better watch out. They fit the profile," Mrs. Noonan said.

"No, no they don't," Sarah insisted. "They're just having a little trouble because the babies are so much work. They're already sorting things out." At least Sarah hoped this was true. The twins' birthday, El Dia de los Angelitos, flashed into her mind and she shivered. Then she remembered how normal Helen and Scott looked after sleeping through the night. And how miserable Sarah had felt. Helen and Scott would be fine. "Anyway, I think a lot of jobs offer life insurance. We're not the only ones."

"That's interesting," said Mrs. Noonan. "Maybe lots of people have these big policies. Maybe it's not so unusual."

"Right. And Helen isn't dead," Sarah said and shivered again. "What's unique about all these cases, Joseph and Shelley Stalk, David and Serena Evans and Paul and Andrea Blackwell, they all have million-dollar insurance policies and a dead spouse. *That* is unusual." Sarah vowed to check in with Helen to make sure she and Scott were sleeping, were coping, and to see if she could help.

"Yes," said Mrs. Noonan. "So I'm going to write to Serena and ask if she wears rose perfume. I'll send her these pictures from the resort and see if she knows how Spencer Tremaine heard about her case. His main offices are here in California, but he has other locations. I wonder if he had an office in Illinois already. Or not. I think it would make a difference in how skeptical of him I am."

"Skeptical's not the word I'd use," said Sarah. "He's downright disturbing. Plus, he met Helen and Scott, and not at their best."

Chapter 51

His father was home for once. The house was filled with cigarette smoke. His parents both smoked, but his mother smoked more when his father was around. It was because she couldn't drink. As much.

"I want to see some behavior out of you when your aunt and uncle are here."

"Yes, sir." It went without saying that if he didn't, there would be a switching. His father's switch was stiff and painful.

He loved it when his uncle came. His father and his uncle were nothing alike. His father had always been the way he was, Uncle Morris told him, wore his shirt buttoned to the top even in high school. Uncle Morris wasn't mean about it, just said they were different.

Uncle Morris was a fireman and worked a week, then was off a week. He and Aunt Eunice were staying for the entire week, and his mother had cleaned and cooked for days.

His father was still able to find the dresser in the guest bedroom undusted, and he came to dinner wagging his dust-covered finger. His mother jumped right up and ran upstairs with her dust cloth. His father also said her stroganoff was too salty, and she'd better not serve something like that to his brother.

When Uncle Morris and Aunt Eunice finally arrived, they brought presents for everyone plus a basket of fruit and a basket of homemade cinnamon buns. There was a light blue sweater for his mother, a political book for his father, and a soccer ball for him.

"Soccer's a sissy sport," his father said. He said it quietly to Uncle Morris but not quietly enough.

"Builds teamwork and endurance," Uncle Morris said.

"Sissy sport," his father said.

It didn't matter because the first time he kicked it, he cracked the window of the garden shed, and his father took the ball away.

Uncle Morris showed him a book with pictures from all the national parks in the country with a map to see where each one was. He taught him how to tie fishing flies and to whistle and to throw a curve ball. He showed him how to jump into the water without holding his nose with his fingers, and he let him start the coals on the backyard grill.

Uncle Morris did all this in the week he was there. It was more than he'd learned from his own father in his entire life.

Chapter 52

Alma Gordon waited with Sarah and Frances Noonan for Chantrelle to return from her weekend with Baby Owen. Chantrelle and her sister had recently had a reunion, and into this tenuous situation Mrs. Gordon handed over Owen.

What if Chantrelle and her sister got along? What if the sister was nice? Would Chantrelle move back to San Francisco and move in with her? Would this be a good home for Owen? Would Alma get to see him?

What if Chantrelle decided to take Owen back to Los Angeles? Zach was already out of the picture, broken up in the few days he and Chantrelle had spent alone together. What if Chantrelle decided a toddler was just the thing to fill the empty space?

What if Chantrelle was able to take Owen back? Because Alma Gordon was tired. It had been easy when Owen was a baby. But he was a toddler now and toddlers were nonstop. She spent all day trailing behind him, keeping him safe, entertained, fed, happy.

He was such a happy little boy. Her heart squeezed, and though her heart test had been normal, her heart hurt just the same.

Chantrelle would make a good mother. Wouldn't she? In time? With lots of coaching?

Los Angeles was so far away.

A sharp knock at the door made her jump. She

couldn't manage to get off the soft couch, and Sarah went to open it.

"She's here." Enid Carmichael strode into the apartment. She homed in on the plate of brownies on the table supplied by Frances Noonan and helped herself.

"Saw her from my window. She's having a hard time getting the kid out of his car seat."

"Oh, dear." Alma Gordon couldn't believe it. She'd gone over this and over this with Chantrelle. They'd practiced several times. She and Frances had no trouble with the car seat themselves.

"She's swearing like a banshee. I opened my window to get the breeze and I heard her." Mrs. Carmichael took another brownie.

"Oh, dear." It was freezing outside, and Alma doubted Enid had wanted a breeze, more likely wanted to spy on Chantrelle. Still, Alma was glad for the information.

"She called him a little sh—well, you know. I don't use that type of language myself. I'm just telling you what I heard." Mrs. Carmichael licked the chocolate off her fingers.

"What!" Frances Noonan cried.

Alma sat stuck in place on her squishy sofa. She felt her face get squishy, too, and she started to cry.

"She doesn't seem very suitable," Enid Carmichael said. "Do you have anything to drink?"

"Alma, Alma, don't worry. We will find a way. We have to find a way. Owen cannot go with her." Frances Noonan put her arm around her shoulder. Alma knew she meant these words as a comfort.

Mrs. Gordon couldn't tell them the truth. That

she'd hoped Chantrelle had matured into a mother. That she got along with her sister and had a home to go to with Owen. That Mrs. Gordon really was too old and tired to take care of a toddler.

Owen. Her Owen.

The buzzer shrieked. Sarah buzzed them up and waited by the open door. The elevator opened and the hall filled with screaming.

Chantrelle spilled into the apartment. She pulled Owen along by his arm. His face was maroon, and he tried to plant his feet to keep from moving. Then he saw Alma and broke free from Chantrelle. He ran to the couch on his short legs and flung himself at her so that she fell backward deeper into the cushion.

Up close, Owen's face was grimy and tear streaked. He stopped screaming and tried to speak, but he could only cry.

"We lost the bear," Chantrelle said. "I told him it's only a bear, and he's too old anyway, and we can get another, and why won't he just shut up?" She shouted now. "First it was the food, he didn't want what we had, then he wouldn't go to sleep, then it was the park and not wanting to leave, then it was the jacket, which he refused to wear."

"Sit down, dear, you must be exhausted. Have a brownie." Mrs. Noonan offered her the plate.

"My sister was exactly how I remembered. She'll never change. She knows everything. I'm a failure. My life is a waste. She'll never take in my kid. She'll never take in *me*. I don't need her. She's been out of my life for years and I've done fine."

"You sure about that?" said Enid Carmichael.

"It's Owen. That's the problem," Chantrelle

continued. "I can live on my own in LA. But Owen takes so much work. I can't get a job. I can't do anything."

Chantrelle was crying now, not shouting. "I'm too young to be a mother. It's too hard. I can't do it, I can't do it, I can't do it."

Neither can I, Mrs. Gordon thought. I'm too old to be a mother. The courts won't let me, and I can see why.

Owen had calmed in her lap. He lay limp against her chest. She dried his eyes with her handkerchief, smelling its lilac scent and trying to calm herself.

"Wing, wing," Baby Owen suddenly shouted, climbing off the couch and toddling over to Sarah. She bent her arm, and he held on and lifted his feet and started swinging.

"That's what he wants?" Chantrelle's voice rose again. "He said it all weekend. He kept trying to grab my arm. I couldn't figure it out. I thought he wanted me to flap like a bird. How was I supposed to know this is what 'wing' means?"

"Oh, dear," Mrs. Gordon said. "It means 'swing.' I'm afraid this is Harold's fault. He taught Owen this ages ago."

"Owen will swing until your arm feels like it'll fall off," Sarah added.

"Men don't notice things like that. Stronger. That Harold could probably do it for hours," said Enid Carmichael.

"Wait a minute, wait a minute." Frances Noonan waved her hands in the air. Alma looked at her. Everyone was silent.

Mrs. Noonan pointed to Sarah, with the toddler

swinging on her arm.

"Harold. Harold and Sylvia. No one would turn down Harold and Sylvia. They can adopt Owen."

And she was right. Mrs. Gordon called Sylvia. She knew immediately from the tone of her daughter's voice that this would work out. Sylvia said she would talk with Harold. They called back a few hours later. They sounded so happy.

Chantrelle met them the very next day, visiting their house and seeing their town. Jonathan put through the papers and said they could start any time. The papers were simply a formality as long as everyone was in agreement.

Mrs. Gordon planned to take Baby Owen to Sunnyvale as soon as Sylvia and Harold made arrangements. Which somehow took them no time at all. Sylvia shifted her hours at work. Harold painted the spare bedroom blue. They said they were ready before the week was out.

"I can't believe I'm going to be a mother," Sylvia told her. "I only hope I can be anywhere near as good a mother as you."

Mrs. Gordon's heart squeezed again. A squeeze of joy.

Chapter 53

Sarah was there the day Baby Owen moved out of Alma Gordon's apartment. She remembered the awful day last summer when he went with Chantrelle to Los Angeles. Chantrelle was here today, too, standing to the side and looking lost. Harold and Sylvia and Alma Gordon and Baby Owen all left together, the trunk of Harold's car stuffed with bags. Mrs. Gordon would stay with Sylvia and Harold for a while, for as long as it took, as Sylvia said. Mr. Glenn planned a visit the very next day in case Alma forgot something.

Everyone had smiles. Even Chantrelle smiled, though Sarah saw her lip tremble. Mrs. Gordon got out of the car and came back to her and took her hands and whispered in her ear.

The remaining Fog Ladies and Chantrelle and Mr. Glenn stood together on the sidewalk and waved. As soon as the car was out of sight, Chantrelle mumbled good-bye and left.

Sarah rode the elevator up, saying good-bye to Mr. Glenn at the second floor. She'd forgotten to push the third floor and ended up at the top with Frances Noonan and Harriet Flynn.

"Come in at least for some scones," Mrs. Noonan said.

Sarah laughed and happily followed her.

"What's all this?" Sarah asked. Mrs. Noonan's

kitchen table was strewn with pill bottles.

"Oh, my, this is embarrassing," said Mrs. Noonan.

Sarah couldn't read the labels on the bottles. Was one of these medications embarrassing? Some ailment Mrs. Noonan didn't want her to know about? That didn't seem like her.

"To tell you the truth, I've been practicing."

"What?" Sarah said.

"Watch." Mrs. Noonan picked up a bottle, held it firmly in her left hand and gripped the lid with her right. Her fingers were bent at the tips from arthritis, making it difficult to turn the cap.

"Oh, here, let me." Sarah reached out her hand to help.

"No!" Mrs. Noonan yanked the bottle away.

Mrs. Noonan's cat flew out from under the table. Sarah dropped her hand.

"I'm sorry, Sarah. I didn't mean to shout. But I've been practicing and practicing, and I've pretty much got it." She pushed and pinched the bottle lid and twisted her right hand.

Mrs. Noonan's fingers strained, but Sarah kept her hands at her side. The lid popped off and a few pills flew out. The cat meowed and ran back under the table.

"There. See? I can do it myself. Bill used to do this for me. I've struggled with these lids for years. Now I've got it down."

Sarah picked a pill from between the scones and held it out for Mrs. Noonan to put back.

"My hands are really getting strong. It was watching Baby Owen that gave me the idea. He doesn't know how to do anything, but that doesn't stop him trying. He practices. And practices. And then he can make a block tower taller than he is. Or put the square block in the square hole and the triangle in the triangle. Well, now I can open my own pill bottles."

Mrs. Noonan nodded with satisfaction. She looked so triumphant. Sarah didn't have the heart to tell her the pharmacist would be happy to give her medication bottles without the child-proof caps.

"What an accomplishment." Sarah took a scone. "They call that 'growth mindset,' thinking you can do anything, within reason, as long as you put in the time and try hard enough."

"Growth mindset. That's me. Have some blueberry preserves." Mrs. Noonan set a jar on the table, brushing her medication to one side. "I made them myself."

"Oh, this looks yummy. Preserves. Pill bottles. Is there anything you can't manage?"

"Well, I confine myself to baking and canning. And I do like casseroles. And I went through a soup phase, and I make a pretty mean meatloaf."

"I guess that's a 'no.'" Of all those talents, Sarah guessed Mrs. Noonan was most proud of her pill bottle opening skills.

Sarah headed back down to her apartment with a plate of scones. Andy was stretched out on her couch, legs crossed and looking comfortable. She set the scones in his lap.

"New parents," he said. "How exciting for Harold and Sylvia to be new parents."

Sarah cocked her head. He'd never said anything like this before.

"I hope they don't end up dead like all these other couples you've been telling me about. Parenthood must be hard. I'm glad I'm not a parent."

Oh, well, Sarah thought.

He went on. "By the way, you can rest easy regarding Marco the chef. He had a nasty divorce and custody fight, but there's no mention of bloodshed. Here or in France. I found a blurb about his wife from a year ago."

"Oh, thank goodness. Mrs. Noonan found out from Shelley Stalk's sister that Shelley liked to try all different kinds of perfumes, so she might have been wearing one with roses that summer. Seems such a little thing to make a man go berserk. I'm glad his family is alive. But that doesn't let him off the hook. His wife could be safe in France, and he could still hate rose-scented women here in the United States."

"Motive maybe. But means? San Francisco is three hours from Big Sur. And Shelley Stalk died in Philadelphia." Andy bit into a scone.

"I know, I know," Sarah said. "And David Evans definitely didn't wear rosewater perfume. If Marco is killing because he hates fragrant women, David Evans must have gotten in the way somehow. Maybe he was protecting Serena. That would be too sad."

"It's impossible," Andy said. "Philadelphia. Chicago. How would he do it?"

"Okay. Just Andrea Blackwell, then. He could drive here and back all in one long night."

"One very long night," Andy said, taking another bite of scone. "By the way, I can also find out about Tremaine's Illinois license. Mrs. Noonan was wondering about that. There's probably a record of when it was first issued."

Sarah leaned down and kissed him. "You are amazing. Too bad you don't have the blueberry preserves for those scones. Mrs. Noonan made them herself."

"They're pretty good just like this. That woman sure can cook."

"For two kitchen doofuses like us, we're lucky to have her," Sarah said.

"Speak for yourself. Are you calling me a doofus?" Andy pulled her down and she lost her balance and landed laughing in his lap on top of the scones. He drew her in for a quick kiss.

"You taste even better than the scones," he said.

"That's 'cause you don't have the jam." She brushed scone crumbs off the two of them.

He kissed her again, this time longer. His arm circled around her waist and he stroked her hair.

"I wish we could lie here all night, but remember what we're doing?" Sarah reluctantly sat up. She was doing her best to make sure Helen and Scott had some time together, alone.

"Agh. Babysitting. I forgot. Here I was gearing up for a nice, leisurely evening. With you."

"It will be with me, but it will be anything but leisurely." Sarah twined her fingers in his. "Unfortunately."

They arrived at Helen and Scott's to hear both babies crying and Scott shouting at Helen to hurry up with the bottles and Helen shouting back she was moving as fast as she could. They hadn't rung the buzzer downstairs because the front door of the apartment building was held open with a newspaper. Now Sarah wished she'd given them some warning. She gave Andy's hand a quick squeeze and then knocked on the door.

The two adult voices fell silent, but the babies kept crying. Scott came to the door with a baby in each arm. Their faces were bright red.

"Come on in, if you're sure you want to," he said. "We tried to get them fed before you came. It didn't happen."

Helen came out of the kitchen with the bottles. She used both hands to stick one in each baby's mouth and the room became silent.

"Bliss," she said. Scott rolled his eyes.

Sarah took a twin from Scott, the one dressed in pink. Emily, she assumed. Then she looked at the other baby as Scott brought it around to his front. It wore pink too.

"Which is which?" Andy said.

"Helen didn't get to the laundry today, so everyone's in pink," Scott said. "We're not sure who's who."

Helen gave him a mock slap on the arm. "You've got Aidan," she said to Sarah.

"We'd better put something blue on him so we know," said Andy. "I'll never be able to tell them apart."

"He has a little blue cap from the hospital," said Helen. "I've been looking everywhere for it, but I can't find it. I think we left it in Big Sur."

"Something else, then," said Andy.

"Everything's covered in vomit and crap," said Scott.

"Scott! Watch your mouth! They'll hear you." Helen seemed serious. Scott rolled his eyes again.

"Wait, I know what to do." Andy took a blue pen out of his shirt pocket. He lifted Aidan's little hand from the bottle and drew a smiley face on his lower arm.

Helen gasped. Scott looked wounded. Sarah couldn't help herself and started to giggle. She felt Helen and Scott's glares.

"You don't draw on babies," she finally managed.

By now Scott was laughing too. Then Helen.

"I think this will suit our purpose just fine," said Andy. "This is Aidan."

"Here, see what you can do with this one." Scott handed Emily to Andy. Andy held her out in front of him, her lower half dangling. The bottle fell to the floor.

"Uh, I don't, I've never…" said Andy.

"It's easy," Scott said. "You'll get used to it. She won't break. Bring her in and give her some support around the head." Emily's head had lolled sideways.

"Uh, how?" Andy said.

"Sit down," said Helen. Andy sat. Helen readjusted the baby in his arms, laying her sideways with her head resting in his elbow. She wiggled around until Helen gave her the bottle. "There. Now don't move."

"I've got to change my clothes," Scott said. Sarah looked at him now that he was free of babies. His shirt was wet with spit up and his pants were wet too. He saw her staring. "You'll both look like this when we come home. And you won't have any spare clothes."

On cue, Emily turned her head, burped, and spit up onto Andy's arm. Andy grimaced, but he didn't move, his muscles tensed to keep his arm bent.

Helen dashed back with a cloth. "I'm so sorry." She wiped off his arm and tucked the cloth under Emily's head. "We have to get moving or we'll be late for our dinner reservation."

They left Sarah and Andy with the babies and went to get dressed. Andy sat stiffly on the couch. Sarah laughed. "Andy. Relax. She's not going anywhere. Relax your arm."

He let his arm sag. Emily started to whimper. He tensed his elbow again and she stopped. "This baby stuff is hard," he said. "Who knew?"

"Scott, for one," Sarah said.

They could hear Scott, his voice rising, looking for something he couldn't find. He hissed at Helen and she hissed back. By the time they came out dressed, they were bickering again.

"Have a lovely time," Sarah said.

"Right," Helen said. She led Sarah into the kitchen to show her where the emergency telephone numbers were. "I've been looking forward to this all week," she whispered. "Now look, we're just going to fight all night."

"No. You'll see. By the time you get to the restaurant, you'll have forgotten what you were arguing about and you'll be fine."

"We never do argue about anything important. That's the problem. We never talk about the *real* problem."

"Good luck, man," Scott said to Andy, and he and Helen left, Scott walking in front and Helen walking behind.

Chapter 54

He had to kill them. He had a higher purpose. He didn't want to do it. In fact, the first time he couldn't look. Just held up the gun and pulled the trigger with his face turned away.

But he heard a whimper, right before.

After that, the killing was easy. Only the man had been harder. He had to give him quite a whack in the neck to subdue him. Before he did, he thought the man might actually overpower him.

The kids were never around. He made sure of that. Usually they were out of the house or asleep in another room. The Philadelphia woman had been different. But he liked a challenge. He planned on killing her in the car as soon as he saw how the father stormed into the building every time he arrived home with his family. But that left the boy in the car. He tried to steal a front door key from the old neighbor lady. Her giant purse contained everything except what he was after. Then he noticed the keypad. The mother said the numbers aloud to the little boy when they went in: four...two... six...four. Anyone on the block could hear if they were listening. Getting the kid into the building after he hit her on the head had taken less than a minute. The kid hadn't made a sound. Just like he'd thought.

It took him no time to finish her off in the back of the car. She was petite and the car was a huge

American model with a roomy back seat.

Still, it was better when he didn't have to deal with the kids. He sometimes thought of the look on the little boy's face. But he had to do it. It was for the best.

He had tried several different methods of killing. He did this from necessity, he told himself. Didn't want things to look too similar. He thought about it a lot ahead of time, what to use, a gun, a machete, a scarf, a hammer. And he thought about the sounds he'd heard and might hear, a whimper, a plea, weeping, terror. This last woman had actually cursed him, not profanity but an actual curse.

"Your black soul will never find peace."

She'd managed to get that out in a loud enough voice for him to hear after he'd already left the kitchen.

Her threat didn't bother him. At least not during the day. Sometimes at night he thought of it. But not very often.

Chapter 55

Enid Carmichael slowly opened her window, keeping her eyes on the well-dressed man to make sure he didn't notice. The breeze felt pleasant. She settled back into her chair. She had already eliminated the Snowball problem with one of Frances Noonan's soup bones she'd purloined for exactly this purpose. The small dog's face was hidden in the marrow. She wouldn't hear a peep from him anytime soon.

The front door gave its telltale opening squeak. If you had sharp ears. Fancy Bad Guy Man was down the street a bit. He stood still, staring at the front door. Mr. Glenn came into view.

The man gasped. Mrs. Carmichael heard him, but Mr. Glenn did not. Mr. Glenn started down the sidewalk. He used to be stooped and shuffling. Now he walked straight upright. He was still slow, but weren't they all.

He was slow enough that Bad Guy was across the street in no time. Mr. Glenn, with his lack of awareness of his surroundings and inferior hearing, obviously didn't know he was a target. Fancy Bad Guy Man headed straight for him.

Should she call out? Warn him? What if this suit-man was a killer? But what if he wasn't? He'd know she was here. She had waited in her duck blind for months for the denouement to this man's story. She couldn't miss it now by giving herself away.

She held her tongue. Bad Guy held out his hand in a "Hold on a minute there" sign. Mr. Glenn stopped. They were at the edge of her view.

Mrs. Carmichael was on her feet, leaning as far as she could out the slim window without losing her balance and tumbling out. She held tight on to the window trim, but her fingers were not strong enough to hold for long. She dropped to her knees, bones grating on the hardwood floor, and stuck her head out the window. Much safer. And she could see everything.

Fancy Man had obviously asked Mr. Glenn the time. What a lame opening. Everyone knew a man his age would have a pocket telephone with the time printed right on it. But Mr. Glenn wasn't as astute as she was, and he fell for it. He pushed his jacket sleeve back and twisted his wrist toward the man so he could read the watch.

"Thanks," Bad Guy said. His eyes were locked on Mr. Glenn's. Mrs. Carmichael could feel the intensity all the way up on the second floor.

Mr. Glenn must have finally noticed because the two men stood there staring at each other. How long could this go on? Why weren't they talking?

"Albert Glenn?" the man finally asked.

"Lionel?" Mr. Glenn said.

"What?" Mrs. Carmichael shrieked. Her upper body catapulted forward like a clown spring-loaded in a box, arms flailing helplessly in the air, body held in place by the wall and the windowsill.

Both men gaped at her, but she didn't care. The Glenn's long-lost Lionel had returned.

Chapter 56

Frances Noonan and Sarah heard the whole story from Enid Carmichael, who interrogated poor Mr. Glenn ceaselessly until she'd heard it all.

"The kid, man, whatever, is corporate now, comes to San Francisco on business, gets put up in a fancy hotel and everything." Mrs. Carmichael helped herself to zucchini bread.

Frances had set out the whole loaf so she wouldn't have to replenish the plate. Thank goodness Alma was at Sylvia's. She didn't need to hear this from Enid Carmichael. Mr. Glenn would tell her himself. Probably already had.

"So, first he's a drug addict, then the Glenn's are part of the problem and he divorces them and moves to Oregon and denounces the material world, now he turns up all expensive-shoed and staying in a hotel I've never set foot in in my life, probably ordering exorbitantly priced drinks at the bar." Mrs. Carmichael took a large bite of bread.

"And he didn't know how to approach Mr. Glenn, so he loitered outside our building when he was in town, hoping Mr. Glenn would appear. I set Mr. Glenn straight on this, though he still thinks they bumped into each other by serendipity. Men are so thick." She chewed and swallowed.

"So now they're going to be buddy-buddy, and Mr.

Glenn is gaga because he never thought he'd see his son again. Watch out, that's what I say."

"How sad Bessie Glenn didn't live to see her son come home," Mrs. Noonan said.

"What a surprise. What a shock for Mr. Glenn," Sarah said.

"I remember those days, what a tough kid Lionel was. I hope he's changed," Mrs. Noonan added.

"Doubt it," said Mrs. Carmichael.

"How long has it been?" Sarah asked.

Mrs. Noonan made a quick calculation. "Well over twenty years. Probably over twenty-five. Seems like yesterday, but it wasn't yesterday." My goodness, how time marched on.

Twenty years was the total amount of time Serena Evans would be in prison. Her girls would be all grown up when she was out, maybe changed as much as this corporate son of Mr. Glenn's.

A letter from Serena arrived just before they set out on Friday for the card game at Olivia Honeycut's. Mrs. Noonan tucked it into her purse to share with the ladies. She was not fond of the trek to Mrs. Honeycut's apartment as it required driving from their building to Olivia's a few blocks away on a steep street that never had parking. Today she, Enid Carmichael, Harriet Flynn, and Alma Gordon, now back, circled three times before a space opened up, which was actually less than usual.

Olivia Honeycut had years ago purchased a special card table with cup holders at the sides, and she was proud to show it off. She clunked their lemonade in and commented on the convenience every time they visited. It was far easier when the card games were at Frances's or Alma's, but the fancy card table kept them voyaging to Mrs. Honeycut's more often than Frances liked. The lemonade was too sugary, and the table had a tendency to jiggle on the uneven floor with an annoying rattle, but they didn't have the heart to tell her.

Mrs. Honeycut passed around glasses of the too-sweet lemonade.

"I have some news," Frances Noonan told the group. "I heard back from Evelyn Ringley. She was able to contact her brother-in-law in Philadelphia. Spencer Tremaine was not his lawyer."

"So much for the pattern, then," rasped Olivia Honeycut.

"I knew it," sighed Alma Gordon.

"And she and her husband were vacationing in Hawaii when they heard about Shelley's death. So it does not appear that Evelyn's husband is a killer," said Mrs. Noonan.

"I tell you, it's just what it appears, anger and jealously. Believe me, I know." Enid Carmichael reached her hand toward the tub with Mrs. Honeycut's favorite cream puffs, retrieving four miniature pastries in her large hand. She jammed two into her mouth and chewed thoughtfully.

In the silence that followed, Mrs. Noonan mused that it was a good thing Stanley Carmichael had never turned up dead.

Mrs. Honeycut set a small blue tin on the table and opened it.

At first Frances Noonan could not place the smell. Then she inhaled sharply, engulfed in memories. The scent of her husband wafted out of the tin.

"Maybe you will like these," Olivia Honeycut said

to the group. "Too strong for me. When did mints stop coming in rolls?"

Mrs. Noonan sat paralyzed. She smelled Bill and his wintergreen breath as he leaned over to kiss her cheek. She smelled Bill sitting next to her reading on the couch, his feet touching hers. She smelled Bill at the kitchen table working on the crossword.

A cream puff was halfway to Enid Carmichael's mouth, but she dropped her hand and grabbed at the tin, knocking a few mints out onto the table. "I'll try one," she said. "Alma, Harriet? Someone's breath was mighty fragrant in the car. Who had onions for lunch? Frances, I think it was you. Here."

The mint was tiny in Enid's oversized hand. Tiny. But packed with reminiscences.

Frances inhaled again. The wintergreen was overpowering. She breathed it in, and her uncertainty and panic fell away, leaving her happier and happier. She reached out her hand, seized the mint, and popped it in her mouth. She sucked in, savoring the intensity of the wintergreen flavor. Bill was with her and always would be. Every memory was a blessing, to hold and to cherish.

"Maybe take two," Enid Carmichael said, shoving the whole tin closer. "It's definitely your breath."

"Oh, dear," Alma Gordon said, but Mrs. Noonan took a second mint feeling lighter than she had in months.

She smiled to herself. Enid Carmichael would never change. Take Harriet Flynn. The woman did look good with her new hair. But Enid had been her usual blunt self in the car on the way over.

"Why's your hair so dark?" Enid must have just

then noticed it. As if she should talk, with her dyed hair that was never the same shade of red.

Unfortunately, Enid didn't stop with her question. "Your hair may be dark, but your face is still old," she'd said.

Frances didn't agree. She had watched Harriet's hair slowly change, a little less gray, a little more brown, until now when she frankly looked ten years younger. Heck, twenty years, especially if you had Mrs. Noonan's bad eyesight and couldn't see the wrinkles. Harriet's mouth, previously always pursed, smiled often now, hiding the wrinkles in the creases. Frances Noonan smiled across the card table at her, hoping her own wrinkles disappeared too.

Alma was back from her babysitting, her fluffy white hair unchanged. Mrs. Noonan smiled at her too. Alma's plan was to take the train to Sylvia's on Sundays and watch Owen while Sylvia worked Monday, Tuesday, and Wednesday. She'd finished her first week and was full of stories, telling one now, her arms waving in animation. Owen learned how to kick a ball, and Sylvia made giant soap bubbles for him to attack in the backyard.

"You should see him, a yard, his own room…" Her voice trailed and she took out her handkerchief and wiped her eyes. She waved it dismissively. "These are happy tears."

Mrs. Noonan smelled the lilacs and felt so happy for her friend.

"What kid can't kick?" said Mrs. Carmichael.

"I brought something to show you." Mrs. Noonan held up Serena's letter. Enid Carmichael had no tact.

"'Dear Frances, Thank you for your letter. I look

forward to them, as you know. In answer to your questions, Spencer Tremaine approached me. He said he had followed my case since the beginning, and he was certain he could mount a better defense. As far as I know, he had offices in Chicago already. I only ever saw him at the jail.'"

Mrs. Noonan looked up. "Sarah said Andy confirmed Tremaine's office has been in Chicago for ten years, so that part's correct." She continued reading.

"'There is one other thing about him. I don't like to talk about this because it is an unpleasant memory, one of the worst of a very unpleasant time. When I fired Spencer Tremaine, he was very angry. He said it didn't matter because it was impossible to defend someone who wasn't straight with him. He said he knew I was guilty and that he could have gotten me a lesser sentence if I'd let him plea bargain. He said it was my fault he lost because he was dealing with lies.'"

"So Spencer Tremaine thought she was guilty," Harriet Flynn said.

"Indeed. That means, if he truly thought she was the killer, and that's a big 'if,' that he couldn't have been the murderer himself," Frances told them.

"I always knew she was the one," said Olivia Honeycut.

"This doesn't mean she was the killer. It only means Spencer Tremaine thought she was," said Mrs. Noonan.

"Oh, this is so confusing," said Alma Gordon.

"All this talk of guilt, yet nobody admits their sins," said Mrs. Flynn.

"What a woman," said Mrs. Carmichael. "What else does she say?" She snatched the letter from Mrs.

Noonan.

"'He also blamed me for a downturn in his career. He was filming a new series in London when he heard about my case, and he said the time he wasted with me was time away from his television career. They canceled the series after the first season, and it took him a while to reclaim his celebrity status.'"

"I remember that series," Alma Gordon said. "*Law Across the Pond.* He did live commentary on active cases in Britain and explained to the Americans and the Brits the similarities and differences in our two legal systems. He was wonderful." She had that dreamy look again.

"I remember too." Enid Carmichael stuffed another cream puff into her mouth. "Seems to me the show was canceled due to Spencer Tremaine's off-screen antics. I read about it in my celebrity magazine. Now it's coming back. I remember a situation with one of the barrister's wives. Seems she preferred a man who didn't wear wigs."

"Celebrity magazine? Wigs? This sounds like a sordid affair," Mrs. Flynn said.

"'Torrid' is the word they used," Mrs. Carmichael said.

"Oh, dear. Spencer Tremaine? Are you sure?" Mrs. Gordon said.

"Live commentary?" Mrs. Noonan said. "Enid, you remember this in the gossip columns? If he was in England at the time of David Evans's murder and making headlines in the gossip columns, then he was not in Chicago, and he is definitely in the clear."

"I still have the magazines," Mrs. Carmichael said. "Never throw anything out. We can check the dates."

"Good heavens. Who would think such an unseemly matter would ever get a man off the hook for murder?" Mrs. Flynn said. "It doesn't seem right."

"Alma's probably pleased he's not the murderer," Enid Carmichael said. "Unseemly, sleazy, decadent. But not a murderer." She waved the letter in the air. "Let's see what the true murderer says."

"Enid! Enough." Mrs. Noonan tried to get the letter back, but Enid was so darned tall.

Mrs. Carmichael held the letter above Mrs. Noonan's head and read on. "'I looked at your pictures. I don't recognize any of them. If you have others, I'd be happy to look at those.'" Mrs. Carmichael glanced at Mrs. Noonan. "So much for your big theory about Big Sur." She went back to the letter and read the rest to herself. "Nothing more here about the murder. Just some personal stuff for you, Frances. She really took to you."

She finally handed the letter back, and Mrs. Noonan folded it and put it in her pocket for later. Serena didn't know the men at Paradise Cove Resort. Maybe there was no connection.

"What do you think, Frances?" asked Mrs. Gordon. "I was at the resort and it sure seemed a lovely place. I was thinking of recommending it to Sylvia, but I wanted to wait to see what we found."

"Well, it seems a strange coincidence that both Paul Blackwell and Shelley Stalk were there. But lots of people go to resorts. If we knew about everyone who went to Disneyland and then got killed, we might have the same suspicions about Disneyland," said Mrs. Noonan.

"Don't go bringing Disneyland into it," said Mrs.

Flynn. "It's a bastion of good family fun."

Mrs. Noonan agreed. She and Bill went to Disneyland once and enjoyed it every bit as if they had children in tow. She still had a picture of the two of them, posed with the big castle in the background. She remembered the trip fondly, no sadness.

"They have those giant turkey drumsticks at Disneyland," said Mrs. Carmichael.

"It could be anywhere popular. It doesn't have to be Disneyland," Mrs. Noonan added.

"But how many people get killed at all?" said Mrs. Gordon.

"According to Andy, a lot," said Mrs. Noonan.

"I think it's much more likely that these cases are just what they seem," said Mrs. Honeycut in her low voice. "Dissatisfied spouses who kill their life partners for money and freedom."

"Marriage is a sanctity," said Mrs. Flynn. "For better, for worse, for richer, for poorer, in sickness and in health, until death do us part. They took marriage vows. These people are defiling a sanctity."

Mrs. Carmichael plucked the last cream puff from the tub. "Till death do us part? Sounds to me like they followed the vows. Death parted them, all right."

Chapter 57

Some people weren't cut out for marriage.

He watched them come out. Fighting again. It was obvious from their posture. She said something, and he was close enough to see the man roll his eyes. A sure sign of a marriage in trouble. He knew he'd chosen well, as well as he always did.

Things usually fell into place very nicely. Last time, when he thought he might have to let them go, the man's mother arrived, and he saw the bond between her and the boy. A simple phone call pretending to seek employment and inquiring about benefits confirmed the amount of life insurance. For the Philadelphia couple, the woman fortuitously mentioned their high policies while trying to placate her husband about a lottery ticket.

This time, things were going so well he knew his path was right. No one would dispute that they were an unhappy couple. He knew she had insurance, enough insurance. He had heard them talking.

The apartment building would pose no problem. The front door was propped open now, as it had been the time before when he'd come by. People came and went at all hours, people of various ages. If he wore a white doctor's coat or bright blue scrubs, as so many of these doctors did despite being outside the hospital, he would blend right in.

He had to decide exactly what to do. He was itching to use a hammer. Helen would die and Scott would be blamed. The spouse was always blamed.

He was anxious to get started, but a second killing in the city might not go undetected. He was a patient man. This one was important. He had to plan carefully.

Chapter 58

"Sarah?"

Mr. Glenn leaned against the table in the lobby, reading a newspaper. Sarah wondered if he'd been waiting for her to appear, like Lionel had waited outside their building, according to Enid Carmichael. Sarah was on her way to work, but she'd seen him up this early before.

"Wonderful to bump into you. Could I ask you something?"

Sarah was pretty sure now. "Of course," she said.

"It's about Bessie. And Alma." He took off his large glasses and set them on the table. His blue eyes were bloodshot, and he had bigger bags than Sarah on her post-call day. "Do dreams mean anything? Are they subconscious signs?"

"What?"

"You know. If you dream something, is your brain trying to tell you something you can't admit to yourself during the day?" His voice was very soft.

"Mr. Glenn, I think you'd better tell me a little more." Sarah didn't know much about dreams, but she could see he was tormented.

"I knew Lionel immediately when I saw him. His nose, his mouth. Bessie's nose and mouth. He looks just like her. He always did. How many times did I study that boy while he was sleeping? I'd know him anywhere. Time didn't change that."

Sarah stepped closer to him, he spoke so softly.

Mr. Glenn sighed. "I love Alma. You know I do. But since I saw Lionel, all I can think about is Bessie. He bites his lip like she did. His mouth curves up the same way hers did. Bessie is in my dreams. Sweet, beautiful dreams. She's alive when I sleep. Then I wake up and she fades away, and I can't keep her image in my head, her voice, her smell. I want to sleep all the time. I want to see her."

He turned his head away. "Am I being unfaithful? To Bessie? To Alma? In my dreams? Does that count? Should I not be with Alma?" He hung his head in his hands.

Sarah touched his sleeve. He turned back to face her.

"She was the love of my life," he whispered.

"Of course she was."

"I can't tell anyone. I can't tell Frances Noonan. She and Alma are so close. I don't want her to think less of me. What do you think, Sarah?"

Sarah's heart tugged for him. He was so sensitive, he cared so much. She spoke slowly so she could think carefully of what to say.

"Mrs. Gordon is away at Sylvia's now. Lionel was just here. It's clear why Bessie is on your mind. That doesn't mean you love Alma any less. That doesn't mean Bessie is telling you something. You will always love Bessie. What it means is that you are lucky enough to love twice."

He looked at her and she hoped he believed her.

"It's not betrayal? To Bessie? To Alma?"

"It's not betrayal. It's very natural, with such two

lovely women."

Mr. Glenn stood up taller. "I am very lucky."

"Enjoy your dreams. Enjoy your days. Enjoy your luck." Sarah left him in the lobby, and she saw him look in the mirror like Mrs. Flynn had and smile.

She got to the hospital before seven thirty and climbed the stairs two at a time. She never took the elevator. It was too slow. If she waited for the elevator whenever she changed floors, she'd never get any work done. Besides, she didn't have much time for exercise, and this seemed the perfect solution. Most of the residents were the same. The staircase was usually crowded.

She slowed as she approached her sixth flight of stairs. Her head was down, so she didn't see Helen until they were passing.

"Hey, Sarah, I haven't seen you much this week."

"Helen. Hi."

"I'm glad I ran into you. My birthday's coming up. Do you want to go for a little trip? I really want to get away, but Scott's glued to football. It's the first year he's gotten to see the playoffs and all the hoopla that surrounds them because he's stuck home with the kids. But my birthday is on all-important Super Bowl weekend, and he's so invested. I got a nursing student I know from Level Seven, Susie, to come and watch the twins during the day so he can watch his ball game, and he's sending me away anywhere I want to go. Two days, one night."

"Wow," said Sarah.

"Yeah, we could have a girl's weekend. Except where I'm going is back to Paradise Cove Resort because I loved the place, plus I left Aidan's hospital cap there. They couldn't find it and I'm desperate in my new mommy, hormone-flaring way to find it myself. So I'm going. That's what sealed the babysitter deal. We were going to go somewhere together, all of us, but of course there's no television at Paradise Cove. So when Scott heard that's where I wanted to go, he came up with this solution. It's probably better than going somewhere and having him sit in the hotel room watching football while I amuse the babies."

"He thought of this?"

"Yeah, pretty resourceful when football's involved, huh?" Helen said.

"How's he doing with the kids? Any more dual poo situations?"

"Ha. That sort of thing happens all the time. One spits up and you change your shirt, then the other spits up on the clean one. Scott's very good with them, knows more tricks about soothing and things than me, probably because he's with them so much. I'm a little jealous, to tell you the truth."

"Is he getting any writing done?"

"No, not a bit. He's not thinking much about it right now because he's got football on his mind and it turns out so do a lot of other people, talk show hosts, sports commentators and such. I think once that's over and he's there all day with nothing to do but unable to work, then I think we're in trouble."

"You might be right."

"And another funny thing, I'm almost back to my pre-baby weight, all this running around, I guess, but Scott's actually gaining weight."

"What?" Sarah remembered Mrs. Noonan noticing this as well.

"Yes. It's ironic. Don't tell him I said anything. I don't actually care, but he does. We've eaten so much takeout since the babies were born because no one has time to shop or cook. And he doesn't get out much, certainly isn't running like before the babies. I try to get him to go at night when I get home, but it's so late and he's so tired, and it's the first time he's able to actually relax without two little tyrants wanting something from him. So he doesn't go. I bet he's gained fifteen pounds, maybe more."

"Poor guy."

"I know. It's always been a problem for him, and I can tell it bothers him. Anyway, do you want to come with me back to Big Sur? I'm usually not this sentimental, I don't know why this baby cap means so much to me. Also, I have such good memories of the place, we had such a good time there. That's where Emily first smiled. I'm looking forward to going back."

It was clear Helen was hell-bent on going. "Let me check with Andy, make sure he didn't make any plans. If not, I'd love to come."

Good memories? Helen must have blocked out the entire beginning of the weekend, much of the middle, and the end, Sarah thought.

Chapter 59

"Thanks for taking in my mail," Alma Gordon said. "Enid asks me all the time if she can do it. I know she just wants to snoop through everything."

"It's no problem for me. You get a lot of mail, don't you?" Frances Noonan said.

Alma laughed. "I'm a sucker for filling out those little cards. Each one seems to get me several new catalogs. Once it gets started, there's no stopping it."

"Lots of baby catalogs."

"Yes, but I also get fliers for exercise equipment and sports cars and mortgage companies and skiing at Tahoe. I think they think I'm younger than I am."

"The wrong demographic," Mrs. Noonan said. "You fooled them."

"I fooled them all right. Last month I got a coupon for an inexpensive weekend package to Calistoga, and Sylvia and Harold are going to go. That reminds me, I'm watching Owen for them, so this week I'll go down on Friday. I won't be home until next Wednesday." Saying it out loud made it sound longer.

"That's a long stretch," said Mrs. Noonan.

"Yes. I think I'll be pretty worn out by then. Owen's so active. My usual three days a week are perfect. They were thinking of day care, there's a good one right down the street, but this has worked out so well. It suits me just fine." She didn't mention that she was also very happy on Wednesday afternoon when Sylvia came home, and Alma got to relax on the train back to San Francisco knowing Albert would be waiting at the station.

"Maybe I could come down for a visit, help you out," Mrs. Noonan said.

"I'd like that." Alma could count on Frances Noonan to know what she needed before she knew herself.

"I bet Mr. Glenn would like to come too," Frances said. "We can both help with Owen. Which reminds me. You know Sarah's friend, Helen?"

"Hmm?" Alma was thinking of Mr. Glenn. Harold had a big-screen TV. Maybe Albert could watch the Super Game on it. "Oh, yes, of course. With the twins."

"That's her. Her husband watches them while she works, but he's supposed to be writing his PhD in Japanese history."

"Oh, dear," said Mrs. Gordon. "That's impossible." She couldn't even read the front page of the newspaper with Baby Owen charging around the house, wanting food, wanting a story, wanting to sing or paint or build towers with his blocks.

"Exactly," said Mrs. Noonan.

"I know what you're thinking," said Mrs. Gordon. She knew her friend, how she always wanted to help where she could. "I'm afraid I won't be able to participate. I think my three days is enough. Owen moves so fast, I have to keep getting up and down. Sometimes I get dizzy if I do it too fast. It's my blood pressure medication. I don't think I could handle twins too."

"Oh, I know, Alma, I wasn't counting on you.

Between Olivia Honeycut, Harriet Flynn, and me, I think we could help a lot."

"It's a lovely offer. I'm sure Helen and Scott will appreciate it. But does Harriet babysit?"

"She told me she's up for anything. You wouldn't believe how she keeps asking me about new projects. She mentioned babysitting specifically, thinking of little Ben Blackwell. She's a whole new woman."

"Like Lionel is a whole new man. I'm so happy for Mr. Glenn. He's beside himself."

"Things are going well, then?"

"Extraordinarily. For now. Fingers crossed." Alma worried about Lionel, that Albert would get hurt, but for now, the two seemed smitten.

"I'll talk to the group on Friday about the babysitting. I wish you were going to be there. I'm making chocolate fudge."

"I'll miss you too. And the fudge. Maybe you could bring me a piece. Don't talk about anything important while I'm not there."

"Not much to talk about these days. Looks like I was wrong on all accounts. No guardian killed for insurance money. Spencer Tremaine is in the clear. Paradise Cove seems as charming as you thought. It doesn't leave Julia Blackwell feeling very happy because her son is left as the murderer."

"I can't imagine raising a child into adulthood, doing the best you can, then having something like this happen." Mrs. Gordon's heart squeezed, and she was happy she'd had it checked out. "Look at Lionel. Look at Baby Owen. All the love, all the worries. And then to have it turn out like it did for Julia. So sad."

"I still don't think Paul did it," Mrs. Noonan said.

"I just don't have any idea who did."

How could they? Mrs. Gordon wondered. How could they know anything about all these sad families?

Chapter 60

*Families. Blood was all that held them together.
Blood.*

*They'd had a fight just before the man came
outside. He could hear it from the yard. The girls had
been sent to a friend's, and as soon as they were alone
the shouting started.*

*The man had stormed out and was headed for his
car. It didn't take much to trip him up and get a few
slices in. He fought hard, though. There was a lot of
blood before it was over.*

*The yard was private, and the alley was empty. He
had planned this well. Mechanic coveralls always made
a good cover-up, and he could get them on in seconds.
A careful wipe of the face and a baseball cap and he
was in his van driving slowly and looking perfectly
respectable.*

*He left his job a few weeks later. The money didn't
matter, of course. Another career change, another
name, another town. He'd had experience now with lots
of work. Neighborhood pizza parlor, country club. Each
with opportunity to observe family dynamics.*

*But this resort was much easier. Now his families
came to him.*

Chapter 61

Sarah added a rainproof jacket to her weekend bag. Andy dropped her at Helen's on his way to work.

"Have a wonderful time." Andy kissed her behind her ear. "Tell Scott I'm going to try to catch the game too, if he wants a change of venue. It might be hard for him to watch with the babies right there."

"That's sweet, I'll tell him," she said.

Everything seemed normal when Scott first opened the door, but when she told him Andy's invitation, he slammed the door shut behind her, turned on his heel, and walked away.

Helen came out of the bedroom carrying a small suitcase. "I'm not sure what to do," Helen whispered. "Susie called and she'll come today, but her boyfriend's parents are making a last-minute trip and she's never met them. She can't come tomorrow. So Scott's on his own for the Super Bowl."

"Oh, Scott, that's too bad," Sarah called out to him. To Helen, she said, "I could stay, I could watch them."

"No, I offered to stay too. We had a huge fight, of course. You and I are going. Happy birthday."

They looked in on the twins, who were both asleep. Helen leaned over and gave each a kiss. She shut the bedroom door softly.

Scott stood in the living room with a large bouquet of red roses tied with a ribbon. He thrust them at Helen, muttering, "Happy birthday."

Helen buried her nose in the flowers and breathed deeply. She lifted her face with a smile, but Scott had already turned away. "Thank you," she said. "They're beautiful."

"Yeah," he said, slumping onto the couch.

Helen leaned down to kiss him. He barely looked up.

Some birthday, Sarah thought. Poor Helen. Poor Scott.

Sarah was thankful that the family resort did seem magical to Helen, far away and like a whole other world. By the next morning, Helen's tense face and strained voice were gone. She seemed her normal self, smiling and relaxed.

They lingered over breakfast, sitting at a table by the window. The room was almost empty. The sun warmed their arms as they drank their coffee.

Sarah caught Marco the chef staring at them. Glaring, really. She'd seen him watching them when they arrived the day before, too, watching so intently that he hadn't noticed George calling out to him. She turned back to Helen, who stirred sugar into another cup of coffee. Sarah started to point him out but couldn't bear to break Helen's mood.

"I can't believe I had to give up coffee for so long while I was pregnant." Helen sipped loudly. "Boy, it tastes good in the morning."

Sarah turned her face to the sun and inhaled deeply. Helen had brought her bouquet of roses, and the flowers sat on the table between them. Sarah felt so peaceful sitting there with the sunshine and the beautiful rose scent. "You didn't like coffee when I first knew you."

"You're right. Scott used to tease me because I had to put so much cream and sugar in to be able to drink it. Now I can drink it black if I need to. That's what internship did to me. And those foggy mornings."

Sarah was sorry Helen mentioned Scott because her expression changed briefly, then her smile was back.

"Today's the day. Super Bowl Sunday. I wonder how he's doing," Helen said. "No way to call him from here to check in. I hope he got to relax yesterday at least. Get out of the apartment." Helen took another sip of coffee. "Actually, I definitely hope he got out of the apartment. Susie's pretty cute, full of energy, bubbly, not like me these days. I was a little worried about them there together all day both days. I was happy to hear she has a boyfriend. Scott and I aren't even sleeping in the same bed. Most nights he's with the babies and I'm on the couch."

"Oh?"

"I know, it's awful. I wasn't getting any sleep, and I actually made a mistake at the hospital. Wrote for too much potassium. Thank goodness the nurse caught it and asked me about it. But, of course, Scott can't stand it, me on the couch. He doesn't understand about the hospital, how hard it is."

"No one can really understand." Sarah remembered a mistake she made the year before. A single mistake could haunt you forever.

"It's one of the things we fought about yesterday. He accused me of staying later than I need to at the hospital just to avoid coming home."

"What a thing to say."

"I know. But sometimes I actually do. I sit in the residents' room and read up on a patient because I know if I went home, I wouldn't be able to do it."

"That's different," said Sarah. "You're still working. Reading about patients is working."

"And he said I was selfish and that I thought my career was more important than his."

"Oh, Helen."

"Maybe I do." Helen's voice was soft. "And he said some other things." She looked out the window. She bit her lip.

"Oh, I'm so sorry. I'm sure he didn't mean it. He's just frustrated."

"I know. But there's a kernel of truth in everything he says. He's making such a sacrifice. He didn't even want children yet. Not until we were settled in our first jobs. We had a plan. He's probably not going to finish his PhD. And there I'll be with my doctor career and he won't have anything, and this will be our life forever."

Sarah leaned forward and took Helen's hand.

"I thought about taking a year off or even dropping out, but Scott says I have to finish and finish on time because I have so much debt from medical school. We could never pay it back if I'm not a doctor. I'm even paying some now. We need my income."

This was true for so many residents, and Sarah was grateful her inheritance had been enough to cover her own education.

"And if Scott does somehow miraculously finish, what's he going to do with a PhD in Japanese history? He wants to be a college professor, but it's such a hard road. No harder than medicine, he says. I don't know…And that's assuming he finishes."

Sarah couldn't contain herself. She hadn't wanted to say anything until it was certain, but Helen looked miserable. Frances Noonan had spoken to her before she left and told her the Fog Ladies' tentative plan. She told Helen about the Fog Ladies' offer to babysit the twins.

Helen looked at her in disbelief. "This would be a miracle. It would solve everything."

Sarah doubted that but she didn't say so. Childcare would certainly help, though.

"Why would they do this?" Helen asked.

"They like projects," Sarah said. "Your babies could be their project."

Helen sat back and drank her coffee, silent and smiling. Sarah hoped the Fog Ladies would come through. She had never known them not to.

They walked slowly back to the room. There was no one around, though they could hear children laughing near the garden. Helen's head was down, and Sarah didn't know what she was doing until she let out a shout.

"Here it is! I knew I could find it!" Helen knelt and pulled a small blue cap from under a bush. Aidan's hospital cap. She held it close to her chest and repeated her phrase. "This place is magic."

It was cold outside, but their room was warm because of the sun. Sarah yawned and let her body relax.

Helen looked wide awake, wired. She must have had more coffee than Sarah realized. "I can't wait to tell Scott about the Fog Ladies. I'm so excited I could run all the way home. I think I'll go down and see if Karl the sea lion is still with the group or if they ate him."

"I might take a nap," Sarah said.

Helen laughed. "When I first met you, you couldn't sleep during the day."

"That's what internship did to me," Sarah said. "Now I never pass up an opportunity to doze."

Chapter 62

No one could be more surprised than he to see them show up. He had planned on meeting Helen alone at her own apartment. With his hammer.

But not yet. And not here.

A smile and a nod were all he could muster for a greeting. He wanted to say, Where are the children? What have you done with the children? Drinking alcohol, popping pills, deeming a career more important than babies, now leaving them for a frivolous weekend. What kind of mother are you?

Chapter 63

"This one's not mine."

Frances Noonan looked over at Alma Gordon, who held out a gray envelope. They sat in the backyard of Sylvia's house, enjoying the unseasonably warm day, drinking iced tea in the shade of an orange tree surrounded by plants and trees of all shapes and colors. A hummingbird flitted in some red flowers nearby. Harold had dug a sandbox in the corner, and Baby Owen sat in the middle piling sand into the back of a yellow plastic dump truck. Mr. Glenn squatted next to the sandbox, unwrapping a set of small garden tools he brought for Owen. Mrs. Noonan couldn't help but smile. The spot was so relaxing, and the child looked so happy.

The envelope was addressed to her. She recognized the print immediately. It was from Serena.

Alma Gordon's apartment was 4-A. Frances Noonan's was 5-A. The postman must have mixed this letter in with all Alma's junk mail. So much for not snooping. After Alma's comment about Enid Carmichael and how Alma didn't trust her with her mail, Frances never so much as peeked at the letters and fliers and catalogs, just bundled them up with a rubber band and put them in a paper sack from the gourmet grocery store. Sarah had brought her some lemons and Frances saved the bag, it was so pretty. Imagine buying lemons at the gourmet grocery.

She liked to respond quickly to Serena's letters, as the mail took extra long to get through the prison screening system. She didn't want Serena to have to wait forever. This one might have been in the bag since Friday. She slid her finger under the flap.

"Owen!" Mr. Glenn howled. He fell back on his haunches, hands to his face. "We don't throw sand!"

Frances set the letter on the table and hurried to help him.

Chapter 64

As Sarah closed the drapes to block the sun, she saw Helen turn the corner at the end of the garden. Just as the drapes shut, a form flashed past the window. Sarah yanked the drapes back to see Marco storming down the garden path where Helen had just walked.

Was he after Helen?

Sarah shoved her shoes back on and plunged back out into the sunshine. It was so bright, she couldn't see. Then she caught sight of the chef rounding the corner after Helen.

Sarah sprinted down the path and around the corner herself. She slammed into Marco. He was stopped dead, searching around. Helen was nowhere to be seen. Sunlight glinted in the woods. Sarah saw Helen between the trees.

Marco saw Helen too. He lunged in her direction. Sarah shouted and grabbed his arm, trying to slow him down. He spun around, his face red and furious.

In his large hands were Helen's flowers.

"Roses," he sputtered. "Roses."

Oh, no, Sarah thought. He's coming unhinged because of the roses.

She stepped back, putting some space between them. Marco was breathing hard. He looked to be in shape. He couldn't be out of breath from the running. His face was red, but maybe not furious.

He held out his hand with the bouquet. "Your friend left her roses," he said haltingly between breaths. "Will you give them to her?"

He started to cry, his hand still extended with the flowers. The rose scent wafted between them. "I miss her. I miss her so much."

Sarah knew who he was talking about. His body shook. The flowers fell to the ground. Sarah bent to pick them up. Before she straightened, he shuffled away.

Chapter 65

Sarah walked slowly back to the room feeling sad and weary. She set the flowers on the bedside table and slipped off her shoes.

A knock at the door stopped her just as she threw back the covers. Glenda and her housekeeping cart were outside.

"I know you're checking out today, but I'm here to see if you need anything," Glenda said.

"Oh, my, thank you, no," Sarah said.

"Dylan told me you were back," Glenda leaned in conspiratorially. "I think he's got a little crush on you."

Sarah groaned inwardly. Of course. That's why he was always watching her. He couldn't be more than eighteen or nineteen. Sarah was twenty-eight. What was it Mr. Glenn said? Men could always hope?

"He don't mean nothin' by it. Don't worry. He's a good kid," Glenda said, as if reading her mind.

Somehow that didn't make Sarah feel any better.

"Nice you girls could come by yourself."

All Sarah wanted was her bed. Glenda still stood in the door, so Sarah felt she had to keep making small talk.

"Yes, it's been very peaceful," she said.

"Where are the children?" Glenda asked.

Sarah explained about the birthday and how she and Helen were enjoying the relaxation. She looked pointedly at her bed, but Glenda was in a mood to talk.

"It is relaxing, isn't it? I find it relaxing even with all the hubbub of the families. It saved my husband, you know."

She must be referring to his heart attack. Maybe this resort, even with all its chaos, was less stressful than whatever he used to do.

"George's heart stopped on Christmas Day four years ago. I thought that was the worst thing that could ever happen."

The same Christmas Sarah's boyfriend dumped her. Sarah thought at the time her own heart had stopped, but she realized this was ridiculous hyperbole once she started her clinical rotations and saw what the expression truly meant. It had happened to George.

"He pulled through, thank the Lord, but then the dark times really hit. George couldn't work for a long time. And he didn't want to go back to his old job. Dylan was having problems, and we were at our wit's end. Dylan couldn't get a job because he had a record for drug possession, and he didn't want a job anyway, was barely sober. I was the only one working. George needed me, Dylan needed me, and we all needed health insurance. Lordy, Lordy, what a dark time. My brother said he'd take Dylan back, *if* he shaped up, and by God, I almost said yes."

"That must have been very hard," Sarah murmured. She shifted her tired legs, trying to be inconspicuous.

Glenda didn't notice. "George had worked for Mr. Allen before, and when he wrote that the resort needed a Jack-of-all-trades like George, we jumped at the chance. Came out here as soon as George was up for it. George is a new man now, like he has a new life. We feel blessed."

"That's wonderful," Sarah said.

"I'm so ashamed I even considered sending Dylan back. George is so good with him, loves him like his own son. Dylan looks up to him. They've done well by each other."

Sarah stood shivering with the open door. "That's wonderful," she said again.

"Well, honey, you don't want to hear all this. I'll leave you to your relaxation."

Sarah finally felt just that as she pulled the down comforter up under her chin.

Chapter 66

Mr. Glenn's eyes washed out, they all settled back in their places, Mr. Glenn a safe distance from Owen and the sand, Frances Noonan and Alma Gordon back under the tree, now enjoying some of Frances's cheese biscuits.

Frances saw Serena's letter and picked it up.

"I looked one more time at your pictures," Serena wrote. "I'm not sure, but the one of George the maintenance man looks familiar. We had a groundskeeper at our country club that looked a little like him but was much heavier. He would have had to lose a lot of weight. I don't remember his name. I'm embarrassed to say I may not have ever known. But I heard from a girlfriend who used to visit me in jail in Chicago (when I still had girlfriends that would visit me), that he had a heart attack and was pretty sick. He might even have died. So it's probably not him anyway. I know you wanted anything I could remember."

Mrs. Noonan handed the letter to Alma. "What do you think of this?"

She watched Alma read the letter. Alma lifted her iced tea glass to her lips and took a sip. Then her eyes opened wide. She dropped the glass. It shattered on the gray stone patio.

"What, what?" Mrs. Noonan said.

"It's him!" said Mrs. Gordon.

Mr. Glenn rushed over at the sound of the glass breaking. "Alma, are you okay?"

"Albert, this is the man you talked to about his heart attack. It's him!" Mrs. Gordon thrust her hand out to him, passing him the letter. "Your oh-so-fit maintenance man is the killer! He was in Chicago with Serena and he's here now at this resort where the Blackwells and the Stalks stayed. Oh, dear. Oh, dear. Those poor children."

"Sarah. Helen." Mrs. Noonan's mouth was dry. "Sarah and Helen are there."

"What?" said Mrs. Gordon. "They're back there? Now?"

"We've got to reach them. Alma, where's the telephone?"

"It won't help," Mrs. Gordon said. "Sarah tried to use her cellular phone while we were there, and she didn't get any reception. The only telephone is the one at the desk."

"Okay, but if *he* somehow answers, hang up," Mrs. Noonan said.

Mrs. Gordon retrieved the resort brochure she'd given to Sylvia, and they all crowded around the phone while she dialed.

"Please leave a message."

"Oh, no. This happened to me before. It's a small place. There's no one there," Mrs. Gordon said.

"How about the police?" said Mr. Glenn.

"The police?" said Mrs. Noonan. "I don't know what we'd say. We think this man is a killer because a convicted murderess remembers a man who looked like him but was much heavier and might be dead anyway? Oh, it's too complicated. I don't think the police can help."

"Oh, dear. Oh, dear," said Mrs. Gordon.

"I guess we don't really have much to go on. And the Stalks were at the resort, but Shelley was killed in Philadelphia. That's a long way away. George would have had to travel to Philadelphia for there to be a connection. But if we're right, Helen is in danger. We have to make sure they're all right."

"Philadelphia?" Mr. Glenn said.

"Shelley and Joseph Stalk in Philadelphia. She was strangled in her car," Mrs. Noonan reminded him.

"George is from Philadelphia, remember? He's a Phillies fan." Mr. Glenn practically bounced up and down.

"What?" Mrs. Noonan felt like fainting, herself.

Mr. Glenn burst out in excitement again. "He's a Phillies fan. From Philadelphia. Still goes to ball games there. That's your connection."

Mr. Glenn stopped bouncing. They all stared at each other.

"Oh, dear. Oh, dear," said Mrs. Gordon.

Baby Owen toddled over, and Mr. Glenn held out his arm to keep him from the broken glass. Owen reached up and touched the letter. "Oh, dear," Owen said.

"Everybody, quick, get in the car!" Mrs. Noonan's heart pounded. "We'll drive there!"

Chapter 67

He did it for the children.

Before his first liberation, he gave this careful consideration. He had to get rid of both parents, get a fresh start for the children. He knew full well from his own family. Marital discord is never one-sided. It always takes two. Fathers aren't around, wives have affairs, fathers never wanted children to start with, wives nag. The whole air of the household is poisoned. Neither parent could remain. The children deserved a clean break.

Take Dylan. He might be a different boy if he'd left his father sooner. Not the disillusioned, dejected, angry, hopeless, broken teen who arrived, barely speaking, using drugs, drinking alcohol, involved in petty crime, arrested for possession. That was Dylan then. Now look, sober for years, a job giving him a purpose in life, surrounded by beauty and love.

He'd had nothing to do with Dylan leaving his father. But what an opportunity to see if his theories were correct, to see how a child could change if given different circumstances, different parenting. An experiment playing out before his very eyes. And Dylan had indeed changed.

It would be satisfying to finish things off with Helen now, but that was not his style. Patience.

Though he'd covered his tracks, with enough

digging, the police could find his travel to Philadelphia, his connection to Chicago and San Antonio.

He wasn't afraid to die, but he was terrified of getting caught. If his deeds were discovered, the surviving parents would go free. Then all his work would be in vain.

These babies were important. Two more young souls to free. He would wait.

Chapter 68

The car crawled around the tight curves. Frances Noonan didn't want to waste gas by braking. The gauge was on empty, and there were no gas stations at all. She hunched over the steering wheel, struggling to see farther ahead than the corners allowed. Her whole body was tense from holding back on her speed when all she wanted was to rocket forward. As she drove, a fog started to swirl around them, and then she had to strain to see the corners at all. She slowed further, willing the weather to improve.

"This is just like when we drove down here, remember Alma?" said Mr. Glenn.

"Oh, what a drive that was. No apple juice for Owen today." Alma Gordon tousled his hair. Mrs. Noonan saw Baby Owen in the mirror, beaming back at Mrs. Gordon.

"When we get there, keep your eyes open for George." Mrs. Noonan addressed this to Mr. Glenn. "You're the only one who knows what he looks like. We'll go to the office to try to find out what room they're in. But if George sees us all, he might figure out why we're there. It's already going to look odd to be coming at all."

"Why are we there? What exactly are we going to do?" asked Mr. Glenn.

"Well, now, I don't actually know," said Mrs.

Noonan. "Find Sarah and Helen. Make sure they're all right. Bring them back with us."

"You mean us go back with them. We don't have any gas," said Mrs. Gordon.

"Whatever. However we can, we will all leave together," said Mrs. Noonan.

"And what about the proprietor? Will we say anything to him?" asked Mrs. Gordon.

"No. We don't really know anything for certain," said Mrs. Noonan. "It's more of a hunch and speculation. We'll leave it all to the authorities. We can tell them everything we know in as coherent a way as we can and see if they can make something of it. Maybe start with Spencer Tremaine. His team may be able to put this together even better than the police. That's what he's paid for, certainly."

"Spencer Tremaine." Mrs. Gordon sighed sadly from the back seat.

"So, when we get there, just one of us should go in. Maybe me, and you, Mr. Glenn, can look around. If you see George, let us know somehow and keep him occupied," said Mrs. Noonan.

"Okay, I'll whistle," said Mr. Glenn.

"I'll try to find out the room number as fast as I can so we can track them down," said Mrs. Noonan.

"Oh, dear. Oh, dear," said Mrs. Gordon. "I hope they're all right. That young mother. Those babies need her."

"Look, there's the sign," said Mr. Glenn. "It says one-half mile. I think you can speed up now."

Mrs. Noonan pressed on the gas pedal. The car did not accelerate. They were going up a hill. The engine sputtered.

"Ease off, ease off!" said Mr. Glenn.

She lifted her foot as the car reached the top of the hill. She left it off as the car slowly picked up speed heading down. "I think we're running on fumes," she said.

"But we're going to make it!" said Mrs. Gordon. "Yippee!"

"Yippee!" said Baby Owen. Mrs. Noonan smiled. He mimicked everything he could these days. His vocabulary was better every time she saw him.

Mrs. Noonan's foot was back on the pedal. The car inched around the corner into the resort and across the parking lot. She coasted to a stop near the office and they tumbled out. They waited while Mrs. Gordon leaned back in to unfasten Owen from his car seat. The fog danced in the wind like a living creature, moist and chilly. Mrs. Gordon pulled the toddler toward her chest under her sweater.

"Come on, come on," hissed Mrs. Noonan. "We've got to find them."

"I'm coming, I'm coming." Mrs. Gordon stood, the baby hanging on with his hands around her neck. She reached out to steady herself. "Not so tight, Owen." She adjusted his position with her other hand. She still gripped the car door handle. Her face was pale next to Owen's rosy cheeks.

"Alma, are you all right?" Mrs. Noonan kicked herself for hurrying her friend.

"Just stood up too fast. I'm a little dizzy."

"Here, let me." Mr. Glenn hoisted the toddler into his arms.

"Tuck him under here." Mrs. Gordon brought Mr. Glenn's jacket around and zipped Owen in. "He's just getting over a cold."

"We've got to hurry." Mrs. Noonan stomped her foot, desperate to finally take action.

"I'll just stand here a moment and equilibrate," said Mrs. Gordon.

Forgetting what they discussed, Mrs. Noonan and Mr. Glenn both piled into the office, their voices loud from talking above the wind. They stopped abruptly when the proprietor appeared from the back room and stepped to the counter.

Mrs. Noonan recognized him from the photo. He smiled at them, eyebrows raised.

"May I help you?" he asked. "I'm afraid we don't have any rooms."

Mrs. Noonan tried desperately to think of something to say that didn't sound idiotic.

He looked more closely at Mr. Glenn. "You've been a guest here before, am I right? If you really need a place to stay, maybe we can accommodate you in some way. We don't open all our rooms in the winter, but we could arrange something today. We do suggest reservations, however."

"We're out of gas," blurted Mrs. Noonan.

"Oh, certainly, out of gas. We can help you there. I'll ask George to help you. It's his day off, but I can easily fetch him from his cottage. I won't be a moment. Please have some tea." He motioned to the hot water pot and the selection of tea.

Quite a generous selection, thought Mrs. Noonan. The place *was* nice. As soon as he was out the door, she craned her head over the counter to look for some sort of registry. Right on top of a neat stack of papers was the listing for the day, and she immediately saw

"James, S" written next to room twelve.

"While he gets George, we can get Sarah and Helen. Room twelve," she said. "Which way?"

"I think we were in room twelve," said Mr. Glenn. "It's on the other side of the building."

"Let's go," said Mrs. Noonan.

"Let go!" said Baby Owen from Mr. Glenn's chest.

"Shouldn't we wait until he comes back?" asked Mr. Glenn. "Won't he think it's strange if we leave?"

"Let's write him a note. Say you wanted to show me around." Mrs. Noonan grabbed a memo pad and a pencil. She scratched a quick note and left it on the counter. Mr. Glenn opened the door and she waved him through. "Lead on."

Mrs. Gordon was shuffling across the parking lot when they came out.

"It's our same room," said Mr. Glenn.

Mr. Glenn and Baby Owen led the way, then Mrs. Noonan. Mrs. Gordon slowly followed.

"Alma, Alma, a little faster," said Mrs. Noonan.

"My foot's got a crick in it from the drive. It won't bend right. You go on ahead. I'll be along."

Mrs. Noonan charged out in front, searching for the room numbers through the tufting fog.

"Twelve. Here it is." She knocked loudly on the door. At first no one answered. Then they heard a rustling.

"Who is it?" Sarah called from inside.

"Oh, thank God. Sarah, it's us, Frances and Alma. Open up."

Chapter 69

Someone pounded on Sarah's door. In her dream, the Karl sea lion pounded on the rock in triumph after he pushed off the last foe. But this wasn't Karl. This was someone outside her room. Frances Noonan and Alma Gordon, apparently.

Sleepy and alarmed, Sarah flung open the door. "Mrs. Noonan! What are you doing here?"

"Helen? Helen?" Mrs. Noonan called.

"She's not here," Sarah said. "She went down to the beach to see the sea lions."

"In this weather?" said Mr. Glenn.

Sarah looked out past them. "When did the fog come in?"

"How long have you been asleep?" asked Mrs. Noonan.

"What time is it now?"

"Noon," said Mr. Glenn.

"Wow. An hour or two. The weather was nice when I fell asleep. Hmm. Helen's been gone a long time." Sarah shook her head and breathed in the cold air to clear her mind.

"Sarah, we think Helen's in danger." Mrs. Noonan told her about Serena's letter. "George the maintenance man killed all those parents," Mrs. Noonan said.

"George? George, Glenda's husband?"

"Yes, he's lost weight and he looks like a new

man, but he is exactly the same man that worked at Serena's country club at the time her husband was brutally murdered, and he now works here, where two more parents have visited and then been killed. And he's from Philadelphia and still visits there and that's where Shelley Stalk was killed. He's a murderer. We've got to find Helen."

"It's his day off, so he could be anywhere," Mr. Glenn said. "He could be with Helen."

"Wait a minute, wait a minute," Sarah said. Something seemed off. What was she not remembering? "How long ago was Serena's husband killed?"

"Four years ago, the day after Christmas," Mrs. Noonan said.

That's right, Sarah thought, the same Christmas my boyfriend dumped me. She said, "Four years ago on Christmas, George was lying half dead in the ICU after his heart attack. It can't be George."

"What? Are you sure?" asked Mrs. Noonan. "Did we get this wrong? I was so certain, certain that coincidences like this don't happen, three family tragedies, one man with ties to all. But maybe they do."

"No, no." Sarah strained to think. "There's something else."

"Now I feel foolish, racing down here convinced you were about to be murdered. What was I thinking? It's a wonder we didn't drive off the road into the sea," Mrs. Noonan said.

"I'm glad it's not George," Mr. Glenn said. "I like him. He's been through some dark times."

That's just what Glenda had said. She and George had been through some dark times.

"George may not have been the only one who worked at that country club." Sarah rushed to get the thought out. "Glenda said the proprietor here knew George and offered him this job because George was so skilled at what he did. If Serena recognized George from the country club, then that might be where they worked together. If so, the proprietor was in both places as well."

Sarah's mind filled with a vision of Allen Werble, courteous to the point of obsequiousness. She remembered how he hovered in the dining room, being first on the spot when Ben kicked over the water into Andrea's lap or offering his opinions on alcohol and breastfeeding. She remembered him rushing over when Scott started shouting in the parking lot. And how he had all their information on his registration cards. Her head whooshed, and she steadied herself on the doorframe.

"It's the proprietor," she said.

"The proprietor? We just saw him in the office. He knows we're here," said Mrs. Noonan. "We've got to get going."

"We have to find Helen," Sarah said.

"Helen," said Baby Owen. Sarah jumped. She had not noticed Owen tucked into Mr. Glenn's jacket, but now she saw the back of his little head.

If Baby Owen was here…"Didn't you say Mrs. Gordon was here too?" asked Sarah. "Where is she?"

Mr. Glenn whipped around, so fast Baby Owen let out a cry. "She was right behind me."

"I never saw her," Sarah told them.

"Let's go," said Mrs. Noonan. "We've got to find them."

Chapter 70

It was the best day of his life. The idea came suddenly, and once he thought of it, he acted immediately.

His father had come home the night before. He was a day early. His mother was drunk. In all of the things she shouted at him and he shouted at her, the one that stuck with him was, "I don't need you. You're never here anyway. I wish you were dead so I could live off that insurance policy you're so proud of."

They were both hung over the next morning, and he knew they would sleep until at least nine. He was up early, very early.

It was easy to light the cigarette and drop it on the bed. He was a little surprised to see how close together they slept, but that left him plenty of room to get the fire started. He and Buster once played with his mother's hair spray and a match, so he expected the flames to spread quickly once they neared her hair. And they did.

It was the best day of his life when he went to live with Uncle Morris and Aunt Eunice. And the insurance money made them all very, very rich.

Rich enough for him to work or not. When his aunt and uncle died, he was rich enough to buy this resort. He couldn't believe it when he saw the ad. A family resort was for sale. He couldn't have dreamed up a more perfect scenario for his life's work.

Chapter 71

Alma Gordon's toes were kinked and painful. This happened sometimes for no good reason. Even all that stretching with yoga hadn't helped. Her horoscope that morning read, "Your limitations are limitless." At the time, she was annoyed at the lazy newspaper, recycling the horoscopes. She'd read this one before. Now she was just plain annoyed. Limitless. Ha. She couldn't even walk.

She stopped to try to stretch her foot against the ground. She steadied herself with a hand on the side of the building. Ah, that felt better.

Shouts and cries rose from the area near the cliff. Was that Helen's voice? Yes, it was definitely Helen, and she sounded like she was in trouble.

Oh, dear! Alma raced to the cliff, limping because of her foot. She tried to move faster and thought how ridiculous she must look, her body lurching up and down with each step. But the voices sounded frenzied.

She couldn't see them on the path along the cliff. Protected from the edge by a waist-high solid fence, the path twisted and turned with the crags in the cliff, sometimes veering away from the sharp drop-off into forest and bush. Fog obscured any view of the ocean and whispered against her cheek. Even with the wind whistling in the trees and the surf crashing right below, the voices grew louder. She was close. The protective fencing came to a dead end, but Mrs. Gordon could see the path continued. If she could only climb over. No easy feat. She was more limber now after her yoga sessions, and she could hoist her leg over. It wasn't pretty, but eventually she was on the other side. I could never have done that a year ago, she thought.

She saw them as she came around the corner, two ghostly creatures in the fog. Helen held by a man, Helen screaming. Her words were lost in the wind. They stood too close to the edge.

Alma hesitated for a moment. Then she thought of those little babies. In a burst of power which surprised her, she pitched forward and tackled the couple from the side. The three of them flew sideways and landed in a clump of ice plant, safely away from the cliff's edge.

The man was laid out flat but started to sit.

"Helen, run!" Mrs. Gordon shouted. She was down on all fours, and the man was behind her. She could see him through her legs, rising quickly. Helen sat on the ground, dazed, and the man staggered toward her. Just as they practiced in class, Mrs. Gordon thrust her leg out behind her, a faster version of her favorite yoga movement, balancing table with knee-to-nose flow. She caught him under the chin, sending him back down again.

Mrs. Gordon jumped into a standing warrior position. She felt quite proud of herself. Helen looked stunned. Mrs. Gordon reached out her hand.

"Come on, Helen, we've got to get you out of here."

"What? Why?" Helen asked.

"He wants to kill you," said Mrs. Gordon.

"No!" said Helen. "Scott isn't like that."

"Scott? This is Scott?" Mrs. Gordon peered closer at the man on the ground. She'd only met Scott once, and he didn't look like she remembered.

The poor man lifted his head. "I'm just going to lie here. I'm not going to do anything. So you don't have to kick me anymore. But why in the world would I want to kill my wife?"

"Oh, dear. Oh, dear. I am so sorry," said Mrs. Gordon. "It was the fog. I thought you were the maintenance man."

"Helen, Alma, thank God!" Mrs. Gordon turned to see Frances Noonan hurtling toward them through the mist, Sarah behind her, and Mr. Glenn far in the rear, Baby Owen still tucked in his coat.

Sarah ran over and hugged her. She motioned at Scott on the ground. "What are you doing here?" she asked.

"I'm starting to wonder that myself," he said. "I drove down here to apologize."

"Apologize?" said Helen.

"Yeah, I know, it didn't come out right," said Scott.

Mrs. Gordon silently agreed. She was heartened to see Helen scoot closer to him.

Scott sat and turned Helen toward him. "I came to say I'm sorry. I drove all that way in the fog. In case you fell off a cliff or drove off the road, I didn't want that fight to be your last memory of me."

Helen reached out and took his hands.

"I don't know what's gotten into me lately," said Scott. "I think I've got baby brain."

Helen leaned forward and gave him a gentle kiss.

"Where *are* the babies?" asked Mrs. Noonan. "Are

they here?"

"No, I left them with Andy. He was going to watch the Super Bowl with me, but I called him to come early. I borrowed his car to get here," said Scott.

"Andy's with the babies?" said Sarah. "Oh, Lord."

Mrs. Gordon looked down at Helen and Scott. They were covered in dirt and Scott's chin was bleeding. "I'm so sorry." She looked at the others. "I thought he was the maintenance man. I kicked him."

"Maintenance man? We were wrong. It's the proprietor. He knows we're here. We have to leave now," said Mrs. Noonan.

"Maintenance man? Proprietor? What's going on?" said Scott.

"We think he wants to kill Helen," said Mrs. Noonan.

"What? Why?" said Scott.

"We're not sure," said Mrs. Noonan. "But there's a pattern. She fits the pattern. Children, insurance money."

"And an unhappy marriage," piped in Mr. Glenn.

"Oh, dear," Mrs. Gordon said as Scott shot Albert a hard look.

"Anyway, we need to get you out of here," said Mrs. Noonan.

Helen and Scott rose, still holding hands.

"Not so fast." There was a rustling in the bushes. A small man stepped out. A small man with a large revolver in his hand.

Chapter 72

It was a risk, bringing people from his past to work with him in the present. It made everything more complicated. He had to do it. For Dylan.

He met Dylan when George bailed him out after he was arrested for shoplifting, not more than a week after arriving in George and Glenda's home. George needed a ride because Glenda had the car, and as George's boss and a manager at the country club, he felt it was his duty. Plus, he wanted to meet the boy he'd heard about.

And Dylan didn't disappoint. He was as sulky, foul-mouthed, and disrespectful as George had described. He had nowhere to go but to them, and Glenda was determined to show him all the love her brother lacked. Even she was no match for Dylan. It took the both of them to keep him in at night, to force the youth to and from school each day. George confided all this to him as they drove to the jail.

He'd left the country club a few weeks after Christmas, his work there complete, another two girls free of their battling parents. He changed his name, bought the resort and settled into a new life. He'd also done this when he divorced his wife and left San Antonio. He was looking forward to staying put for a while.

He saw George only once after his heart attack,

but he sent get well cards and got letters from Glenda in return. He was able to keep up on Dylan. He heard that Dylan had stopped speaking to them completely, and that he missed more school than he attended.

Then Glenda wrote that she couldn't do it, she didn't know if she could manage both Dylan and George, that Dylan was just too much. She was going to send him back to that father. That father who didn't know how to be a father.

He knew he had to act. It was his call to arms.

He invited them all to Paradise Cove, said he needed skills only George possessed, take as long as he needed to recuperate, Dylan could help out, too, get him away from the bad influences of the city.

He told them he changed his name to honor the uncle whose inheritance bought the resort. The truth was he'd already honored his uncle. When he worked at the country club, his name was Morris Allen.

Within a few months, they were all there together. Dylan was in the loving hands of Glenda and George, but he also had fresh air and new surroundings and work.

He even shared with the boy that his own parents had been alcoholic. It was the first time he shared that with anybody.

In any case, he brought Glenda and George to Paradise Cove understanding the danger that one of his past lives could catch up with his present. His own jobs had always been low profile. No one remembered a middle manager.

He took a calculated risk. He did it for Dylan. He would do the same again.

Chapter 73

Frances Noonan wrenched her eyes away from the gun and assessed their group, standing in a line at the edge of the cliff. The fog was lifting, and the ocean was visible again, the cliff starkly outlined against the blue. She took a step forward, away from the edge, and Alma Gordon pulled Mr. Glenn forward as well. Mrs. Noonan stood on the far end, then Sarah, Alma, Mr. Glenn and Baby Owen, then Helen and Scott. The man motioned for them to move closer together.

"Isn't this cozy," the proprietor said. The wind was loud, and Mrs. Noonan had to strain to hear him.

He waved the gun at Scott. "I thought he might do my dirty work for me. I saw him arrive and was just slipping out the back when you all showed up. I wanted to witness the reunion for myself. Angry husband shoves wife to death over cliff. Or I could help them both to fall, a tragic accident in the fog. It would suit my purposes."

He shook his head. "Not that I would choose to have a death at my resort. I would never have planned to kill her here. Think of the publicity and scrutiny."

He pivoted and pointed at Alma Gordon, who shuddered. "And then you came on the scene. I knew I'd have to let you all go on your merry way. Much safer for me anyway."

He slowly leveled the gun at each of them. "Then

the rest of you appeared. And you know about me. Now we've got a problem."

They all stood silently. Mrs. Noonan measured the distance between him and their group.

"You might have to follow one another off the edge, like lemmings. You just couldn't see the danger in the fog. A heartbreaking end to a vacation weekend. It *is* plausible."

Mrs. Noonan's mind raced. Could they run? Could they jump him? Of course they could, if they could communicate. But he was too far from them for one of them to rush him without endangering the others. And there was Baby Owen. They had to be careful of Baby Owen.

The man regarded their uneven line. She knew he knew they were plotting.

"Don't try to run. You have no gas." The proprietor nodded at Mrs. Noonan. "And your car has been incapacitated." He gestured with the gun toward Helen.

One car. They had Scott's car. Mrs. Noonan looked at Scott. His hands were clenched. She willed him to stay still a while longer. He looked at her and she gave a slight shake of her head.

"Sit down," the proprietor said.

Mr. Glenn and Alma Gordon slowly crouched. The others stayed standing.

He lifted his gun to Helen. "Sit down," he said, and they did.

"Sit, sit, sit," said Baby Owen.

The proprietor jerked his head toward the sound. Baby Owen popped his head out of Mr. Glenn's jacket.

"Shh," Mrs. Gordon said and wrapped her arms around Mr. Glenn and the baby, her body in front.

"You can't possibly kill us all," said Mrs. Noonan. "We have a child with us. These people are parents. They have two small babies at home. You can't kill us all."

"Kill us all," sang Baby Owen.

Chapter 74

After the fire, he thought he would go right to Uncle Morris's house. Somehow things didn't work out that way. Uncle Morris and Aunt Eunice were on vacation, a last-minute camping trip, gone an entire week.

They placed him with a family until they could find his uncle. A family that did this all the time, a foster family who also took in children short term.

There were no foster children there that week, just two teenage girls and the mother.

And the father.

"I can see you like this."

"I wouldn't be doing this if you didn't like it. You know you like it."

"It's our little secret."

"No one will believe you anyway. I am the school principal. I am known in this town."

"A boy who likes this sort of thing isn't normal. If you tell anyone, they will put you in a home for boys like this."

He hadn't thought of this in years. In thirty years. He hadn't thought of this since it happened.

"Your black soul will never find peace."

That woman was right. He was damned for what he'd done. All the things he'd done.

He surveyed the group sitting terrified before him.

They had a child with them. A child. Did he have parents? Or did he only have this grandmother? And Helen and Scott were both here. Sarah, his self-chosen new guardian, was here, along with her apartment building family of helpers. The old lady was right. He couldn't kill them all. He never wanted to kill them all. And if he did, this little boy and the babies would become wards of the state. Like he had been.

He would do anything to prevent that.

Chapter 75

Sarah shifted her eyes left and right. They had to act. Now that they were seated it would be harder. They could overpower him, but someone might get hurt in the trying.

"Why are you doing this?" she said. "Why would you want to kill Helen? Why did you kill Andrea Blackwell?"

The man's face twisted. He looked different. His voice was soft, and she barely heard it in the wind.

"What kind of parents are these? What kind of family life do they provide? People never change. Their children will be forever scarred. My guardians provide love and stability. Not anger and loathing. I do it for the children." He paused. "I *did* it for the children."

He examined the gun in his hand, tilting it one way then the other. He bent and laid the large revolver on the ground.

Scott leaped to his feet. Before he could move forward, the man leaped as well. Toward them. Over them. He sprang over Sarah, diving forward, plunging over the edge of the cliff.

They all sat there, stunned. They didn't hear a sound other than the wind and the surf. But he was gone.

Scott ran to the cliff edge. "I can see him!" He turned back to the group. "There's no question. He's dead."

Helen ran to look and Scott held her back, held her tight, their bodies swaying as if the wind was that strong.

"He's dead, he's dead," sang Baby Owen softly to himself.

Chapter 76

"What do you think?" Sarah asked the Fog Ladies as she took another molasses cookie. They gathered in Frances Noonan's apartment, warmed by tea, fog veiling the view outside. "Do people never change?" That's what the killer had said. As if there were no hope for any of them.

She bit into the cookie and closed her eyes to take in the taste and aroma. Frances Noonan made these molasses cookies all the time now and they were delicious. This was proof that someone could change right here, in these scrumptious cookies. Mrs. Noonan would be the first to admit it.

"Bill used to say the same thing. People never change. He was wrong," Mrs. Noonan said. Sarah watched as she unscrewed a jam jar as easily as if she were turning a knob on her old radio.

Mrs. Noonan cocked her head. "Although, personally, I like to think I've returned to who I always was. I took some detours this year, and now I'm back." She sounded pensive. "Maybe that's not real change."

"I can't believe I missed it," Enid Carmichael burst in. She loomed over Alma Gordon seated next to her on Mrs. Noonan's flowered sofa. "How could you have gone without me? You got to meet the murderer. A real-life serial killer. Oh, I wish I'd been there."

"Oh, dear. Oh, dear," said Alma Gordon. "I wish I

had not been there." She shifted away from Mrs. Carmichael on the couch. "That awful man, killing those innocent people, all because he thought they were unsuitable parents. As if he were God."

"God would do no such thing." Harriet Flynn crossed herself.

"It all happened so quickly, Enid," Frances Noonan said. "Had we known we were setting out to confront the killer, we would definitely have included you in our plans." She winked at Sarah.

"I should hope so. Hmph." Mrs. Carmichael munched her cookie loudly. "Serena Evans didn't even turn out to be a real killer."

"No, she did not," said Mrs. Noonan. "And now she will be reunited with her girls. Spencer Tremaine is already back on the case. He said he would return for no fee. I think it's the publicity he's after, but no matter. Paul Blackwell will be out soon too. Julia's giddy with excitement. Evelyn Ringley said Joe wants to move out here when he's released, make a clean start. So little Joey will stay close to her. There may be more parents, like that businessman in San Antonio Andy found. I hope not, though. I can't bear to think there are more cases, more tragedies."

They fell silent. Harriet Flynn crossed herself again.

"Those poor parents have all changed," Alma Gordon said softly.

"One would hope," Mrs. Carmichael said.

"A bright spot is that Allen Werble left the resort to Glenda and George, so they can all stay on there if they want," said Mrs. Noonan. "Marco the chef left as soon as the police were done with him. He went to France to see if he could reunite with his family."

"Oh, I hope it works out," Sarah said, remembering his anguish.

"Touching," Mrs. Carmichael said. "Anything more about the murderer?"

"We've finished with that topic," Mrs. Noonan said.

"I've changed," Olivia Honeycut broke in with her low voice. "I'm old. Look at this walker. Without it I'd topple over like little Owen when he took his first steps."

"That's different," Sarah said. "That's just aging." She was sorry as soon as the words left her mouth.

"Just? Just? Only a young person can say 'just aging,'" huffed Mrs. Honeycut.

"She's right, Sarah," Mrs. Noonan chimed in. "We don't feel old. Our hearts and minds are exactly the same as when we were your age. It's our hips, our fingers, our teeth."

"Our hearing," added Harriet Flynn.

"Speak for yourself," said Enid Carmichael.

"Yes, I'm sorry. Aging takes its toll." Sarah smiled at the group, taking in each lady, old and older. "Frankly, I tend to forget that when I'm around all of you."

"I have come to terms with my life, my abilities," said Mrs. Honeycut.

"Well, I, for one, am not giving in." Mrs. Flynn reached up and touched her dark hair.

"I didn't say 'giving in,'" snapped Mrs. Honeycut. "I said, 'come to terms.' There's a difference."

"I can't see that any of you are giving in," Sarah laughed. "But it's those hearts and minds I'm wondering about. Do people's hearts and minds change?"

Sarah remembered trying to be less emotional in the hospital and how that had not worked for her. Patients touched her emotionally, and that was all right. For now.

"Well," said Mrs. Honeycut, "I come here now. We used to have all the card games, the quilting, everything, at my house. Now I'm here. That's change."

"I think she had something a little more substantial in mind, Olivia," said Mrs. Carmichael.

"Olivia, you are absolutely right, and we all thank you for your graciousness," Mrs. Noonan said quickly.

"Frances has better treats anyway." Mrs. Carmichael reached for another cookie.

Mrs. Honeycut opened her mouth, but Alma Gordon, thank goodness, spoke first.

"Look at Lionel. He's changed. I remember that boy, sullen and ill-mannered. Look at him now. He seems to be as lovely a man as Mr. Glenn could hope for in a son."

"The jury's still out on that one," Enid Carmichael said.

"Teenagers don't count," rasped Olivia Honeycut. "They're not real people yet."

Sarah smiled at this, and Mrs. Noonan winked at her again.

"Dylan, too, another teenager," Sarah added. "From what Glenda said, he has had a true transformation."

"Sounds like Glenda and George can take much of the credit for that," Mrs. Honeycut said.

"Maybe there is something to this killer's idea." Enid Carmichael bobbed her head up and down, enthusiastically chewing her molasses cookie.

"Enid!" Mrs. Noonan leaped from her chair so fast Sarah thought she might fall over. "That is absolute nonsense. That poor young man had abuse in his childhood. Now he has love and kindness. Abuse is a far different situation from parents who bicker and squabble. None of those families, none of those children, are better off without their parents."

"Amen to that," said Mrs. Flynn.

"Okay, okay," said Mrs. Carmichael, mouth full of cookie.

"Chantrelle has changed." Mrs. Gordon set down her teacup. "She got a job in a clothing store, something she swore she would never do because her despised sister works in one. But she's paying her rent and had money left over for an excursion to Disneyland. She hasn't had a boyfriend since Zach. Says it's *her* time now. She even mentioned the GED. She says she'll come see Owen soon."

"Ha! I'll believe that when I see it," said Mrs. Carmichael. "And when was it not *her* time?"

Mrs. Honeycut said, "Enough talk about teenagers. Has anyone old changed?"

"All right, then, look at me," said Alma Gordon. "In a year, my heart has opened twice, for Baby Owen and for Mr. Glenn. Me. I've changed. My brain sometimes can't believe it. But it happened."

She had indeed changed. Sarah remembered how timid and anxious Mrs. Gordon used to be. And now she'd attacked a presumed murderer without hesitation.

"Look at me," Harriet Flynn said. "My whole

outlook has changed. The Lord put me here for a reason, and I intend to fulfill his will."

Sarah had to agree, she had changed. No one would believe this was the same woman who refused to help at the hospital if unwed mothers or unruly children were involved. Now she was poised to take on any cause.

"Speaking of God's will," Harriet Flynn added, "we need to help that young couple. Marriage is sacred. God has joined them together, and we are all responsible for keeping them from being pulled apart. Sarah, what can we do?"

"We may not have to do much," Sarah told her.

Sarah had ridden with Helen and Scott on the way home. Scott drove the whole way with Helen's hand on his knee, twisty roads or not.

"I almost lost you," Scott said over and over.

When they opened the door, Andy was sprawled on the floor with a baby on either side, their heads on his chest as he sang and they cooed. Sarah pulled him out the door as first Helen, then Scott burst into tears, hugging each other so hard they looked like one person.

"They're going to marriage counseling," Sarah said. "They truly love each other. They just got off track. With the right tools, they know they can change. And they both are ecstatic to have the Fog Ladies' babysitting services. Scott says he's far from the finish line, but he thinks he can do it with your help."

Frances Noonan beamed. Harriet Flynn and Olivia Honeycut beamed.

"Hmph," said Enid Carmichael. "I'm not going. I haven't changed my mind about babysitting. I haven't changed my mind about anything. I don't see that I need to. Why should I change? The world has changed

326

enough."

Sarah looked around at each of the Fog Ladies. Did people ever change? Maybe, maybe not. The Fog Ladies had changed, in their own ways, large and small, save one. That sounded right to Sarah.

A word about the author...

Susan McCormick is an author and doctor who lives in Seattle. She graduated from Smith College and George Washington University School of Medicine, with additional medical training in San Francisco and Washington, DC. She served in the US Army for nine years before moving to the Pacific Northwest. She is married and has two boys, plus a giant Newfoundland dog. She writes cozy murder mysteries and is also the author of *Granny Can't Remember Me*, a picture book about Alzheimer's disease. Visit her at:

https://susanmccormickbooks.com

Thank you for purchasing
this publication of The Wild Rose Press, Inc.

For questions or more information
contact us at
info@thewildrosepress.com.

The Wild Rose Press, Inc.
www.thewildrosepress.com

Lightning Source UK Ltd.
Milton Keynes UK
UKHW020703270223
417728UK00015B/1278